Praise for Arianna Hart's *Devil's Playground*

"Devil's Playground is yet another exciting, heart-pounding romantic suspense novel by Arianna Hart."

~ *Kathy's Review Corner*

"DEVIL'S PLAYGROUND by the extremely talented Arianna Hart is a delicious novel that will delight and enthrall all who read it! ...Her multi-faceted characters are brimming with life and their steamy passion will gratify your need for love and romance."

~ *Nadine, Romance Junkies*

Look for these titles by
Arianna Hart

Now Available:

A Man for Marly
Dark Heat
Leap of Faith
Snowy Night Seduction
Spitfire
Surprise
Take Your Medicine

Devil's Playground

Arianna Hart

A SAṁHAIN PUБLISHING, LTO. publication.

Samhain Publishing, Ltd.
577 Mulberry Street, Suite 1520
Macon, GA 31201
www.samhainpublishing.com

Devil's Playground
Copyright © 2008 by Arianna Hart
Print ISBN: 978-1-59998-802-3
Digital ISBN: 1-59998-201-3

Editing by Sarah Palmero
Cover by Scott Carpenter

First Samhain Publishing, Ltd. electronic publication: August 2007
First Samhain Publishing, Ltd. print publication: June 2008

Dedication

For my mother who is still the epitome of the perfect nurse, even if she is retired. Thanks for all the insights and help with research.

And as always, for my family. Although I don't have any brothers, I know my sisters have my back no matter what. My husband and my children put up with me when I'm neck deep in a story and my parents support me even when I don't deserve it.

Also, to my second family, my writing buddies who listen to me whine, lift me up when I need it and kick me in the pants when I need that too.

It may take a village to raise a child, but it takes a vast global network to get an author through a book. Thank you to all of my friends around the world who get me through this crazy process.

Chapter One

"Help."

What on earth? Caitlyn O'Toole looked down to see a bloody hand holding a badge sticking out from under her SUV. There was a man under her Jeep.

A bleeding man.

She squatted down to get a better look and immediately recognized the coppery smell of blood in the air. Bright red splatters covered her white shoes and made her blue hospital scrubs look black in the dim light from the parking garage. Bending lower, Caitlyn peered under the running board.

"Mac?" Devlin "Mac" McDougal, her brother Tom's partner at the FBI, stared at her, blue eyes filled with pain.

"What are you doing here? Where's Tom? Have you been shot? Let me help you get to the emergency room. You've lost a lot of blood." That was an understatement. There was a pool of it in front of him.

"Undercover. Can't blow it." His voice was weak and his eyes closed with the strain from talking.

"And can't go to the hospital because someone will have to report a gunshot wound." She'd done two of those reports tonight during her shift in the ER. He nodded weakly.

"Let me call Tom."

"Can't put him in danger. Please. Help. Me." Sky blue eyes entreated her from the shadows under her car. Footsteps thundered from the floor above her almost in time to the rapid beating of her heart. The squeal of sneakers on cement echoed in the cavernous emptiness of the parking garage.

"They're. Coming. Will. Finish. Me. Off." He tried to move, but hissed in pain. His breathing was rapid and shallow.

"Who's coming?" she asked, watching as blood spurted between the fingers he had held to his side.

Caitlyn looked around for one of the security guards. Not an officer in sight. She had to do something. She couldn't just leave him here to die. "Come on, you'll have to help me. I can't get you in the back by myself." She'd call her brother, Jim, to ask him for help. By the looks of Mac's injury, she was going to need all the help she could get.

Mac rolled slowly out from under the Jeep, leaving a trail of blood in his wake. She'd better do something about that too.

It wasn't until he had stumbled and groaned his way to his feet that she remembered how big her brother's friend really was. She was close to six feet tall, and he topped her by at least another four inches. And solid. Boy he was solid. She could feel the muscles in his arms and torso as she slipped her shoulder under his arm to support him until she could get the door open.

"Here, get in the back and lay down. I'll put the blanket over you. Try to stay as still as possible." Caitlyn grabbed the beach blanket out of the back and flipped it over him messily. It didn't cover him all the way. Damn.

Slipping off her light jacket, Caitlyn tossed it over the seat, draping it over his head in the process, effectively covering him but hopefully not suffocating him. She grabbed a towel off the front seat and used it to mop up the blood on the floor the best she could. The nurse in her winced at wiping up blood with her bare hands but she didn't have time to find gloves.

Rolling the bloody towel into a ball, she tossed it in back on top of the lump that was her passenger. The more stuff back there, the better he'd be hidden.

She hoped.

Caitlyn's blood pumped with excitement and adrenaline. This was just like the spy games she used to play with her brothers when she was a kid. Looking around the garage she didn't see anyone watching her but even as she tossed her purse into the passenger seat, she heard the sound of running feet coming from around the corner.

Panic churned in her gut, urging her to peel out of the lot

as fast as she could drive but Caitlyn kept her foot light on the gas pedal. She didn't want to do anything out of the ordinary. Nodding politely to the security guard on duty at the gate, she pulled out slowly and cautiously. It wasn't until she hit the straightaway that she leaned on the gas and tried to make up time in the night-darkened streets.

Her mind moved as fast as the buildings whizzing by her. She'd need a bag of IV fluid, some sutures, a probe, some antibiotics, and plenty of trauma dressings. She thought she had everything but the IV fluid and antibiotics at home. Time to call in a few favors.

With one hand on the wheel, Caitlyn reached into her purse and fumbled around, trying to find her cell phone.

"Stupid things. Why do they make them so small you can't even find them?" Upending the purse, she dumped its contents out on the seat until she found her phone.

"Don't tell anyone." Mac's voice came from the back seat, deep and raspy with pain.

"I'm just going to get some help from my brother, Jim. You remember him, don't you?"

"No one. Can't let anyone else know." She looked through the rearview mirror and could see his hand on the door handle. Caitlyn just knew he'd try to jump out if she didn't agree to keep quiet. He'd rather kill himself than let her get help.

"You aren't making this very easy." She waited for him to say something else but he remained quiet, his hand still on the door handle. Stubborn man. "Fine, I won't tell him but I still need to call him so he can get me some supplies from the clinic."

"Don't tell him." Mac's face was ghastly white in the glow of the passing streetlights.

"I'll make up something. Don't worry." What, she didn't know but she'd think of something. She needed those supplies.

Dialing Jim's cell phone while keeping her eyes on the road, she prayed he was back from his last paramedic run on the ambulance.

"O'Toole."

"Jim! I need a favor. A big favor."

"I am not taking any more shifts at the ER. The last time I worked in there I ended up with a fat lip from a drunk."

"I don't want you to work, I need your help."

"What do you need?" he asked, his voice wary.

"I need a bag of ringers and a bag of antibiotics, plus the needles, tubes, and catheters to go with them. And I need them now."

"Now?"

"Yes. Please, Jim. Do this for me and I'll put in a good word for you with Maggie." Jim had been working on getting one of the other night nurses to go out with him for weeks.

"Come on Cat, it's after midnight, can't it wait?"

"Would I be calling you if it could? And don't give me 'it's after midnight' you know you'll be up for hours still. All I'm asking is just this one tiny favor. I'll replace them. Please."

"Cripes." She could hear his heavy sigh of exasperation. "All right. Is this another one of your strays?" Caitlyn had a habit of taking care of sick and stray animals and nursing them back to health.

"Uh, you could say that."

"I can't believe I'm going to have to beg medical equipment for some stray dog that got hit or something. How big?" he asked.

"What?"

"How big a dog? I need to know how many bags of ringers to bring."

"Big, real big." Caitlyn remembered the feel of Mac's body against her side. "Probably close to two hundred pounds."

"Two hundred pounds! Hell! What did you pick up, a stray horse?"

"Just bring me the stuff. Okay?" Caitlyn risked another quick look in the rear view mirror. Mac's hand had relaxed on the door handle but he still watched her.

"Yeah, yeah, I'll do it. Meet you at your place in about fifteen. I've got to finish up this paperwork then I'm off."

"You're the best, Jimbo! Did I ever tell you I loved you best?" she teased.

"Only when you're getting your way."

Caitlyn hung up with a smile. That was one obstacle out of her way. Now, she needed to get Mac into her apartment without making a scene, find the bullet, patch him up, and pray that he survived the night. She'd worry about why she couldn't tell Tom about this in the morning.

Provided he lived that long.

Squashing the thought, she pulled into the driveway of her apartment. She'd park next to her back door and move the Jeep later.

Her hands shook as she got out and unlocked her door. She flipped on lights and pulled down shades as she went through the apartment. Once she reached the living room, she quickly unfolded the futon bed. She grabbed some old sheets and towels from the closet in the bathroom and threw them on the mattress. It wasn't a bed at the Ritz but it would do.

Rushing back outside, she took a quick look around. She didn't see anyone but it was pitch black out. She'd have to take her chances that they hadn't been followed because her patient wasn't going to be able to last much longer.

"Come on, I can't do this without your help. Just a little longer and I'll have you stretched out on the bed."

Those eyes! Those startling blue eyes looked up at her blearily, blinking and wincing at the light over the steps.

"Come on, we've got to hurry. I need you under wraps before Jim gets here. Can you walk on your own?"

"If I have to." His voice, husky and filled with determination, sent chills down her spine.

"You have to. I'll help you, it isn't far."

Again, Caitlyn was surprised by how tall he was. She wrapped her arm around his back and used her body to take as much of his weight as she could.

"You're doing great, just a few more feet and we're there. You can do it," she encouraged him as they stumbled their way through the kitchen. His face was alarmingly pale and sweat dripped from him in torrents. Jim better get here soon with those fluids or she was in deep doo doo.

Her apartment had never seemed so big as it did now that

she was trying to help him across it. Finally they made it and she was able to lower him, a bit gracelessly, to the futon. Stretching the aching muscles in her back, Caitlyn noticed the blood on her shirt. She had to get his bleeding stopped before she could do anything else.

The baggy shorts he wore came off easily, along with the enormous high-top sneakers. She cut off his basketball style shirt with her trauma sheers, and then grabbed a sheet to cover his nakedness.

Turning on another light, Caitlyn eased him over on his side so she could see his wound better. There was a huge, gaping hole to the left of his navel. Placing one of the towels against the wound to stop the bleeding, she rolled him over to see the other wound. He'd been shot in the back, probably not from close range, and it looked like the bullet went clear through. At least she wouldn't have to go looking for a chunk of metal; she'd just have to make sure nothing else was damaged.

Caitlyn grabbed another towel and pressed it against the smaller wound. She pulled on the pieces of the torn shirt that were still trapped under his large frame, until she could tie the ends in a knot. There, that should keep the towels in place for the moment.

Running to the bathroom, she pulled her mega first aid kit off the shelf. This was usually reserved for camping trips when they were deep in the woods and miles away from medical care. God, she hoped she'd restocked it after the last trip. Loosening the buckles on the bag, she hurried back to the futon.

Mac hadn't moved so much as a muscle, his face was deathly pale and his black eyelashes stood out in sharp definition on his cheekbones. She was going to do her best to make sure those eyes didn't stay closed forever.

Digging around in the huge knapsack, Caitlyn pulled out trauma dressings, her suture kit, gauze, and some peroxide. She put everything in easy reach, then cut the ties holding the towels over the wounds. Dumping peroxide over a cloth, she washed out the entrance wound, wincing at the pain it must cause him as it bubbled away the germs.

Mac's hand twitched near her as she continued to dab at the wound. Taking his wrist, she felt for his pulse. Rapid and weak, not exactly the two things she wanted to feel. Where was

Jim? She needed to get some fluids into him or all the cleaning she did would be useless.

The sudden knock on the door made her jump and she sloshed peroxide all over the towel she had on the bed. Speak of the devil. Her hands shook as she put the cap back on and ran to the door.

"Geez, Cat, you didn't even shut your car door. Do you want someone to steal it or something?"

"Sorry, I had my hands full. Do you have all the stuff?"

"Yeah, you need any help? There's blood all over you." Jim tried to look past her into the living room.

"It's his, and no, I don't need any help. He's out cold."

"He?"

Crap. She wasn't used to lying to her brother. "Yeah, you know, the stray. It's a he."

"Oh, yeah, I guess it would have to be, seeing as he's so big. Okay, I'll leave you to your duties, Dr. Doolittle." He craned his head again but she blocked his view as she took the bag of supplies from him.

"Thanks." She kissed him on the cheek and waited impatiently for him to back out of the driveway. At least he hadn't mentioned the blood soaked blanket in the back seat of the Jeep. He must either be really tired or have something to do because he gave up pretty easily. Well, she couldn't worry about that now, she'd just thank God for small favors.

And large. She was going to need all the help she could get tonight.

As soon as he was out of sight, Caitlyn slammed the door and locked it, then ran back to the living room. Mac had turned over onto his back while she was talking to Jim. Blood soaked through the towel she'd used. She'd get the IV started and then go back to work on his wounds.

He had veins like garden hoses. Man, she wished all her patients were this easy to start a line on. In two minutes flat she had the catheter in and the fluids running full speed. That should counteract the shock. Maybe. He'd lost a lot of blood.

Caitlyn focused on the gaping hole in Mac's stomach next. Using every pad and dressing she had, plus most of her towels, she managed to clean out the wound and slow down the bleeding. Thank God the bullet hadn't nicked an artery or he'd be in even bigger trouble.

As it was, without making the injury worse, she couldn't tell if anything had been damaged on the inside. The only thing she could do was hope the bullet had gone through without hitting any major organs. Stopping the bleeding was the most important thing right now. If he lost much more blood, she'd have to take him into the hospital for a transfusion. Or watch him die.

"Thank God you're out, buddy, this isn't going to feel good." Caitlyn strung her needle with the sterile thread and took a calming breath before sewing the ragged flesh back together. He didn't even flinch as the needle pierced his skin.

The wound on his back was so small she could use Steri-strips to close it. He probably wouldn't even have a mark from that one. Must have been a small caliber bullet to make such a small entrance wound.

She finished up her stitches and taped the other wound closed. Once she finished with the bullet holes, she wrapped a roll of gauze around his torso to hold everything in place. That should hold him for a few hours.

Caitlyn started the antibiotics flowing through the IV line, then sat back on her heels and wiped the sweat off her forehead with the back of her wrist. All she could do now was pray.

Standing up, Caitlyn felt the room spin. It was after three in the morning, and she'd been working since noon. It was way past time for bed. She'd put the blood soaked clothes into the wash, then lay down for a little bit.

She tried to take a step towards the washer and stumbled. The room spun dizzily around her. Maybe she'd do the wash later and just take a little nap right here on the futon next to Mac. She'd wake up in a few minutes.

ℬ

Hot, why was it so hot? Caitlyn tried to kick off the covers and realized she didn't have any on. Was the air conditioner off again? Groggily opening one eye, she looked for the clock on the side of her bed. It wasn't there. Or more precisely, she wasn't on her bed.

And she wasn't alone.

She was pressed up against a very hot, very male body in the middle of her living room. Trying to kick her caffeine-deprived brain into gear, Caitlyn forced herself to remember why there was a drop dead sexy, naked, man in bed with her. And why did she still have her work clothes on?

Work. Oh, hell. This wasn't a man, this was Mac. Okay, so he was a man but not in the real sense of the word. He was a patient.

Shaking her head to clear the confusion, Caitlyn jumped off the futon and ran over to the lamp where she had strung the IV bag. It was down to its last two cc's of fluid. Time to switch bags.

How long had she slept? Looking at the clock on the mantle, she figured she'd been asleep two hours. Caitlyn tried to calculate the rate of flow from the bag but couldn't do the math without coffee in her system. It seemed about right for a man with a hole in his stomach. She'd do a chart later to keep things straight.

After switching the IV fluids, Caitlyn felt his pulse again. Heat rolled off him in waves and he was still ghostly pale but his pulse felt steadier. His body fought off the infection by raising his temperature. She'd let it do its work for now but if his fever got much higher, she'd have to intervene. The next twenty-four hours would decide whether he lived or died.

A chill chased its way down her back. How could someone normally so full of life have it snuffed out in seconds?

Caitlyn tried to remember the last time she saw Mac. Tom had been home from Washington D.C. on vacation at Christmas. He'd started working with Mac shortly before that. He was from somewhere up north, Maine maybe?

Tom had gotten a call after Christmas dinner, and the next thing she knew, he was packing his bags. Mac was driving down and would pick him up on his way back to Washington. Caitlyn had only seen her brother's new partner for half an hour or so while he stopped and visited before they were on their way. If it weren't for his eyes, she probably wouldn't have recognized him at all.

Brushing her hand over his forehead, she let her fingertips drift down over his razor sharp cheekbones. His face was all angles and planes with intense eyes that grabbed her attention immediately. Those sky blue orbs seemed to take in everything around him, process all the data and file it away without giving away a hint of what he was thinking.

Jim and her other brother, Liam, had picked on her mercilessly about mooning over Tom's partner. She'd brushed them off with some well-placed insults but the truth was he had made a definite impression on her. An impression that hadn't waned in the ensuing months.

Midnight black hair and light blue eyes were a striking enough combination but paired with an angular face and fabulous body, well, she had no trouble remembering him six months later. Even with a scrubby growth of beard darkening his jaw and skin pale from his adventures, he still looked good enough to grace the cover of a magazine.

Caitlyn's gaze drifted over the muscular frame revealed by the sheet that grazed his hips with only the barest hint of propriety. Corded muscles bulged in his arms, his chest, and across his stomach. Dark hair liberally covered his arms and chest, trailing down to a thin line leading from his navel to—

What was she thinking? This man had come to her for help, trusting her to save his life, and she was ogling his unconscious body! That wasn't exactly something they taught her in nursing school.

Shaking off her irrational thoughts, she checked the rate on the IV fluids again. Must be the lack of sleep getting to her. It was normal to notice his body, she was human after all but becoming fixated on it probably wasn't a good idea.

Still, she'd better get away from temptation. Bending over, she scooped up the bloody towels and used dressings. As she walked to the bathroom, she stripped off her soiled uniform and threw it into the washer with the bloody towels.

She disposed of the dressings before casting a weary look towards the futon. Making sure Mac was still asleep, Caitlyn hustled to her room in just her bra and panties. He might be out of it but she didn't feel comfortable prancing around half naked in front of a strange man.

Especially this strange man. If her brothers found out, she'd have hell to pay.

Collecting a clean tank top and some boxer shorts, Caitlyn wrapped her robe around her and headed back to the bathroom to take a shower. Her brain was starting to kick into gear and questions were running around in her head like a hamster on a wheel.

What did she know about Mac? Not much. Why didn't he want Tom to be called? And what was he doing on assignment in Connecticut anyway? He and Tom worked in D.C. Or at least they had the last time she spoke to Tom.

She'd talk to Jim and Liam when she could function well enough not to slip up. Turning the water on as hot as she could stand it, Caitlyn stepped under the stinging needles and willed her brain to work again. There was something major happening here. She had a feeling she was going to need all her wits about her to figure it out.

Stepping out of the shower, she peeked out the window. The sun was starting to break over the horizon and she still had to clean up the mess from her impromptu surgery, put the wet clothes into the dryer, and move her Jeep so her neighbors could get out of the driveway when they left for work in a few hours. She was never going to get any sleep.

She slipped into clean pajamas, and combed out her dripping wet hair. One last check on Mac showed him to be resting quietly. He was going to have to go to the bathroom when he woke up but he should be all right for a couple hours.

She had so many questions, and wouldn't be able to get any answers for a while. Liam was working days this week, so she'd have to wait for him to get home tonight before she could call him. Jim would be sleeping, and she couldn't call Tom. That didn't leave her many options at five in the morning. She should get some sleep. Mac was going to need a lot of help when he woke up, if he woke up.

Stop thinking like that. He would wake up, and when he did, he was going to need a whole bunch of things. She'd need to get him some pants, loose shirts, and boxer shorts. Eventually he'd want to eat something, so she should go grocery shopping. It was on her list of things to do anyway since she'd eaten her last carton of yogurt for breakfast yesterday.

Thinking of practical things helped ease the worry all the unknowns gave her. One thing at a time, she could only do one thing at a time. And right now, she needed sleep more than anything else.

Chapter Two

Mac woke feeling as if something had crawled up and died in his mouth. His tongue stuck to the roof of his mouth like it had dried onto it, and he had a desperate thirst. Opening his eyes, he looked at his surroundings and remembered nothing.

Where the hell was he? Rolling to his side caused stabbing pains to shoot through his abdomen, taking his breath with the force of it. That's right, he'd been shot.

It was coming back to him now. He'd been walking through the park on his way back to the apartment. It should have been safe enough, or so he'd thought.

Mac had been headed for the place he shared with several other gang members when he'd felt fire burning in his back, then an explosion of pain in his gut. He'd looked down to see blood blooming through a hole in his stomach.

Not knowing if his cover was blown or if it was just a random act of violence that had become so prevalent in the city, Mac had taken off looking for shelter so he could evaluate the seriousness of his injuries. He'd headed towards the nearest parking garage, hoping he wasn't leaving a trail of blood to mark his path. The shot had been more serious than he had thought because he had felt his legs getting weak and his eyesight had gotten blurry. Seeing a familiar SUV parked in the shadows, he'd rolled under it. He'd barely managed to dig his badge out of the hiding place in the sole of his shoe before he'd passed out.

It was just dumb luck that he managed to find Caitlyn's Jeep. Tom's very pretty sister, who happened to be an emergency room nurse. He'd headed towards the hospital garage because it was close and he'd hoped he could find someone to help him on the down low. Tom had mentioned Caitlyn worked nights but it was a one in a million chance he'd find her Jeep when he needed her most.

He vaguely remembered the ride to her place, or at least he assumed it was her place. Taking a better look around, he noticed an IV strung to his arm and clean sheets over his body. The bed he was on was small and hard. His feet hung over the edge and his head was at the very top. *Must be one of those futon things, cheap and practical as it turned into a couch too. The room was dim, with light peeking in from behind drawn shades. What time was it anyway?*

He searched the room for a clock and noticed one on the mantle of a bricked up fireplace across from him. Seven o'clock, but a.m. or p.m.? It was bright outside, but that was no clue. It stayed light out until eight or nine this time of year. Mac tried to turn again and get a better look, but stabbing pains halted him in his tracks. He wasn't going anywhere for quite some time.

There was a funky looking lamp on the table next to him. It looked like a mermaid with her arms out, one of which held the IV bag that dripped into his arm. He pushed the thought of an IV in his arm out of his head. Man, but he hated needles. There was a picture on the table in a seashell-crusted frame which showed Tom, his two brothers, and his sister Caitlyn laughing on a beach somewhere.

Looked like this was her place all right. Now the question was, had she called Tom or not? And where was she anyway? He could turn his head without too much pain at least, and as he did, his nose brushed the soft cotton of the pillow and the scent of baby powder drifted into his nostrils.

Lifting the sheet, he inspected his injury. A neat strip of gauze wrapped around his body, covering a thick pad over his wound. Nothing covered the rest of him.

How'd she manage to get his clothes off? Did she have help? Damn, he wished he could remember something. If he was going to get undressed by a beautiful woman, he wanted to remember it.

And man, was she ever beautiful.

Mac looked at her picture again. Long brown hair blew in

the breeze from the ocean. Her tanned body was displayed nicely in her cut off shorts and bathing suit top. Laughing brown eyes the color of his favorite whisky twinkled from the picture like she found the whole thing funny. High cheekbones and a narrow nose gave her an elegant look. Her mouth was full with generous lips and a dazzling smile. Yup, she had the whole package.

And that package included three older brothers, one of whom was his partner, who wouldn't hesitate to pull his guts out with hot prongs if he so much as looked at her cross-wise. The one and only time he'd asked Tom about her, his partner had let him know in no uncertain terms that she was off limits. There'd be no trifling with the youngest O'Toole, or there'd be hell to pay.

Too bad he'd put her life in danger just by crawling under her Jeep.

He had to get out of here, had to find some place to hole up in until he recovered and could do some damage control. He needed to find out what was going on in the city and there was no way he could do that if it meant putting Caitlyn O'Toole's life in danger.

Getting out of here could be a problem, seeing as he was as weak as a newborn kitten and buck-naked. He couldn't even get out of the bed, forget out of the apartment. There was nothing he could do the day after taking a bullet, and if memory served, tomorrow would be even worse. If he could lie low for a few days, he might be able to get out of here without passing out from pain. It wasn't like he had much choice in the matter at this point.

"Oh good, you're up."

Mac jumped at the sleep filled voice coming from behind him. Caitlyn moved in front of him and looked into his eyes. She wore a white tank top and palm tree covered boxer shorts. Her miles and miles of legs were shown off to an advantage that he wasn't too hurt to appreciate.

"Yeah, I just woke up." She didn't have to know how up he really was. The tight shirt outlined her nipples, and if it weren't so dry, his mouth would have watered at the sight.

"I'll bet you're thirsty. The IV will help to keep you hydrated, but your mouth has to feel pretty sticky."

"You could say that."

"Let's try some ice chips first, and we'll work our way up to clear liquids from there. Until I know how much damage that bullet did, I can't risk anything else."

"You're the expert. You, ah, wouldn't happen to have a spare toothbrush though, would you?" At this point he'd have to chew razor blades to get the nasty taste out of his mouth.

"I might have one around somewhere. Let me get you the ice chips then I'll go hunt it up for you." She brushed her fingers against his cheek and walked towards what he thought was the kitchen.

Her shorts just barely covered her butt and he stared unashamedly. He was in too much pain to do anything more than look, but he'd have to be dead not to enjoy the sight.

Caitlyn came striding back into the room, her strides eating up the floor as she moved. She held a plastic cup with a local pub's logo on the side, and thank the Lord, a toothbrush, toothpaste and a little basin.

"Here, chew on this for a little while." She gave him a spoonful of ice chips. "When you have a little moisture in your mouth, I'll help you brush your teeth."

"Uh, thanks. I think I can handle it though." He'd brush his own damn teeth.

"Ever brush your teeth lying on your back before?"

"I can sit up." Maybe. She had a very smug grin on her face.

"Go ahead and try, let me know when the stitches start to pull."

Those laughing eyes weren't so damn attractive when they were laughing at him. Mac rolled the few remaining chunks of ice in his mouth, then braced himself to sit up.

Flaming arrows of pain shot through his body as he moved his stomach muscles. His skin stretched and pulled with every movement. He probably hadn't moved an inch before the pain got to be too much and he fell back in defeat.

"If you turn your head to the side, I can help you get that taste out of your mouth without you choking on spit."

He was surprised that she didn't say, "I told you so." She

efficiently brushed his teeth and wiped his mouth. Having his teeth brushed like a two year old wasn't something he wanted repeated in this lifetime, but he had to admit having that decaying taste out of his mouth was worth a little slap to his pride.

"If you're up to it, I have a few questions I'd like answered."

Mac considered faking unconsciousness for a minute, but knew he'd have to answer some of her questions eventually. "I'll tell you what I can without compromising your safety or the success of the assignment." There, that should give him some room to tap dance around the truth a bit.

"I know that. I have a brother in the police department and one in the FBI. I know all about 'need to know'. What I want to know is why can't I call Tom?"

How much to tell her? There was a lot at stake here but if he lied outright, she could easily get caught in the middle of a situation he was in no shape to get her out of.

"Tom and I aren't on this case together." That much was true. "If you call Tom and start asking questions, my location could get picked up by the wrong people."

"Tom would never reveal your location."

"He wouldn't but that doesn't mean the people after me can't find out if you call. A twenty dollar police scanner can pick up most cell phone conversations."

"Okay. I'll give you that one. Do you know who shot you?" Her eyes were focused on his, and he worried she could read through his carefully constructed half-truths. He had to make sure she didn't.

"No. I was in the park and thought I was alone. It could have been a drive-by, or it could mean my cover is blown. Until I know for sure, I'm going to act like I'm busted."

"Better safe than sorry. Okay, how did you know it was my Jeep? I've only met you that one time."

Mac laughed a bit, until his stomach hurt and reminded him that wasn't a good idea. "Pure, blind luck. I knew you worked nights there but I was just looking for a secure place to hide until I could get my strength back and find shelter."

"Talk about lucky. You get shot in the back, manage to avoid getting any major organs hit, and find your partner's sister. You must have been born under a good star, Mr. McDougal."

"Under the circumstances, I think you can call me Mac. Normally when I get naked with a woman, she calls me by my first name."

Her laugh was boisterous and full of life. "I hope you normally aren't bleeding that badly when you share a bed with a woman."

"Share a bed?" He watched a blush color her cheeks.

"Yeah, I ah, fell asleep beside you for a little while after you were all stitched up."

"Sorry I missed it. Naked and in bed with a beautiful woman and I slept through the whole thing." Her blush deepened and she moved to check his IV. She obviously wasn't used to getting compliments. He'd have to talk to Tom about that. Damn, he had to get his mind back on the problems in front of him and off the *woman* in front of him.

"It's a good thing Jim was working at the clinic last night too, or I don't know how I'd have been able to get the IV fluids and antibiotics."

"You didn't tell him about me, did you?" His voice was sharper than he wanted.

"No, I told him it was for a stray. I didn't say stray what."

"A stray? Like in dog?"

"Yeah, when I see a hurt animal, I just can't help myself. I try to fix him up the best I can, then let him go. I've been doing it since I was a little kid. I guess that's how I knew I wanted to be a nurse."

"So your brother brought you medical supplies in the middle of the night for a stray animal? And didn't ask any questions?" Mac asked in disbelief.

"No, he didn't. He's done it before. I always pay him back or replace the supplies."

"Then why go to him in the first place?"

"Because it was after midnight and there wasn't a convenient pharmacy open. He could get the supplies from the clinic where he works part-time per diem a lot easier than I could have that late at night."

"What are you doing up north anyway? I thought you worked out of DC?"

"That's one of those things I can't answer."

"Figures." She fiddled with the IV a bit. "Okay, this bag looks like it's almost done. Why don't you relax while I switch it and check your dressings? If things look okay, I'm going to want you to try to walk a little bit tonight. It'll help keep things moving."

"Yeah, I know the drill." And he wasn't looking forward to it either.

"You've been shot before?" She looked up from the IV bag and met his gaze, giving him another one of those jolts.

"Unfortunately."

"Where? I didn't see any scars when I was treating you." She blushed again.

He wondered how much of his body she'd been looking at. "Ah, in my thigh. I got hit in the femur and was out of commission for months."

"Were you hit in the femoral artery?" She calmly and competently, checked his pulse and adjusted the lines running into his arm.

"Yeah, I got caught in the middle of a hostage situation. It wasn't pretty."

"I can imagine. You're lucky you didn't bleed to death."

"Well, I seem to always get shot near hospitals."

"You were talking someone down with a hostage near a hospital?"

"Ah, no, I was the hostage, in the hospital. Ouch!" Caitlyn squeezed his arm so tightly her nails dug into his skin.

"Oh, sorry. I'm just trying to picture someone holding you hostage at a hospital."

"It's old news." News he had no intention of rehashing if he could avoid it. Dealing with a strung out junkie with a gun was part of the reason he'd left hostage negotiations and went into undercover work. He didn't like talking about his past or his reasons for changing jobs. Or what it was like to face down a fifteen-year-old going through withdrawal, holding a gun in his shaking hands.

"Still, that's scary stuff." She looked into his eyes briefly, then looked away. "Okay, I gave you a new bag of antibiotics, so you should be all set for a while. I need to run out and get some stuff. Are you going to be all right if I leave you alone for an hour?"

"I should be fine. It's not like I'm going anywhere." Just thinking about walking made him wince.

"I don't like leaving you by yourself but if I don't go out we won't have anything to eat. You made it through the night, which is something, so I think you'll be okay for a little while."

"I'm sure I'll be fine. Just leave me a phone in case I need to call you."

"No problem, I have my cell. I'll leave the number for you by the cordless phone."

"Ah, do you have something other than a cordless? They aren't exactly secure." Neither were landlines but at least some guy couldn't pick them up with a scanner in his car.

"That's right. Tom's always telling me that. I have a regular phone in my bedroom. I'll drag it out here and plug it in."

"Thanks." If he had his own cell phone with its built-in scrambler, it wouldn't be a problem but that had been lost somewhere along the way. Probably when he was stumbling around after he was shot. He was lucky he'd been able to produce his badge or Caitlyn never would have stopped for him.

Hell, he was surprised a blood-covered badge was even enough to keep her from calling 9-1-1 the second he called out to her. That was one thing Tom hadn't exaggerated when he spoke of his sister, she didn't rattle easily.

Mac waited for Caitlyn to get changed and fought down his reaction to the thought of her undressing one thin wall away. Feigning sleep, he waited until he heard the sound of her Jeep backing out of the driveway and counted to one hundred, slowly.

When he was reasonably sure she wasn't going to be coming back into the apartment, he grabbed the phone and began dialing an elaborate series of numbers that would put him in touch with his boss in Washington D.C.. It was time to start doing some damage control.

෨

That man was hiding something, and it wasn't just to protect her. Caitlyn tore through the grocery store, trying to get as many things as she could in as short a time as possible. She'd already used up half an hour at Wal-Mart buying sweats, boxers, pajamas, and some more bandages and gauze to re-stock her depleted supply. If she actually made it back to the apartment and Mac in the hour she had allotted herself, it would be a miracle.

The fact that Mac was awake and alive this morning was miraculous in and of itself. His condition was far from stable but looked very promising. The fever was down and his wound looked a little better. She wouldn't know for sure that he was out of the worst of it for another twenty-four hours.

Caitlyn wondered about the other bullet he had taken while she waited in the checkout line. What was an FBI agent doing as a hostage? And in a hospital no less. She might have to do some research on the web to find out about that. It didn't look like Mac was going to be very forthcoming with information. The "No Trespassing" sign he had thrown up when she asked him about it came out loud and clear.

Caitlyn paid for her groceries and loaded them into the Jeep. Swinging out into traffic, she checked her rearview mirror to see if she was being followed. It might seem paranoid but Mac had gotten to her with all his secret agent talk. It never hurt to be a little careful, or to take a different route home for a change.

At the next red light, Caitlyn checked her mirror again. It wasn't illogical that the same Honda that was in the grocery store parking lot was headed in the same direction but just in case she'd take a turn around the block. She wasn't being completely paranoid, just safe. Right?

The Honda followed her. Okay, it still wasn't out of the realm of possibility that he was going this way too, no need to be concerned. She took the next right turn without signaling and went down a residential street, looking in her rearview mirror as much as she could without driving into a telephone pole.

Brakes squealed as the Honda took the corner practically on two wheels.

Now it was time to be concerned.

Turning out of the neighborhood, Caitlyn circled around and headed for the highway. She could lose them in the maze of intersecting highways and then double back to go home. Gunning the engine, she took the on-ramp like it was the Daytona 500.

Traffic was light, which made for good maneuverability but lowered her chances of getting away. The Jeep wasn't exactly built for high-speed car chases. Another check of the rearview mirror showed her followers getting on the highway behind her. Caitlyn pushed the Jeep even faster to dart around a tractor-trailer, then pulled over a lane to hide along side of it.

The truck cut off all her visibility. Hopefully if she couldn't see them they couldn't see her either. She ignored the voice in the back of her head that told her she was acting like a two year old with her eyes closed in the middle of the room saying "you can't see me!"

The Honda hadn't pulled out on the other side of the truck yet and Caitlyn was in an exit only lane. If she took the exit and the tail hadn't passed her, they would just follow her again. But, if she waited much longer she'd either have to switch lanes in a hurry or take the exit and take her chances.

The green highway sign indicated the exit was in a quarter mile. Where was the car? She bit her lip in worry. Should she take the exit or not? Caitlyn took her foot off the gas pedal, slowing down to pull behind the truck when a blur of red flew by the truck's front bumper. The Honda! They'd passed her and didn't even know it.

Slowing down even more, Caitlyn exited and took the back roads to her apartment. She was way past the hour she had told Mac she'd be gone but at least she'd get home without being tailed.

How could they know it was her Jeep Mac had hidden under? It wasn't like they had assigned parking spaces and she didn't park in the same spot every night either. Something must have tipped them off. Whoever they were.

She probably should keep this little adventure to herself. If

Mac was anything like her brothers, the minute she told him of it he would insist on leaving to keep her out of danger, and right now he had no place to go. Why that thought made her feel so sad, she didn't know.

Chapter Three

He had no place to go. Mac's bladder was filled to bursting and there was no way he could get out of bed to relieve it. He didn't want to wet the bed but he was getting desperate. The sound of a vehicle in the driveway gave him hope that Caitlyn was home. God, let that be her, because the last thing he wanted to do was piss his non-existent pants.

A key jangled in the lock and Caitlyn breezed through the door loaded down with bags.

"Sorry I'm late. You wouldn't believe the traffic. How are you feeling?"

"Ah, okay, but can you help me to the bathroom?"

"Oh my. You've had three bags of fluids. I bet you're about ready to explode. I don't think it's a good idea for you to walk to the bathroom but I'll get something for you to go in. Hold on a minute." Caitlyn ran back out the door.

Mac wasn't sure he'd last a minute. It was a fight but he managed to hold on long enough for Caitlyn to run back into the apartment with a milk jug. She cut off the top and handed it to him.

"This should work," she said. "Do you need any help?"

"No. I think I can handle this, really." There was no way he was going to let her help him pee too. It was bad enough having her brush his teeth. Helping him take a piss was not going to happen.

"I'll take your word for it then." She politely turned her back while he did his business. When he was finished, she took the nearly full jug away from him without looking him in the eye. What did she have to be embarrassed about? He was the one peeing into a milk jug, not her.

"If I had known I was setting up a clinic in my living room, I'd have brought home a bed pan and a urinal from work."

"That's quite all right. This works for now."

"Good thing I recycle, otherwise you would have been peeing into a soda can." She gave him a laugh, then headed to the bathroom.

"Did you get all your shopping done?" Mac watched her carry some blue plastic bags into the room. Man, she filled out a pair of shorts like nobody's business. She filled out the shirt pretty damn good too. He shook his head to get those thoughts out of it. Tom would rip his head off if he knew what Mac was thinking.

"I sure did. Good thing for you you're the same size as Jim. I got you some sweats, some pajamas, and some boxers."

"I'll pay you back when this is all over."

Caitlyn looked up from where she was pulling things out of a bag and frowned at him. "I'm not worried about you owing me money, I'm just glad you're alive."

"Still, I pay my debts."

"Fine, take me out to dinner when you've recovered and we'll call it even. Now I better put those groceries away before they all melt. It's hot as an oven outside."

Mac thought about how he'd like to take her to dinner and then some but it wouldn't be because of any debt. Watching her move around the kitchen was like watching a domestic ballet. She seemed to flow from cabinet to cabinet rather than walk. She'd disappear from his line of vision occasionally, then come back with her arms full of groceries again.

She walked back into the room carrying a large bowl and some washcloths.

"What are those for?" he asked suspiciously.

"I thought I'd dust the room. What do you think they're for? I'm going to clean you up a bit then give you some more fluids." She said it so professionally, he could've almost believed she looked at him as just another patient if it wasn't for the blush staining her cheeks.

There was no way he was going to let her wash his naked body unless he could return the favor. "I'm all right, really."

"No, you're not. You have dried blood, sweat, and gravel stuck to you. Don't worry, I'm a nurse. I do this for a living."

"I know you're a professional, it's just—different."

"I'm sure you were given a sponge bath the last time you were shot." She poured some baby soap onto a wet cloth and lifted his arm to begin cleaning him.

His last nurse had been a battle-axe and certainly hadn't turned him on when she cleaned him up. "Yeah, but ah, she wasn't my best friend's sister." A fact he'd better keep firmly in mind.

"What does that have to do with anything? I'm still a nurse. A very competent one if I do say so myself."

"Yeah, but—"

"No buts. I promise I won't tell Tom that I saw you naked if you don't. It'll be our little secret." Her eyes twinkled at him over reddened cheeks. "Seems we have quite a few of them now."

She was fishing, he knew it. Too bad. She'd just have to understand that it was for her safety that he wasn't saying anything. "So, did you have any trouble while you were out?"

Mac felt her stiffen for the barest fraction of a second, then move on to wash his other arm.

"Caitlyn, did you have any trouble?" He looked her in the eye.

"Nothing to talk about."

"What's that supposed to mean?" She was evading. What the hell had happened?

"It means what it means. There was no trouble worth talking about. Now hold still so I can scrub off some of this dried blood. It isn't going to feel very good while I'm doing it, but at least you won't be sticky and itchy later."

The shock of her warm hands on his lower abdomen was enough to shut him up. At least for now. He'd find out what trouble she'd had later.

෮

Caitlyn tried to pretend that Mac was just another patient. She'd given hundreds of sponge baths when she worked on the Medical floor. Of course none of her patients looked anything like Mac, and none of them were naked in her living room either.

Washing carefully around the gauze that was wrapped around his waist, Caitlyn tried to focus on keeping the bandages dry instead of on his washboard stomach and the tantalizing trail of black hair that arrowed between those muscles. Her hands seemed to fumble more than usual, and her head felt light from the contact.

Her body's response should have reassured her that she was a healthy, breathing female. A woman would have to be ten days in the ground not to respond to a man like Mac.

Especially a naked Mac.

Right next to her, with an erection.

Whoa Nelly! She needed to get away and get away fast. "I think that's clean enough for now. I'll do the rest when you're not so up- ah sore. Why don't you get some rest? I'll make up some broth for you to have after you wake up."

"Yeah, I am feeling kind of tired. Thanks for the bath." He wouldn't look her in the eye. Probably a good thing.

He seemed as relieved to end the torture as she did. Still, it hadn't been all that bad, touching those glorious muscles and tight skin. Warmth she hadn't experienced in a while started to form in her belly and spread out, bringing a flush to her face.

"Ah, no problem. I have some work to do on my laptop. I'll, ah, take it into the kitchen so I don't bother you. Just shout if you need anything." *For God's sake, get out of here before you make a complete fool of yourself! You're practically drooling.* She scooped up the wet cloths and bowl and dumped them in the bathroom sink.

Keeping her gaze firmly away from Mac, Caitlyn scurried to the kitchen, hoping she didn't look as idiotic as she felt. Running her hands under cold water, she splashed some on her face as well. As hot as she felt, she was surprised it didn't turn to steam on contact. It had been a long time since she felt this flustered.

Long time? Heck, she'd never felt like this before. Caitlyn shook off the weird feelings and dried her hands. She grabbed her laptop out of her briefcase by the door and clutched a handful of cords that were tangled up in the pocket.

Plugging the laptop in and setting it on the table, Caitlyn snagged a soda while she waited for the computer to boot up. Someday she'd get a good computer, and a DSL line too for that matter. It took forever for the modem to connect.

Finally. Now, where to look? A web search of "hostages" turned up over a hundred thousand hits, scratch that idea. *Okay, think O'Toole, think.* A hostage situation in a hospital would be big news. She should be able to find information about it in the archives of any newspaper.

Typing in USA Today, Caitlyn searched the site for its archives from two years ago. She scanned through the by-lines looking for anything that had to do with hostages or hospitals until her eyes were about to cross. The thought of giving up the search and just playing Solitaire instead was very tempting, and Caitlyn almost gave in when a bold headline caught her attention:

HOSTAGE NEGOTIATOR WOUNDED WHILE PROTECTING INFANTS.

Caitlyn pulled up the article and enlarged the screen so she could read the small blurb.

FBI agent and negotiator Devlin McDougal was critically shot in the course of a hostage situation at St. Luke's hospital late last night. A youth being treated for drug addiction broke into the maternity ward brandishing a gun stolen from one of the hospital's security guards. McDougal successfully negotiated the release of five nurses and ten newborn infants but was shot in the thigh during a struggle for the weapon. The assailant was fatally shot. Agent McDougal remains in critical condition.

Ten newborns. Mac hadn't mentioned that, only that he had been shot while being a hostage in a hospital. He'd saved ten babies and five nurses and acted like it was nothing. Caitlyn knew that her brothers wouldn't brag about their achievements, but modesty wouldn't stop them from mentioning them either. She looked for any other articles on the shooting but didn't see anything.

Entering his name into the search box, she scanned the articles for something else about Mac, but came up empty. Shouldn't there be some sort of follow up? It wasn't every day that a man got shot saving babies. Hell this should have been made into a TV movie. *Nada.* It was like Mac disappeared after he entered the hospital.

Pushing herself away from the table, Caitlyn took a long drink of her soda and tried to figure out the puzzle that was Mac. *Here's a guy who works as a hostage negotiator, who apparently does a good job, and then drops off the radar only to turn up a few years later working undercover in Connecticut.*

She needed to walk. Caitlyn always thought better when she moved, and being stuck in the kitchen while a mouth watering man dozed not fifteen feet away didn't help her powers of concentration much.

Peeking into the living room, Caitlyn made sure Mac was really sleeping before she left. Keys in hand, she locked the door behind her and went out into the humid air. The heat almost discouraged her from walking to straighten out her thoughts but there was no way she'd be able to pace quietly enough not to disturb Mac.

A quick look around didn't reveal anything out of the ordinary, so she took off at a half jog. *Okay, let's get all the pieces lined up. Mac used to be a hostage negotiator for the FBI and was shot in the line of duty. The man that took him hostage was also shot but he died.*

Not a man, a kid. The article hadn't released the age but did call him a youth. And he was in the hospital for detox. Could Mac be working on a drug bust? That would make sense. The neighborhood where the hospital was located wasn't the best, and Caitlyn had more than enough reason to know that there were plenty of drugs going around in Hartford. A night rarely went by when they didn't have at least one overdose or someone coming in with severe withdrawal symptoms.

Mac said he was in deep cover. If he were out to take down the drug dealers, he'd have to be extremely careful about his cover. Liam had told her enough to know that the drug dealers the local police force could catch were only the small fish. Maybe Mac was out to catch the shark?

Until he told her otherwise, that was a good enough working theory. If she'd been involved in the same situation, she'd want to go after the drug dealers too. It was probably a good thing she was a nurse and not a cop.

Stepping into the air-conditioned coolness of the corner market, Caitlyn smiled at the girl behind the register and went in search of a bottle of water. Luckily she had stuffed the change from her grocery shopping in her shorts. She was desperately thirsty and hadn't thought to bring her purse. As Caitlyn waited for the girl to ring up her measly two dollar sale, a flash of color out the window over the sales girl's shoulder caught her attention.

The red Honda!

Don't get paranoid, O'Toole. There were hundreds of red Hondas in the city. There was no reason whatsoever to get all freaked out because one was in her neighborhood.

Driving slowly.

Like they were searching for something. Or someone.

Caitlyn bent down as if she were tying her shoes and counted to twenty until she thought the car would be gone. She was about to stand up again when she heard horns blaring and the sound of tires squealing.

"Stupid dudes thinking they're in a racecar or something." The cashier rolled her eyes and snapped her gum for emphasis. "That will be two dollars and eleven cents, ma'am."

"Thanks." Caitlyn handed her the money and moved behind the cover of the lottery machine where she could see out the window without being seen. No sign of any red Honda, but she'd head home in the opposite direction just in case.

She'd have to tell Mac about this now. Being followed once could be any garden-variety weirdo, but two sightings were downright fishy. Caitlyn stuffed the coins and receipt into her pocket and headed back out into the heat of the day. Shading her eyes, she searched again for the red car. The coast looked clear but she'd hustle her butt home anyway.

Caitlyn practiced the best way to tell Mac she thought someone was following her without appearing paranoid. Before she told him anything, though, she'd have to marshal some arguments. He'd want to leave, and there was no way he'd survive on the run.

There had to be some way to convince him that she could not only take care of herself, she could take care of him too.

Fat chance of that happening.

She'd have better luck drugging him into submission until he recovered. She'd yet to convince her brothers that she could take care of herself. She didn't stand a chance convincing her brother's best friend.

Drugging him senseless looked better all the time. Nope, that wouldn't work, she didn't have strong enough painkillers handy. And if they had to move in a hurry, she'd never be able to lift his unconscious body. She'd just have to force him to see reason, and if that didn't work, she'd withhold his clothes.

The image of Mac wrapped in one of her flower sheets running down the street popped into her mind and set her giggling.

Not that she'd mind seeing him in nothing but a sheet again. Or nothing at all.

In all her years of nursing, she'd never had such a problem keeping her emotions in check. She'd had plenty of good-looking patients over the last five years, but she'd always been able to compartmentalize that aspect of the patients and focus on their injuries. Never had the surge of attraction hit her with such force before.

Maybe it was because she'd met Mac before and felt attracted to him? Or maybe it was because it wasn't a hospital setting? Hell, she didn't know why her professionalism deserted her. All she knew was being near Mac made her pulse race regardless of whether she was treating him as a patient or as a man.

Before she could figure out how to ice down her hormones she'd arrived back at her apartment. The old house didn't look like much from the outside but it had charm. Not to mention it was rent controlled.

Unlocking the door and stepping into her kitchen, Caitlyn locked the door behind her and tossed the keys onto the table. Her eyes were still adjusting to the dimness of the apartment after the brightness outside when she went in to check on Mac.

He wasn't there.

Caitlyn rubbed her eyes and blinked a few times. Where could he have gone? He had more stitches in him than her grandmother's quilt. What was he thinking?

As she reached for the phone to call Liam to get his help tracking a half naked man, she saw a foot twitch under the futon. Mac? How could he fit under there? It looked scarcely a foot off the ground.

Better question, why was he hiding under there?

"Mac?"

"Caitlyn, is that you?"

"Who else would it be?"

"How about you help me out from under here and I'll explain?" His voice was muffled but not enough for her to miss the pain in it.

"Hold on, I'll fold up the futon a little so I can get you out easier."

"Thank God. I really didn't want to have to slide out from under here."

Caitlyn folded the futon back and lifted it away so Mac would have room to move. She tried not to look at the naked butt cheek peeking out from the sheet but couldn't seem to help herself. A rear end like that should be bronzed.

It wasn't until she saw the bright red splotches of blood leaking through the bandages that she managed to stop staring at Mac's behind.

"Hold on, let me help you, you're popping your stitches."

"I'm fine. Really." Mac's voice was ragged with pain.

"Shut up. You can be a hero next time. Right now you're ruining all my handiwork, getting blood on my floor and about to lose the IV."

Squatting next to him, Caitlyn got a good hold on the sheet he'd partially wrapped around him and pulled him across the smooth hardwood floor. When he was out of the way, she unfolded the futon again.

"Now, do you want to tell me what you were doing hiding under the bed?"

"Someone was poking around, trying the windows and fiddling with the lock on the back door. I couldn't move very well, so I rolled off the bed and wormed my way under it."

"Busting open stitches along the way. I made sure all the safety locks were on the windows and I locked the dead bolt before I left."

"How was I supposed to know that? The last I knew you were in the kitchen. I woke up when I heard someone at the bathroom window and you were nowhere to be seen."

"I took a walk. I had some thinking to do and I didn't want to wake you up while I paced. I only went down to the corner and back. I was gone ten minutes, tops."

"Did you see anyone on your way out?" The urgency in his voice sent a shiver down her spine. She had to tell him about the car now.

"Not exactly."

"What does that mean?"

"Well, earlier today when I was out shopping, I noticed a red Honda following me, so I hopped onto the highway and ditched him. Just now I could have sworn I saw the same car driving down the street."

"Shit. Why didn't you tell me before? I've got to get out of here before I put you in even more danger." Mac tried to push up off the floor but his arms shook with the strain and he couldn't get his feet under him before he collapsed.

"That's exactly why I didn't tell you. You're in no condition to run out on your own."

"I'll manage." His sky blue eyes were defiant.

"How? Please tell me how you are going to go running around chasing bad guys with a hole in your gut and an IV dripping from your arm? Do you want gangrene? If you take that IV out and stop the flow of antibiotics, that's what will happen. Those stitches can't come out for three weeks and it's going to take at least that long for you to begin to recover your strength."

"Tom will never forgive me if I put you in danger. Any more danger. You don't know what these people are like. They won't ask how much you know, they'll just assume it's too much and kill you."

"Then it really doesn't matter if you leave now or not, they'll kill me regardless. And let me handle Tom. I'm a big girl. He isn't in charge of me, my decisions, or my safety."

"You don't understand—"

"No, you don't understand. You aren't going anywhere and it's time you realized it. I'm going to roll you onto your back and help you get onto the bed. Don't pull away from me, I don't want you to rip any more stitches."

He grumbled something incoherently but did as she asked. Caitlyn tried not to think about how much pain he must be in right now. Rolling off the futon would have been painful enough but the effort it took to get himself under the bed had to have been excruciating. Once she got him back on the bed she peeled the gauze back to check the stitches.

"Well, you only pulled them, you didn't rip them out so I guess I can forgive you. But just this once. Don't do it again."

"Yes, ma'am," he said with a weak smile.

"That's the second time today I've been ma'amed. Do I really look old enough to be a ma'am?"

"It must be an authority thing, because you look barely out of high school."

"Flatterer. But don't stop, I like it." Caitlyn laughed as she wrapped new gauze around his waist, doing her best not to touch his skin.

"I can't believe you don't know how beautiful you are."

"Yeah, that's me. Femme fatale." She rolled her eyes and snorted.

"Honestly, you are one of the most beautiful women I've ever seen." Mac held her chin in his hand before she could turn away.

"You're just buttering me up so that I'll let you out of bed again." He looked right into her eyes, like he could make her believe his words by will alone. His hand felt hot on her face, and his breath caressed her cheek. He was so close, if she leaned in just a little her lips would meet his. Caitlyn's pulse raced at the thought and she licked her lips in anticipation.

The phone by the bed rang, breaking the spell. Mac dropped his hand back to the mattress. She was going to kill whoever was on the other end of the phone.

Chapter Four

Caitlyn reached for the phone, but Mac's hand stopped her from picking it up.

"Tell no one."

"No kidding. Do I look like an idiot?" She rolled her eyes again.

His sky blue gaze fired into her eyes for another breathtaking second before he released her wrist. Her arm tingled from the contact.

"Hello?" She had to clear her throat to get the huskiness out of her voice.

"Cat? Did I wake you up?" Liam's voice boomed through the earpiece.

"No, just had a frog in my throat. What's up?"

"Nothing, just wanted to see if there was anything you wanted to tell me." His voice held a hint of laughter.

"Uh, what do you mean?" What did he know?

"Oh, I don't know. Maybe some trouble you've gotten into lately?" More laughter colored his voice.

"None that I can think of." Or that she could tell him about anyway. "Why do you ask?" Had one of the patrol cars gone by her house and seen her dragging Mac into the apartment?

"Just didn't know if you needed me to fix a parking ticket for you."

"A parking ticket? No, I haven't gotten a ticket in years." At least not since Liam had joined the force.

"That's not what I heard," he taunted.

"Quit the theatrics, Liam. What do you mean?"

"I heard from Sue in dispatch that your plate got called in last night around midnight for a parking violation near the hospital. She told me to tell you to park in the garage. It's too dangerous to be parking in the streets at midnight anyway."

"I did park in the garage." Someone must have gotten her plate, but why go to the police?

"Yeah, right. That's why your plate got called in. What are you thinking anyway? You get free parking, use it. You could get mugged or raped if you don't pay attention. I'm gonna have one of my buddies drive by tonight to make sure you're not on the street, and if you are, I'll have you towed. That'll teach you."

"Don't you dare! Liam Patrick, you will not have my Jeep towed. I'm a big girl now, and I can take care of myself."

Mac eyed her with a half smile on his face. Amusement twinkled out of his eyes and he relaxed back against the pillows.

"Then don't park on the street and you won't have to worry about it."

"I didn't park on the street," she growled. "Is that the only reason you called? To bust my chops about getting a ticket and parking on the street?"

"Pretty much. You going to the firehouse for dinner tomorrow night?"

Oh crap. The firehouse. Almost every Friday night, Liam and Caitlyn met up with Jim at his fire station to have dinner with him and his crew. With the crazy schedules all three of them worked, it was the only way they managed to see each other more than once a month.

"I'm not sure. I might have plans." She looked at Mac. He shook his head.

"Go," he mouthed.

"What plans? A date?" Liam's voice lost its teasing quality and suddenly got more intense.

"No, just some stuff I have to do around the house. If I can get them done tomorrow after work and still get some sleep, I should be able to make it."

"'K. I'm working straight through the weekend but I'll be

there after work Friday night."

"I'll see you there, then."

"Park in the damn garage tonight."

"Yeah, yeah, yeah. Nag, nag, nag. I love you too."

"Whatever, just remember, I'm having someone drive by when you get off."

"Good-bye." Caitlyn hung up with a sigh. Someday her brothers were going to realize she wasn't a baby anymore.

"What was that all about?" Mac asked, looking at her through half closed eyes. He must be getting tired again from his exertions.

"My brother, Liam, the cop. He heard from a dispatcher that my license plate was called in for a parking violation and was calling to give me a hard time."

"Parking violation? When?" His eyes were wide open and wary now.

"Last night. Looks like someone grabbed my plate and called it in."

"Did you see anyone when you were leaving?"

"Just the security guard manning the exit." The memory of running feet and squealing sneakers popped into her brain. "Oh! But I think I might have heard someone in the garage before I pulled out. It's possible someone spotted me and took down my plate. But why would they call the police? Wouldn't they want to stay as far away from the police as possible?"

They would—unless they were working with the police. But Mac couldn't tell her that. The reason the FBI was involved at all was because of that very possibility. And with her brother on the police force, he couldn't take any chances. He felt like a shit keeping her in the dark about the investigation but this was too big an operation to risk family loyalties getting in the way.

"Well? Wouldn't they?" Caitlyn looked at him with an eyebrow raised in question.

"You'd think so. Maybe someone misread another plate and they got yours instead." Even to him, that sounded lame.

"I don't think so. It would explain why someone tried to get into the house and why someone followed me earlier."

"What kind of car did you say it was again?"

"A red Honda, tinted windows and souped up wheels."

Adrenaline shot through his system, his blood raced through his veins, and his heart pounded. Carlos! It had to be him. Damn! He had to get out of here before Caitlyn got even deeper into this mess. "Looks like you've been tagged as helping me. Three things in one day are a little too much for coincidence."

"True, but there's not a whole lot we can do about it. We'll just have to be especially careful until you're well enough to travel." She brushed off his concern with a wave of her hand. "I wish I didn't have to work tonight but there's no way I could find coverage now."

She had to work tonight? This could be his chance. He'd get out somehow while she was at work.

"No, you need to go in, make things look as normal as possible. I'll be fine here." He thought about what he'd need to survive on the street. Very little, actually. "I don't suppose you have a gun, do you?"

She bit her lower lip a little nervously. "I do, but I don't know what kind of shape it's in."

"What do you mean?"

"Tom gave it to me for my twenty-first birthday. Except for the occasional practice sessions at the range, I haven't used it much."

Mac couldn't picture her with a gun. Something about her just seemed too nurturing to even conceive of aiming a weapon with the intent to shoot. "Let me see it, would you?"

"Sure, I'll get it out of the safe. Stay here, I'll be right back."

"Trust me, with this hole in my gut I'm not going anywhere." Wouldn't hurt to make her think he was weaker than he was. Not that it was much of a stretch. His whole body ached and the pain from the wound shot fire through his torso with every movement. *How the hell was he going to get out of here in one piece?*

He must have dozed off while Caitlyn retrieved the gun.

When he woke up, she sat next to him dressed in hospital scrubs. Her long hair was pulled back into a braid.

"Hey, I have to get going soon but I wanted you to have some broth and try to get up and walk around a bit before I leave. You need to keep your body moving or you won't heal."

Her eyes were warm and sympathetic. She really was a beautiful woman, even with her hair scraped back and in the shapeless uniform.

"Yeah, I know. Have to get up to remind your insides you're not sleeping." He'd been through this before when he'd been shot. It wasn't a memory that he wanted to revisit often.

"We'll just walk to the fireplace and back, then I'll give you some water and broth."

"What time is it?"

"Three-thirty. Here, let me help." She slipped her arm around the uninjured part of his torso and helped him to stand. "One step at a time."

Hot, screaming agony tore through him as he stood upright. Each foot felt like it was made of lead. Sweat popped out on his forehead and slid down his face. "What time does your shift start? I thought you did twelve hour shifts?" He tried to distract himself from the nausea rising in his throat. The room spun like a carnival ride and he wanted to get off.

"Not tonight. I work two twelves and two eights. I go in from four to midnight tonight, and then have the next four days off. Come on, one more step then we'll turn around. You're doing great." Her voice held the same cheerful tone one would use with a child taking its first steps.

Mac gritted his teeth against the pain and leaned against her harder than he had too. If he didn't leave tonight, he wouldn't have another chance until she went back to work in four days. That was more than enough time for Carlos and his gang to track her down for sure. There might be plenty of red Hondas in the city but Mac was sure the one tailing her had belonged to the leader of Satan's Children. Things weren't looking too good for his cover.

It had taken Mac months of working his way up in the ranks of Satan's Children to get to meet Carlos. He'd sold drugs, ridden on drive-bys, and shot someone to get past their rigid initiation but he'd done it. The person he'd shot had been an undercover FBI agent in a bulletproof vest but the Children hadn't known that.

For months he'd lived in squalor in a tiny apartment with six other gang members, barely daring to sleep in case they tried to snoop through his personal belongings. Always on guard, he'd watched his every move until it became second nature to suspect everyone and every action.

And still his cover had been blown.

No one on the Hartford Police Department knew there was an FBI investigation going on. Who could have spotted him? Could Liam have recognized him? Was it possible that he was involved somehow?

Mac thought he'd been careful to not to let any cops get a look at him, but who knew when he could have been caught unawares? Maybe one of his "family" took his picture and brought it to the police in Carlos' pay?

But the only cop in the state who knew him was Liam. Could Tom be involved too? Mac's mind rebelled at the idea as Caitlyn eased him back down on the futon. Tom couldn't be involved. It went against everything Mac knew about him, everything he believed in.

Still, he couldn't discount any possibilities. No matter how repugnant.

"Here, eat some of this slowly. If you can keep it down, I can take out the IV tomorrow." Caitlyn handed him a mug of broth.

He fully planned on being gone by tomorrow, even if he had to roll naked down the street.

"Thanks." The watery broth was weak but felt good going down. He hadn't had anything to eat in what felt like days. "What does your brother Liam do for the police? I mean, is he on vice? Homicide?"

"Doesn't he wish?" Caitlyn laughed. "No, nothing so exciting. Liam has been stuck in the traffic division for the past two years. He's been looking for a transfer for a while, but he can't move up until someone leaves."

Traffic division? The chances of him being involved with Carlos in traffic weren't that great but maybe someone in vice recruited him. God knew cops didn't make much money. Maybe he'd gotten an offer he couldn't refuse?

"Tom must bust his stones about being a traffic cop," Mac said to cover his inquiry.

"Like you wouldn't believe. And they both bust on Jim for working on a 'hip wagon'. You'd think they'd have better things to do than argue constantly. Honestly, I don't know how my mother put up with it."

"It's just the way guys are. It's how we show affection. The more we rank on someone, the more we like them."

"Then my brothers must lo-ove each other dearly." She got up and brushed her hands briskly on her legs. "I need to get going or I'm going to be late. Are you sure you're okay? I'll bring you the milk jug in case you have to pee again, and I'll leave the phone nearby too." Her whiskey brown eyes radiated concern.

"Leave me the gun and I'll be fine." The bags of clothes she had dropped earlier were still on the floor by the futon. He could get those on as soon as she left.

"Oh, that's right. You were sleeping when I got it out of the safe, so I put it back in my room. I don't really like guns, and seeing them lying around unnerves me." She disappeared into the bedroom and quickly returned with a small pistol in her hands.

"I loaded it while you were sleeping." She passed it to him like she was handing off a poisonous snake, then wiped her hands on her pants. "I haven't used it in a while but I do keep it cleaned and oiled so that Tom doesn't nag me."

Mac inspected the gun. It was a semi-automatic Walther. A lady's gun, but it would work.

"Hopefully I won't need it, but it makes me feel better to know that it's handy."

Caitlyn drew her lower lip between her teeth. No wonder it was so full and red all the time. The thought made him want to bite it and see if it was as berry sweet as it looked.

Down boy! Get those thoughts out of your head right now.

"I could have one of Liam's buddies drive by occasionally, just to make sure you're okay."

"No! It's not necessary and might raise suspicion. No one

can know about my presence here. No one. Do you understand?" He gripped her hand.

"Yes. I get it. I won't say anything." Her eyes still looked worried.

"I can't put your family in danger."

"If you say so. I'll keep my mouth shut. Do you need anything else before I leave?"

Mac felt like crap for yelling at her but it was for her own good. He didn't know what he'd do if Liam was involved with the Children. Or Tom. It would kill her.

He couldn't think like that. Something was going on with the city's gangs and thousands of lives could be at stake. Caitlyn would have to deal with the fallout if her brothers were dirty. He couldn't risk a mission or a city because of one woman's feelings.

"No, I think I'll take a nap. I'm as weak as a kitten." He yawned for effect.

"Good. Eating and sleeping is the best way for your body to heal itself." She brushed her hand over his forehead and checked his IV before smoothing down the sheet and standing.

"I'll be back a little after midnight. I'll knock twice before I come in, so don't shoot me."

"I won't. I promise." If it were up to him, he wouldn't be there when she got home.

He feigned sleep as Caitlyn checked all the locks on the doors and windows. Her footsteps came closer to the futon, then stopped by his head. Mac had to force himself to keep breathing deeply and evenly as she stood there. What was she waiting for anyway? Didn't she say she had to go to work? Why was she just standing there? Did she suspect him of faking it?

A feather soft caress brushed his cheek before she crossed the floor and the door shut firmly.

She'd kissed him on the cheek before leaving. He was stunned. Mac couldn't remember the last time a woman had kissed him with genuine affection when she wasn't trying to get in his pants.

Hell, he couldn't remember the last time he'd kissed a woman when he wasn't trying to get her into bed either. What kind of woman took in a bleeding near-stranger and patched him up without looking for something in return? Then kissed him good-bye?

Maybe he was too jaded. There could be good Samaritans in the world. He didn't tend to run into many in his line of work, though. Junkies and drug dealers had been his companions for so long it was hard to imagine someone who didn't have an ulterior motive.

Could she, though? Maybe she was trying to lull him into a false sense of security to see how much he knew before reporting to her brother?

No. That didn't ring true. Yes, she had fished for information but she hadn't pushed him when he told her he couldn't say anything. His gut said she was on the level and he tended to agree with it.

Though his gut had been wrong before.

Damn. He didn't want to think about Tom being involved with the shit that was going down in the city's underworld. The gangs were uniting under someone and the police were doing nothing to stop it. Someone on the inside was in on it, and Mac had to find out who.

Mac dozed on and off for a few hours, giving himself a little more time to recover. When the sun dipped below the horizon, he knew he'd put it off as long as he could.

Averting his eyes, Mac pulled the IV out of his arm. Without looking at the needle, he slapped a bandage over the spot and held some pressure on it until he was sure it had stopped bleeding.

With a deep breath, he focused on the next Herculean task. Every muscle in his body cried out in misery as he reached for the bags of clothes lying on the floor. He was out of breath and sweating by the time he snagged the plastic bags and dragged them to him. Sweatpants might be stifling hot but they were easy to put on.

Or should have been. His stomach was on fire with pain as he tried to bend over enough to pull the sweats on. Panting, he took a break before he attempted to pull the T-shirt over his head. How the hell was he going to get out of the apartment and find a safe hideout if he couldn't even get dressed without almost passing out?

He'd find a way. Somehow. He had to go on the assumption that Carlos knew he was a fed and knew Caitlyn was helping him. No matter how much it hurt, he had to get away from Caitlyn to keep her safe.

Gritting his teeth in agony, Mac wrestled the T-shirt on. Luckily it was loose enough so he could hide the gun. That it was black was another plus. He'd be able blend in with the night and blood wouldn't show up as well. Rolling to his side, he used the end table for leverage and stumbled to his feet.

The room spun and more sweat dripped down his back. Mac could feel the nausea rising in his throat and he swallowed rapidly. He could do this. *One step at a time was all it took. The door through the kitchen looked so far away. How was he going to get out of here without passing out or falling down?*

"One step at a time, McDougal, one step at a time." With shuffling steps, he made his way to the kitchen table before collapsing.

Rivers of sweat ran down his face. He was as exhausted as if he'd run a marathon. The door was only steps away but he didn't know if he could make it. If he did make it out the door, he'd be a sitting duck for any punk who wanted to kill him.

"Shit. What now?"

The crash of the bathroom window breaking took the decision out of his hands.

Chapter Five

Caitlyn looked at the clock for millionth time that night. Normally, shifts in the Emergency Department flew by. A city hospital was never dull, especially the night shift. Not tonight though. The hands of the clock seemed stuck in place, crawling slowly by as worry gnawed her insides and twisted them into knots. She still had hours left to go, and it felt like an eternity.

What if Mac decided he was strong enough to get up and popped his stitches? He could pass out and hit his head on the corner of the table and be lying unconscious and bleeding to death on her floor. Her hand reached for the phone but she snapped it back. She couldn't call him from here, there were too many people milling around. During her break she'd use the pay phone outside. Surely she could wait that long.

"Cat!"

Caitlyn jumped at the hand on her shoulder. Spinning around, she stared into Jim's amused eyes.

"Cripes. Could you cough or something? You scared the life out of me."

"If you weren't sitting here daydreaming, you would have heard me call you ten times before I reached you."

"Sorry, I was just thinking. What's up? What'd ya bring me this time? I don't think I can handle another psychiatric tonight." Jim's ambulance had been to the hospital twice already.

"Nah, just a shortness of breath. It's too early for the drunks to come out. Whatcha thinking about? The stray?"

Caitlyn looked at him blankly, then remembered she'd told him she needed the supplies for a stray dog. This was why she rarely lied, she couldn't keep them straight in her head.

"Yeah. I'm worried he's gotten up and pulled his stitches."

"You can't save them all, you know."

"I can try." Especially when her "stray" stood over six feet tall, was deliciously muscled, and had dazzling blue eyes.

"Mother Teresa, at it again," he teased. "So, you coming to the station tomorrow night? Liam said you might be busy."

"Just doing some stuff around the house. I'll be there." As long as Mac didn't get worse. "Hey, have you heard anything from Tom lately?"

"No, but that's not unusual. You know when he's in deep cover he can't call home every weekend." Jim's gaze drifted over her shoulder.

"I know. I just worry sometimes."

"Uh huh." He was clearly distracted.

Caitlyn glanced over her shoulder. One of the nurses, Maggie, stood behind her, writing out a chart and shooting flirtatious looks at Jim. If he was caught up in chasing after Maggie, then he wouldn't be showing up at her place unexpectedly. A devious smile crossed her face.

"Why don't you invite Maggie to the Firefighter of the Year banquet? You need a date, don't you?"

"That's a month away, why should I bring it up now?" He looked back at her for a brief moment.

"Men. Because she'll need to get a dress and this gives you an excuse to invite her out on a date another time so that you can get to know each other better." He still looked doubtful. "Do you want me to bring it up? I could ask her for you..." she trailed off, knowing that would goad him into action.

"I can get my own dates, thanks all the same." He looked down at her. "I'll see you tomorrow at the station."

Gotcha!

With Jim distracted, that was one less brother to worry about interfering while she tried to figure out what was going on with Mac. If any one of her brothers knew she had a man staying at her house, the fat would hit the fire in seconds.

Caitlyn sighed and gave one last glance at her brother who was openly flirting with the red headed nurse. Maggie didn't seem to mind the attention. How come it was all right for *them* to flirt and sleep around but not her? She'd called Liam on any number of occasions and had a woman pick up the phone in a sleepy voice.

Did she yell and scream about it? No. But God forbid a man ever answered her phone in the morning. There'd be ten squad cars, four fire trucks and probably a SWAT team at her house within minutes. The city was always complaining about the inability of the municipalities to work together. All it would take would be a man coming out of her apartment in the morning and every one of Hartford's emergency services, plus the feds, would cooperate like a well oiled machine.

Pushing the unfairness of it all out of her head, Caitlyn went to check the vitals on her patients. Maybe because their parents died when she was a teen they felt like they had to keep protecting her? But come on, she was pushing thirty, it was time to drop the big brother routine.

Her thoughts were distracted as she filled out a patient's discharge instructions. There wasn't much she could do to change how her brothers saw her. She'd just have to work around them. Maybe she could find someone for Liam to chase after, then he'd be off her back too. It still pissed her off that he threatened to have her Jeep towed.

"Caitlyn, phone for you," the secretary called from her desk. "It's the P.D. on line two."

"Thanks, Nancy." Caitlyn picked up the extension on the hall phone. What did Liam want now? She'd parked in the garage.

"What do you want, Liam? I didn't park on the street."

"Caitlyn O'Toole?" an unfamiliar voice asked.

"Oh. Yes, this is Caitlyn O'Toole."

"Officer Brown, Hartford P.D."

"Can I help you?" Caitlyn racked her brain trying to remember if she'd ever met an Officer Brown. The name didn't sound familiar but she hadn't met everyone on the force by a long shot.

"I'm sorry to tell you this, but someone tried to break into your apartment tonight. A passing patrol car saw a youth attempting to enter through a broken window and chased him off. We'll need you to come in and check the place out and fill out a report."

"I'll be there as soon as I can. I might be able to find someone to cover for me."

"Very good. Don't enter the premises until the officer waiting for you can check it out."

"Sure. Thank you." Caitlyn's thoughts chased themselves around her brain, scattering in a million directions.

Did someone spot Mac? Could he be hurt? What if he heard the kid at the window and tried to run away?

"Maggie?" Caitlyn called to her friend who was still flirting with Jim.

Oh crap. Jim. If she mentioned the break-in around him he'd insist on coming with her. Hell, he'd know about it soon enough anyway. She was sure Liam had already heard about it. News traveled fast when family was involved.

"What's up?" The redhead flipped her ponytail over her shoulder and winked at Caitlyn.

"Can you cover for me? Someone tried to break into my place and I need to go check everything out and fill out some paperwork."

"Someone tried to break in? I knew you should have gotten an apartment on the second floor," Jim railed.

"Shut up, Jim." She waved him off. "Can you do it?"

"Sure, no problem. Go on home, I'll be fine here. Let me know what happens, okay?" Maggie pulled her in for a quick hug. "Give me a call in the morning."

"I will, thanks." Caitlyn headed for the locker room to grab her coat but Jim grabbed her arm and stopped her.

"I'm coming with you."

Oh great. Just what she needed, cops and an over-protective brother.

"You can't, you're still on duty. Besides, an officer is waiting for me, he'll go in before I do."

Jim opened his mouth to argue, but before he could get a word out, his pager went off, sending him out on another call.

"At least call Liam, will you?" Jim shouted over his shoulder as he headed back to the ambulance.

Caitlyn smiled and waved without promising anything. Once he was out of sight, she grabbed her jacket, signed out, and bolted for the parking garage. She needed to get to her apartment before Liam did.

It didn't matter that it was late and he'd been working all day, as soon as Liam found out about the break-in attempt, he'd be on his way to her place.

And he had a key.

She ran faster.

ⅎ

Liam had just pulled up to the curb as Caitlyn made it into her driveway. His hair was mussed as if he'd been sleeping—or doing something else in bed. Maybe she didn't have to find him a girl to chase after all.

"Hi, Mark," she called, recognizing the officer walking towards her.

Mark was one of Liam's buddies from the police academy and a regular visitor to the O'Toole family get-togethers.

"Hey, Caitlyn. I was just doing a drive-by when I saw someone trying to wiggle his way through the window. I tried to chase him but the kid was too fast."

Caitlyn shot a warning glance at Liam when he opened his mouth to berate her. "I'm glad you were here. The officer who called me said you needed me to check some things out and fill out some paperwork?"

"Yup. If you'd open the door, I'll take a look around to make sure it's safe. You can tell me if anything is missing, then we'll do some paperwork."

"Sure. Hold on."

Her hands shook as she undid the dead bolt. She tried to peek through the lace curtain covering the window on the door but couldn't see anything.

"Just wait out here with me while Mark checks the place

out." Liam grabbed her wrist and kept her from going into the house.

Great. Now she'd have to listen to Liam nag her too.

"What the hell is going on, Cat?"

"What do you mean? Someone tried to break into my apartment. What does it look like?" She wiped her sweaty palms on her pants. She was a terrible liar. Lying made her flustered and nervous.

"Yeah, today someone tried to break into your place, and yesterday someone called your plates into dispatch. And last night Jim said you asked for enough medical supplies to patch up a horse. Spill it."

"What? Are the two of you having conferences about me now? I'm twenty-seven years old, if you haven't noticed."

"We aren't talking about you behind your back. It's just that I was talking to Jim about tomorrow's dinner and when I said you might not make it, he asked if it was because of the stray. Don't get so defensive."

"How can I not get defensive when you question my every move?" The best defense was a good offense, right? Maybe if she attacked him, he'd forget about all the weird things happening lately.

"We don't question your every move. We just...just worry. You're the only little sister we have." He stuffed his hands into his pockets and scuffed his feet on the ground. Talking about feelings other than anger was not an O'Toole male strong point.

"And you don't think I worry? I've got three brothers and all three of them risk their lives every time they go to work. Do I nag you to quit your job? Do I call you all the time to see if you made it home from work safely? Do I follow you when you go on dates to make sure no one takes advantage of you?"

"It was only that one time! And you were only sixteen. Would you get over it already?"

"That's not the point." She took his face into her hands. The tirade had started as a way to distract him, but if a little of what she was saying sunk into his thick skull it was worth it. "You've taught me well, no man is going to take advantage of me. I know every dirty street-fighting trick in the book and then some. And if that doesn't work, I'll sic the three of you on him.

You have to let go sometime."

"Says who?"

Caitlyn rolled her eyes. "Stupid, stubborn, Irish—"

"Hey, you're just as Irish, and just as stubborn." He mock-punched her in the arm. "I hear you, I hear you. I'll lay off. But I'm still going to worry."

"Fine. Just do it quietly. Now go back home. Maybe if you hurry you can finish what you started before Mark tattled to you."

Liam had the grace to blush, confirming her suspicions.

"I'll see you tomorrow. And have Mark board up the window before he leaves. I'll have Jim come over and fix it before he goes to work."

Great. So much for her reprieve. "Good night." She waved him off.

He pulled her in for a quick hug, then tickled her.

"Coast is clear, you can come in now," Mark called from the kitchen, his silhouette outlined by the overhead light.

"Coming." She waited until she was sure Liam was really going before climbing the steps. If Mark had found Mac, he would have come running out, so that must mean he hadn't found anything. Right?

But if he hadn't found anything, where the hell was Mac?

"I don't think he got in but you might want to take a look around." Mark had a sly grin on his face.

"Okay." What was so amusing? Had he found Mac?

The gnawing in her stomach got worse as she walked through the kitchen. One chair was askew but she could have bumped it on her way out. Butterflies the size of jet planes swarmed in her stomach as she moved into the living room. She smiled over her shoulder at Mark to hide her nervousness.

The room was empty. Some of the clothes she'd bought Mac were strewn about on the floor but there was no sign of him.

"I'll, ah, go check my bedroom." Caitlyn scampered to her room, looking under her bed and in the closet but he wasn't there either.

"Everything check out okay?" Mark asked from the

doorway.

"Yup. Doesn't look like anything's missing. Why don't we go to the kitchen and I'll give you the info for the report." Where was he?

Mark sat at the kitchen table and pulled a worn notebook out of his chest pocket.

"Would you like some coffee?" Caitlyn forced her hands to stay still and not fidget with her necklace. It wasn't easy.

"Nah, I'll pass. Once I get done here, I'm off duty and headed for bed."

"Well then, I won't hold you. What do you need to know?" Caitlyn sat across from Mark and folded her hands in her lap. Her gaze darted nervously around the room. Where the hell had Mac disappeared?

A tiny slash of red on the white pantry door caught her attention. Where did that come from? Could it be blood? Mac's blood?

"Full name?"

Her attention snapped back to Mark. "Caitlyn Rose O'Toole."

"Date of birth?"

"October 12, 1981."

"I've got your address and telephone number." Mark scribbled away on the pad, filling in the information.

Caitlyn's mind spun in circles. Could Mac fit in the closet? The pantry was an old-fashioned one and pretty big but so was Mac. Oh crap, was he in there, bleeding to death while she sat here with Mark?

"You'll have to come down to the station to sign the report when I'm all done, but that can wait until tomorrow. If you give me your work number, I should be all set with this for now."

"Sure." Caitlyn rattled off her work number and tried to focus on Mark and not the door behind him.

"That should do it." He pushed the chair back and stretched before putting the notebook back in his pocket. "Oh, and I'll keep quiet about you having a guy staying here, don't worry."

Panic! "I don't know what you're talking about." Caitlyn

tried to sound innocent, but she knew she must look like a spooked horse. Damn it, she had to learn to lie better.

"Whatever you say, Cat. You just suddenly decided to start wearing men's clothes and sneakers. Don't worry, I won't tell Liam. Your secret's safe with me."

"Thanks." She smiled weakly. He must have spotted the clothes she'd bought for Mac. Well, having him think she had a boyfriend was probably better than him thinking she was hiding an undercover FBI agent.

She walked him to the door and waved as he left. *Come on, come on hurry up.* He seemed to take forever to get in the stupid car and leave. When he was finally gone, Caitlyn yanked down the shades and bolted to the pantry door.

"Mac? Are you in here?" If he wasn't, she was going to feel like a real idiot.

"Is he gone?" Mac squinted at her from behind the garbage can and under a pile of grocery bags. Caitlyn helped him to crawl out of the closet. His hand was held to his side and blood leaked out between his fingers.

"Yeah, he's gone. Come on, I'll help you back to bed. Let's hope you didn't pull any stitches."

Mac grunted but didn't say anything. His shirt was sticky with blood and he leaned on her heavily. Caitlyn tried to take as much of his weight on her shoulders as she could, but he was heavy. Sweat dripped down his face and he was pale again.

"Come on, just a little farther."

Mac stumbled the last few steps to the futon and collapsed on it.

"What happened?" Caitlyn asked as she inspected the wound. He hadn't ripped the stitches but they were red and puffy and blood leaked from the site. "Where's the IV?" He'd ripped out the IV, and she was going to have to put it back in.

"Under the bed somewhere. I took it out when I got dressed."

"And why were you getting dressed? I thought you were going to go to sleep while I was at work?" She knew he'd try to leave, just knew it. Stubborn man.

"I've put you in enough danger. I can't allow you to get hurt

61

because of me."

"Allow? You don't allow me anything. I'm an adult and I make my own choices. I choose to help you, and I don't appreciate all the work I went through to patch you back together getting destroyed. Now tell me what happened."

"I was in the kitchen, working up the energy to leave when I heard the window in the bathroom break. I didn't have time to do anything more than hide behind the garbage can in the pantry closet. I take it whoever tried to get in got scared off before they made it inside?" Mac winced as she inserted the needle under his skin.

"Yeah, Mark was driving by and saw someone trying to climb through the bathroom window. He said it was a kid. You want to tell me why a kid is after you?"

"He's no kid. At least not inside where it matters. I can't tell you any more but be on your guard. Just because someone looks sixteen doesn't mean they can't or won't kill you. I've seen thirteen-year olds shoot people for their shoes. They wouldn't hesitate to shoot you either."

Caitlyn frowned in concentration as she restrung the IV bag and added a dose of antibiotics to the line. "I work in the ER, remember? I've seen plenty of thirteen-year old gunshot victims. We get patients from drive-bys every night. I'm careful."

Mac grabbed her hand, preventing her from getting up. "Be even more careful. Don't trust anyone. Anyone."

He stared at her intently. What was he trying to tell her?

She nodded once and moved to get away from the disturbing feelings he created in her. His hand was warm and sent flutters through her body, yet his words scared her. Surely he didn't mean she couldn't trust her brothers? Did this have something to do with them?

"You need to get some sleep. Rest now, I'll be right in the next room." At least one of them would get some sleep tonight. Caitlyn knew it wasn't going to be her.

Chapter Six

Caitlyn bolted upright from a nightmare. Cold sweat dripped down her back and her heart raced like she'd run a marathon. For a minute she felt like she was still being chased and her legs felt weak from the adrenaline rush.

"Just a dream, a nightmare." Her voice was weak and breathy and sounded absurdly loud in the pre-dawn darkness.

There was no way she was going back to sleep now. Hell, she'd probably only gotten a few hours of good sleep anyway. She'd tossed and turned for what seemed like days before settling down.

Something about having Mac in the next room kept her from relaxing. It was more than worry about his injury, although that was on her mind. She was just hyper aware of having such a virile male mere feet away.

It was ridiculous. He was injured. She should be looking at him like a patient, more concerned about his injuries than about his body. But man, just one touch of his hand on hers and her pulse quickened and her mouth went dry.

Caitlyn sighed and got out of bed. She sure knew how to pick 'em. Was she attracted to Mark? No. Nice safe Mark who was friends with her brother, had a good job, went to dinner at his mother's every Sunday after church. No, she couldn't be attracted to him. That would be too easy.

Instead, she had to get all hot and bothered by an undercover FBI agent who kept secrets from her and traveled all over the country doing God only knew what. Figures. The only guy her brothers couldn't scare off, that she liked, and he was doing his damnedest to get away from her to keep her "safe".

Would she ever have a man in her life that wouldn't try to wrap her in bubble wrap?

Okay, deep breath. There was nothing wrong with being safe. Mac was obviously in a bad situation. A deadly situation, and he didn't want her killed. That wasn't going overboard. She'd just have to prove to him that she'd be okay until he was healed enough to go back and do whatever it was he needed to do.

Fear formed a cold knot in her stomach at the thought of him going back out on the streets. How could he do his job with a hole in his side? There was someone after him and they suspected he was here. It was only a matter of time before they caught him. Then what?

She needed to get some help. But how? He didn't want her to get involved, and he didn't want her telling her brothers about it either. Where else could she turn?

A thump jolted her out of her whirlwind thoughts. Caitlyn hurried out of her bedroom and into the darkened living room.

"Mac?" The futon was empty. More banging came from the bathroom. "What the hell are you doing?"

Mac stood on a chair, trying to nail up the board she'd set in front of the window last night.

"I wanted to secure this board so no one could get in."

"I could handle it. Get off that chair before you kill yourself." He had his IV bag propped on the shelf near the window and hammered with his free hand. At least he hadn't ripped that out again. Idiot.

"It's almost done, hold on." His face was white with pain and he was hunched over, protecting his side.

"Get down now and back into bed." Caitlyn's temper was ready to shoot through the roof. "What is wrong with you? Do you have a death wish? Or do you just delight in tearing apart all the work I've done?" Exasperation colored her words. It was like dealing with a two-year-old.

He pounded the last nail in and got slowly off the chair, stumbling a bit. "I feel much better today and I wanted to do something. Laying in bed was killing me."

"It's called recuperating, you should try it some time." She was going to kill him herself if he didn't stop trying to pull out his stitches with his stupid antics.

When Mac stumbled again, Caitlyn automatically slipped his arm over her shoulder and helped him back to bed. He'd taken off his shirt, and his naked chest felt warm under her hands. For the first time it hit her that she wore a thin tank top and a pair of boxer shorts, and he was in nothing more than a pair of sweat pants.

Her nipples tightened in reaction to his nearness, which annoyed her more. If he'd stayed in bed like he was supposed to, she wouldn't be touching all this glorious naked skin and wouldn't be getting hot and bothered over someone she could never have.

She dropped his arm a bit more roughly than was absolutely necessary and Mac practically fell into the bed.

"I'm going to grab a shower and get dressed. Stay. Here. I'll get you some breakfast when I'm done."

She stalked off to her bedroom to grab some more clothes. She'd need to wear a winter parka and ski suit if she was going to hide her reaction to him.

∞

Mac watched Caitlyn through half closed eyes as she stalked to the bathroom. He knew she was pissed at him for getting out of bed again but he'd had to. Lying in bed while the city went to hell in a hand basket was enough to drive him insane.

First he'd stood to see how much mobility he had. When the room only spun a few times, he'd crossed to the bathroom to take a leak like a man, not an invalid. He was smart enough to take the IV bag with him instead of ripping it out of his arm again. If he'd taken it out, Caitlyn probably would have throttled him instead of just stabbing him with verbal barbs.

Okay, so he probably shouldn't have nailed the board in place. That wasn't the brightest idea but he couldn't help it. He hated being helpless, hated being weak and injured. Nailing a board in place was just a small thing he could do to keep Caitlyn safe, since it looked like he wasn't going to be able to leave her.

The pain in his side flared again as he tried to move. He'd exhausted himself with just the trip to and from the bathroom but he didn't dare ask Caitlyn for pain meds. With the mood she was in now, he'd be lucky if she didn't poison him.

He couldn't help but smile at that. Tom had told him she had a temper but he'd never believed it. Fire had practically shot from her eyes when she caught him on that chair.

God but she was gorgeous, even in the morning. Her streaky hair was mussed from sleep and her eyes blazed with fury. It was a potent combination. He'd had to hunch over so that she wouldn't be able to see the erection he'd gotten from looking at her barely covered breasts in the thin tank top.

Steam puffed out under the bathroom door, and Mac pictured Caitlyn naked in the next room. Hot water would make her skin rosy and she'd be slick with soapsuds. He closed his eyes and groaned as his body reacted to his overactive imagination.

How would he spend the next four days with her without touching her? She was so beautiful and honest and courageous. All the things he looked for in a date, and he couldn't do a damn thing about it. Tom would kill him if he fooled around with Caitlyn and Mac wasn't in a position to have anything more than a temporary affair.

He'd just have to bite the bullet and get the lustful thoughts out of his head. The mission was still on and he'd have to focus on that, not on Tom's sexy little sister. Besides, he was so sore from this hole in his side, he couldn't do much more than drool over her anyway. By the time he recovered enough to do more than pant after her, he'd be long gone.

"Keep that in mind, buddy," he reminded himself. In another few weeks he'd be out of her life for good. From what he could gather, whatever was going to happen in the city was no more than a month away. He'd lie low for another couple of weeks. By then he'd be able to move about a bit more easily.

Once he nailed the guy that was supplying guns to the city's gangs, his job would be over and he'd be reassigned to another case in some other city. The only time he'd see Caitlyn again would be if he ran into her with Tom.

For some reason, the thought of never seeing her again left an empty feeling in his gut. Her laughing eyes flashed in his mind, making the empty feeling even stronger. He must be hungry, that was it. He hadn't had solid food in days. That would explain his sappy feelings.

It definitely had nothing to do with the woman standing naked in the shower in the next room.

Yeah, right.

A blanket of steam accompanied Caitlyn as she opened the bathroom door. It smelled of flowers and soap and Mac recognized it as the same scent he'd breathed in when she helped him to bed. It traveled through his nostrils to his brain and reminded him of the feel of her breasts pressed against his side.

Great. Just what he needed, a multi-sensory attack on his control.

"If you can hold down breakfast, I'll take out the IV today. But only if you promise not to be a stupid macho idiot."

"It'll be hard, but I'll try." He smiled at her, glad to see the laughter back in her eyes.

"If you can't behave, I'll be forced to stay home with you tonight, then my brothers will be all over me about why I missed Friday dinner."

"Friday dinner? Isn't it Sunday dinner?"

"Not when everyone works weekends. With a nurse, a cop and a firefighter we get together whenever we can. At least twice a month we meet at Jim's station and do dinner there. Well, try anyway. Every once in a while we actually finish dinner before they get a call."

"Doesn't he work on the ambulance too?"

"Yeah. He does some per diem work for a local clinic and alternates shifts on the ambulance for the fire department. It's easier to pick up ambulance shifts for overtime though, because most of the guys don't like medical calls. The ambulance is busier than the engine, so he rarely switches on a Friday or we'd never get together."

She disappeared into the kitchen and Mac could hear her banging around. In a few minutes she was back with an English muffin and some coffee.

"You do a lot with your family, don't you? They seem to be over here all the time."

Caitlyn snorted as she put the food down in front of him and helped him to sit up.

"Yeah, sometimes I think I do too much with them. With the three of us living and working in the city, we're always running into each other."

Mac bit into the buttered muffin and sighed. Nooks and crannies had never tasted so good. Amazing what a few days of hunger could do for his taste buds.

"It's more than that. You get together for dinner and stuff. Jim dropped everything to bring you supplies for what he thought was a stray dog. Liam came over last night when he heard your house had been broken into. You're helping me because I'm a friend of Tom's."

"Well, yeah. That's what family does for each other." She seemed puzzled by his observations.

"Not all families."

"Don't you have brothers or sisters who would step up if you needed help?"

"Nope. Only child of a single mother. She died years ago, so it's just me."

Caitlyn's face softened and she laid her hand on his arm. "I'm so sorry. I complain about my brothers but I don't know what I'd do without them."

"It's no big deal, really. I'm used to being alone. I like it that way." His words sounded falsely cheerful even to himself.

"What do you do on the holidays? Didn't you come down from Maine or something to pick up Tom on Thanksgiving?" She took a sip of her coffee, removing her hand from his arm.

"I was on assignment then, but I usually visit friends for the holidays when I'm not working." Yeah, but when was the last time he hadn't worked a holiday?

"Well, next holiday, you'll spend it with us." She nodded, as if settling it in her head.

"Let's just get through the next month, then I'll worry about Thanksgiving." He didn't have the heart to tell her he'd probably be undercover in another state by November.

"You think this will be done in another month?" Caitlyn pounced on his slip.

"Maybe. I don't know for sure, we'll see what happens when I'm back on my feet."

"That won't be for at least another week, you know. And even then, you won't be in tiptop shape for months. You were lucky that the bullet didn't hit any vital organs, but you lost a lot of blood and tore muscles."

Her words made the ache in his side flare even more painfully.

"I heal fast. I'll be fine in a week. Maybe a little sore but nothing I can't handle."

"I thought you were going to stop acting like a stupid macho jerk?" She raised one eyebrow.

His laughter made his side hurt even more.

ॐ

"What do you mean, you don't know? Was he there or not?" Carlos forced himself not to grab the punk in front of him by the throat. If he wanted something done right, he'd have to do it himself.

"I didn't get a good look before the cops came, but from what I saw there was no one in the place. I tried to go back after, but by then the chick was home."

"From what you saw, huh? You were too busy staring at some girl in short shorts and not looking for Diego."

"I'm telling you, he's dead. He has to be. I shot him in the park, there was blood everywhere, man."

"Blood but no body. Until I see a body, I'm going to count on him being alive."

"Where could he go? If he went to a hospital they'd have to report it."

"Are you questioning me? You're the one who said the woman could have taken him home." Carlos didn't like this pup questioning his authority. This punk was a smart one and eventually would try to take over the operation. He hadn't been around this long without knowing how the gang mentality worked. Little fish got hungry for power, and as soon as they saw their chance, a quick bullet in the head and Carlos would be no more.

He wasn't going to let that happen. Carlos fingered the knife on his desk and stared the punk down. The kid tried to hold his gaze but it dropped to the knife after a few seconds.

Good, he still feared his leader.

"We plan for Diego being alive and a cop until we find a body. And keep an eye on that girl. It's possible she's helping him in some way, even if he isn't at her place. Now go, out of my sight."

The kid scrambled to get out of the chair and out of the room before Carlos threw the knife.

What the fuck was he going to tell the Man? Carlos felt a shiver of fear slither down his back. The Man said Diego wasn't really Diego and he was a fed. If that was the case, and he had no reason to doubt the Man, Carlos was in deep shit. Diego had gotten in tight with the Children. If Diego was a fed, he knew enough about their day-to-day operations to put them away for a long time.

But if he was a fed, why hadn't he busted them already? He had all the leaders and had enough information to nail them on drug charges. Was he after the Man?

Ha! Fat chance. The Man was so secretive no one even knew his real name. All they knew was that he had the dough and the connections to get them out of jail, warn them of busts, and get them phat weapons. If the Man wanted to run the show from behind the scenes, that was fine by Carlos. The Children were making money hand over fist now that they didn't have to worry about protecting their territory from other gangs.

That part still chaffed his ass, though. The Man insisted the gangs stop fighting each other and focus on one thing. The Children had drugs, the Black Hands had loan sharking and enforcement, and the 525s had prostitution. They all had their territories and no one was to step a toe over the line.

The few who did were disposed of quickly and brutally.

Carlos shivered again as he remembered what was left of his former rival from the 525s. He hadn't wanted to follow the rules. He liked getting the weapons and finding out about the busts but hadn't wanted to stick to just prostitution. With a small group of handpicked men, he'd launched an attack on the Hands' headquarters and stolen half a mil in cash.

He hadn't lived long enough to spend a dime of it.

No, Carlos was smarter than that. He'd do things the way the Man wanted him to until the time was right. The Children were stock piling their weapons, waiting for the other two gangs to screw up. When that happened, there would be all out war in the city streets. The Man thought he was so smart, but Carlos was smarter.

He'd keep his mouth shut and play good little boy until he found out who the Man really was and how much power he had. There was no harm biding his time and making money while the Man was supplying them with weapons. Then when they had enough guns and money stored, they'd make their move.

An evil smile crossed his scarred face. And if the Man got hit in the crossfire, well, that was just too bad.

Chapter Seven

Two weeks later

Mac wiped himself down with a towel and dove under the sheet just as he heard Caitlyn pull into the driveway. He grabbed a nearby magazine and tried to slow down his breathing before she unlocked the door. If she caught him exercising again, she'd rip him up one side and down the other.

Short walks and gentle stretching were his only approved exercises, and that was only because he'd begged her to take the stitches out early. He was still sore, but it felt good to be moving again.

As long as Caitlyn didn't catch him.

Two soft knocks preceded her entrance and Mac's heart rate sped up. He wanted to think it was only because he hadn't seen anyone for twelve hours, but deep in his gut he knew it was because it was Caitlyn walking through the door. Somehow he didn't think he'd be quite so happy to see Tom after twelve hours.

"Mac? It's me." Her voice was pitched low and it slid over him like soft velvet.

"I'm up." He put down the magazine, covertly wiping sweat off under the sheet as Caitlyn walked into the room.

She smiled and sat in the battered recliner next to him. Toeing off her shoes, she curled her feet under her and let her hair out of the clip that held it back. Golden-highlighted strands caught the dim lamplight and looked like liquid sunshine.

"I've got you on my screwed up schedule now. Sleep all day and up all night." Her smile brightened the room. A heat that had nothing to do with his illicit exercise filled his body and traveled straight to his groin.

"Actually, I'm used to being up all night. For some reason most illegal activities don't stick to a nine to five schedule."

"Go figure." She stretched and her uniform top pulled tightly across her chest. Mac's pulse kicked up another couple of notches. "I'm going to get some water, do you want some too?"

"Sure, thanks."

"You probably need it after working out." She shot him a saucy look over her shoulder as she strutted to the kitchen.

"Can't get anything by you, can I?" Mac gave up any pretense of resting and sat up.

Handing him a bottle of water as she came back, she winked at him and collapsed back into the chair. "You left the light on and I saw your silhouette against the shades as I came in."

Shit. That was a rookie mistake. What was happening to him? He knew better than to leave enough light to throw a shadow.

Some of his annoyance must have shown on his face, because Caitlyn quickly reassured him. "It was only your arms, but I could tell you were doing jumping jacks. And that's only because I suspect you. No one else would be able to see you."

"Unless they were specifically looking for me. Which they are." He gulped down the water, pissed at the risk he put Caitlyn in.

"Or they'd just think you're my new boyfriend. That's what my neighbors think anyway."

"Great, so now I have to worry about the gangs and your brothers."

"I'll worry about my brothers. I'm a big girl now." She yawned and stretched again.

Mac didn't need the reminder of how big she was. His body knew she was an adult and responded forcefully. Looking anywhere but at the way her mouth moved on the bottle of water, Mac tried to distract himself.

"You look tired, bad night?" Lame attempt at conversation

but anything was better than thinking about how his mouth would feel on hers.

"No worse than usual, it was just long. We had a lot of psychiatric evaluations tonight and they take up a lot of staff."

"That's tough." He tossed the water bottle between his hands. "Any more gun shots?" he asked as causally as he could.

"Surprisingly, no. We've had fewer than normal drive-bys lately. In fact, now that I think about it, other than domestics, most of the violent injuries have been down. Weird. Usually summertime is when the gangs fight their turf wars and we have our hands full."

Mac's gut clenched. If the gangs weren't fighting to defend their turf it was because they'd already divided it up. He'd been shot before he could find out more about why Satan's Children were told to hold fire, but he was sure there was someone behind the truce.

Someone who wasn't interested in stopping the violence.

"Maybe it's too hot to fight," he offered, just for something to say.

"Maybe. Lord knows I don't want to do more than I have to. I'm going to take a shower, then head to bed. Do you need anything?"

He wished she wouldn't say need. Her showers were torture for him. Every night he lay in bed listening to the water, knowing it was spraying over her naked body on the other side of the wall. His imagination pictured soapsuds gliding over her breasts and trailing down her abdomen to her thighs before sliding down her legs. It was a path he followed in his mind avidly wishing it were his hands soaping her up instead of hers.

"Ah, no. I'm all set. I think I'll just read a bit then call it a night." His voice was husky with suppressed desire. He faked a cough to cover it up.

"Okay, goodnight then."

Mac steeled himself for what came next.

She leaned over and absently gave him a peck on the cheek before crossing to her bedroom, blithely unaware of the havoc her innocent gesture inflicted. He fought back the urge to follow her as she walked into the bathroom carrying her clothes.

Caitlyn was a toucher, and didn't realize that the merest brush of her hand against his face drove him to distraction.

At least he didn't think she realized it.

Could she know that every time she gave him a hug, or kissed him good night, he wanted to pull her down and show her how far off her aim was? Was she trying to drive him crazy on purpose?

The water rattled through the pipes, and Mac's body reacted to the sound with a vengeance. Next would come the smells. The fragrance of her shampoo would drift out under the door with the steam, reminding him of what it felt like to have his arm around her and her breasts pressed to his side. His dick reared up, pushing against his shorts painfully.

And she wondered why he needed to exercise? He had to find someway to burn off all this extra testosterone running around his body. With every breath he took he was reminded of her. Everywhere he looked he saw evidence of her, from her quirky decorations to pictures of her with her brothers.

Her brothers. And that, my friend, is the problem.

If Caitlyn were any other woman, he'd have made a move to relieve the agony he was suffering on a nightly basis. But she wasn't. She was his best friend's sister and he'd been warned off her from the start.

Mac had too much respect for Tom to betray him by screwing around with his little sister. But it wasn't easy.

Sweating, Mac looked at the clock. He still had another five minutes before she'd shut the water off. His mind painted a picture of her actions. Once she shut the water off, she'd take another five minutes to dry off and wrap her hair up in the towel. Then came the scented lotion she wore.

He hadn't actually seen her applying the lotion, but he'd found the bottle in the bathroom and recognized the scent when she was near him. After the lotion would come the baby powder, then she'd get dressed and—

What was that? Mac's attention immediately shifted to the rattle of the doorknob. A crunch of footsteps sounded outside. Rolling out of bed, he clicked off the light and pulled Caitlyn's gun from under the pillow where he kept it. Crawling on all fours to stay below the window line, he crept his way to the bathroom.

The water was still running and he could hear Caitlyn singing softly. Reaching up, he turned the handle to the door and crawled through.

"Caitlyn," he whispered.

"Mac? What are you doing? Is something wrong?" She shut off the shower and poked her head out.

"Someone's at the door. Grab a towel and get down." Mac turned to give her some privacy and save his sanity.

The bathroom window was boarded up—the landlord swore the glass was on backorder—so Mac couldn't look out to see who was trying to get in. If ever he needed a visual distraction, it was now. With nothing to look at but the wall in front of him, his ears picked up every single movement Caitlyn made. And his imagination supplied the pictures all too vividly.

"Who do you think it is?" she asked.

"I don't know, but I think if it was one of your brothers they would have knocked or called first." He didn't dare look over his shoulder. Her clothes were on the counter in front of him, so he knew only a towel covered her. One yard of terry cloth and about six inches of space was all that separated him from a naked Caitlyn.

At this point, he almost hoped it was one of the Children, just so he had a reason to punch someone.

Another crunch of footsteps on gravel sounded loud in the silence of the night. Mac heard Caitlyn's breath catch as someone pushed against the board covering the window, testing its strength. He released the safety on the gun, readying himself for an attack.

Seconds ticked by as he waited for something to happen. The board bulged as someone pushed on it harder. There was no way the half-inch plywood would hold up against a concentrated attack.

Mac shoved Caitlyn farther back and stepped to the side. If someone was going to slam into the board, he didn't want to be crouching underneath it. Sweat dripped down his back and every muscle tensed as he waited for something to happen.

And waited.

A horn honked and Caitlyn gasped. The footsteps retreated and tires squealed off into the night. Mac clicked the safety back on the gun and put it on the counter in front of him for good measure.

"Oh God, I don't ever want to go through something like that again." Caitlyn dropped her forehead to his shoulder, and tension of a different sort shot through Mac.

He cleared his throat to hide the huskiness from his aroused state. "You're fine now, everything's okay."

She laughed weakly. "I know, it's just, that was really tense, ya know?"

Mac could feel her shaking. Probably a reaction from the adrenaline. Hell, he was none too steady either. Without thinking, Mac turned and pulled her into his arms for a hug.

He'd forgotten she was only wearing a towel.

Caitlyn wrapped her arms around him and buried her face in his chest. The only thing holding the towel up was the press of her body against his.

"I was so scared. I thought they were going to come right through the window."

"Shh, it's okay. You're safe now." He tried to hold his lower body away from her to hide his growing erection, but she snuggled closer. Her delicate shoulders shook, so he couldn't let go. What started out as a way to comfort her quickly turned into a disaster.

Her skin was so soft, and he could feel a great deal of it. Mac closed his eyes. He was in hell, absolute hell.

Mac's arms felt like heaven around her. Caitlyn had been dying to touch him for days now. To finally have his strength surrounding her sent a delicious warmth straight to her toes.

Among other places.

She could feel his erection pressing against her stomach, even though he was trying to hold his body away from her. So he wasn't unaffected. But then why didn't he take the next step? She was practically naked for God's sake. And she was more than willing to go wherever he wanted to take her.

Having Mac in her place was slowly driving her crazy. She wanted him so badly her teeth ached. As he healed, she had a harder time relegating him to the "patient" category. Not that it had been all that easy to keep him there in the first place.

Something about Mac called to a part deep inside her that she'd never felt before. Caitlyn took a deep breath and drew his scent into her lungs. He smelled like sweat, soap and her laundry detergent. The combination sent little flares of heat zipping through her blood stream straight to her core.

What was he waiting for? His hand stroked her back gently, giving her goose bumps. She could feel his heart beating rapidly in his chest and his breath blew hot and heavy against her cheek. What more did he need? A personalized invitation to kiss her?

Maybe he was waiting for her to make the first move? He'd struck her as a take-charge kind of guy but maybe he was nervous around her. Caitlyn was willing to try anything to ease the growing need inside her. If nothing else, at least she'd know where she stood with him.

With a nervous flutter in her belly, Caitlyn reached her arms up to his neck and pulled his head down to hers. Standing on tiptoes she was able to meet his mouth and draw him into a kiss.

Soft lips caressed her own as Mac responded. She gasped as the towel loosened. He took advantage of her open mouth and dipped his tongue in for a taste.

Heat shot through her, straight between her legs. His hands were everywhere, running over her shoulders and down her back. The ends of the towel slipped between her breasts and fell to the floor as she pulled him even closer.

The soft cotton of his shirt rubbed against her nipples, teasing her with the contact. Her breasts felt full and heavy and ached to be touched by him. As if he could read her mind, one large hand cupped her, gently stroking the underside of her breast.

A groan slipped from her lips at the touch and Caitlyn rubbed her hips against his. She was dying to see him naked, feel his skin against hers. Her hands slipped under his shirt and she ran her fingers across his abdomen. She was reaching for the elastic on his waistband when he stopped her.

"Caitlyn, we can't." He held both her hands in his now.

"Why not?" She vibrated with desire for him. Every atom of her being screamed to finish what she'd started.

"It isn't right."

"If it got any more right my bones would melt." She stared into his eyes. Eyes that were still dilated with desire. He wanted her, she knew he did.

"That's not what I mean. It wouldn't be right to lead you on. As soon as I'm able to, I'm out of here. Hell, I should've been out of here a week ago."

His words sent daggers of pain into her heart. "A week ago you could barely stand for more than five minutes, forget walk around the block. You're still in no condition to leave."

Anger burned away the desire that had flooded her system. She knew he was going to leave when it was time, she shouldn't be angry because he pointed it out. Or because he was gentleman enough not to lead her on.

She was still pissed.

"It doesn't matter, I have to go. I've put you in enough danger already. Doesn't tonight prove it?"

"Tonight proved a lot of things, but that you should leave isn't one of them."

Caitlyn reached around him for her pajamas and stalked off, not caring that he could see her naked butt. If not for his misplaced sense of chivalry, he'd have seen a lot more.

"Don't leave like this. It's for the best," Mac called from the bathroom.

"You know something? I'm getting really sick and tired of other people telling me what's best for me. How about you let me make my own decisions?"

She made it to the safety of her room before tears of frustration dripped down her cheeks. Throwing herself on the bed, she punched the pillow and pretended it was Mac's stubborn face. Her body still hummed from the emotional roller coaster it had been on all night. She'd gone from exhaustion, to fear, to excitement, to anger, all in an hour's time.

No wonder she felt like a wet noodle. Her feelings had been twisted in so many directions she didn't know how to react anymore. Kissing Mac had felt so good, so right. How could he ignore that?

Maybe he wasn't feeling the same connection she was?

Bull. He'd sported a hard-on that could pound nails. He'd felt something. Could he be commitment shy?

Gee, ya think?

But cripes, she wasn't looking for a ring and a white picket fence. Rolling onto her back, she hugged the pillow to her chest and stared at the ceiling. What did she want? Her body pulsed with a surge of heat.

Okay, what did she want besides sex? As much as she wasn't ready to settle down and play house, she wasn't into one night stands either. Did she want more than a good time with Mac?

Butterflies danced in her stomach at the thought. Yeah, she wanted more. Too bad she wasn't going to get it. He was probably right to stop things before they went too far.

Damn it.

Caitlyn threw the pillow across the room. Next time she'd stick to picking up stray dogs.

Chapter Eight

Caitlyn woke to the melodious sounds of splashing and swearing. With a yawn, she followed the cursing until she spied Mac standing at the bathroom sink wearing only his boxers. He was trying to shave his thick beard using her cheap, disposable razor.

It wasn't very effective.

"Should I get out the IV fluids again? If you cut yourself anymore, you'll need a transfusion." She wasn't sure if she should be embarrassed after last night or not, but she was too busy staring at him to care.

No wonder her body went into overdrive every time she was near him. He had muscular legs that were as thick as tree trunks. His torso rippled with more muscles and his shoulders were broad and well defined. Caitlyn's mouth went dry at the sight of all that skin just a few feet away from her. Her hands itched to run up his back and follow every dip and curve.

"Sorry. Did I wake you?" Mac dropped the razor and grabbed the sweatpants that were lying on the floor.

"No, I was getting up anyway when I heard the cursing. You can't shave that thick of a beard with a disposable razor." Caitlyn averted her eyes as he covered himself. What a shame.

"No kidding. Unfortunately I don't have an electric razor handy, and I can't take this beard anymore. It itches." He dabbed at a nick with a washcloth.

"I have a set of clippers that might do the trick. I use them to give Liam haircuts, but they might trim your beard enough for you to shave the rest off."

She slipped by him to get the clippers out of the linen closet. Her body tingled as her breasts brushed against his back. All her good intentions of last night went down the drain as her nipples tightened and licks of flame shot to her core. Her mind might know having an affair with him would lead to nothing but heartbreak but her body didn't give a damn.

"Here, try these." Her voice was thick with need.

"Thanks." He plugged in the clippers and turned them on without looking at her.

Caitlyn knew she should get out of the tiny bathroom and leave him alone. The space was too intimate, too homey. A memory of her mother sitting on the edge of the tub while her father shaved flashed into her mind.

"Do you think you could cut my hair with these? If I'm getting rid of the beard I might as well get rid of this long hair too."

"You want me to cut your hair?"

"Yeah, my cover's been blown so there's no sense staying in character. In fact it might be better if I didn't look like Diego anymore."

The harsh reality of the situation burst Caitlyn's daydream. She was thinking about playing house and Mac was thinking about staying alive. Kind of put things into perspective.

"Diego? Who's Diego?"

"Me. Or rather my cover, but since they know I'm not really a drug dealer now, there's no sense having all this hair and being uncomfortable. So, can you cut it?"

"Ah, I only know how to give buzz cuts. I'm not a hairdresser or anything. Liam's hair is only half an inch long, so it's easy for me to keep it like that. I can't do a style."

"That's fine. When I'm not on assignment I wear it almost that short anyway."

All that thick hair and he wanted it chopped off? Caitlyn wanted to argue with him but bit her tongue. If he thought he'd be safer with his hair cut, who was she to tell him otherwise? "Okay, when you're done shaving, bring the clippers into the kitchen and I'll take care of it."

Caitlyn grabbed a couple towels, carefully avoiding contact

with him this time, and fled the bathroom. With shaking hands she made a pot of coffee. Water sloshed over the sides of the coffee maker and splashed on her shirt.

Pull yourself together, O'Toole!

She should not be reduced to a quivering mass of hormones just because she saw him in a pair of boxer shorts and brushed up against his back. He was just a man, for heaven's sake. She'd touched plenty of men in her life. Until she went away to college she'd played basketball and football with her brothers and their friends. It wasn't like she was unused to casual touching.

But touching Mac was a whole different story.

Too bad. After last night's fiasco, she knew he wasn't going to act on the attraction zinging between them. It didn't matter that every time she was within five feet of him sexual tension filled the air and her body hummed with desire. If he wasn't going to act on it, she wasn't going to beg him.

Slipping a mug directly under the filter, Caitlyn waited for her first infusion of caffeine. Nope, throwing herself at him once was more than enough. She'd laid her body bare for him, she didn't need to lay her soul bare too. He didn't want her, end of story.

She had a bitter taste in her mouth that had nothing to do with the coffee she'd made.

"Yum, smells good. Can I have a cup?" Mac asked from the doorway.

Caitlyn jumped, spilling coffee on her hand. She shot a look at him while running her hand under cold water. "Can't you cough or something to warn me you're coming? You scared me half to death."

"Sorry, I didn't mean to sneak up on you. I didn't realize you were so jumpy. Is your hand okay?"

"Yeah, it's fine. And I'm not jumpy. I'm just not used to having people trying to break in on a regular basis."

Mac's face hardened briefly. "I know, and I apologize for that. I'll be out of here soon and you'll be safe again."

Caitlyn's heart dropped to her stomach at the thought of him going back out onto the streets. She poured him a cup of coffee to cover her distress. "Let's make sure you're fully healed before we talk about you leaving. Right now you're recovering nicely, but it will be a while before you're up to running around chasing drug dealers."

Handing him the cup, her fingers brushed his and another electrical jolt shot through her. Her breath hitched and her pulse throbbed in her veins.

"Here, sit down. I—I need to go brush my teeth before I cut your hair. I'll be right back." Caitlyn scurried to the bathroom. Maybe she should take a cold shower while she was at it.

After washing her face with cold water and brushing her teeth, she felt marginally under control. If she just thought of him like a brother, maybe she could get through this without jumping him.

Yeah, right. Keep telling yourself that O'Toole.

Caitlyn grabbed a comb and the spray bottle she used for her plants on the way back to the kitchen. Mac sat in the chair drinking his coffee with a pensive expression on his face. His chin, devoid of the layer of black stubble, looked even harder and more stubborn.

And devastatingly sexy.

Think of him like a brother. Think of him like a brother.

"Here, wrap this towel around your neck so you can catch the hair that falls." And cover up all that temptingly naked skin.

Mac did as she directed without a comment, and she stepped behind him.

"You're sure you want me to do this?" she asked, running her fingers through the shoulder-length strands. "I could take you to my hairdresser and she could give you a real haircut that isn't quite so short."

"Why don't I just take out an ad in the paper announcing my location instead?"

"You don't have to get snippy. If you want all this cut off, then fine. Just don't complain to me when you can wash your hair with a bar of soap." She sprayed his hair down with the water bottle, smiling when he flinched at the cold water.

"I'm more used to short hair, I only grew it out for the assignment. Besides, I'll be harder to spot with short hair."

Caitlyn didn't think even shaving his head would make him

harder to spot but kept her mouth shut. Long hair or short, Mac's very presence drew attention. Especially female attention.

Grabbing her kitchen shears, Caitlyn hacked away at his hair to get it short enough to use the clippers. Thick, silky strands fell to the floor as she snipped away, and she bemoaned the waste. At least she was getting to play with it a bit before it ended up in the garbage. It might be the only chance she'd have to run her fingers through his hair.

With every clip of the scissors, Mac felt Diego disappear. He wanted to urge Caitlyn to hurry and cut it all off as fast as she could. He'd been Diego the drug dealer for so long that it was a relief to get rid of him. Losing the long hair made him feel like his old self again. A fine upstanding citizen, not a scummy druggie. He didn't relish the idea of going back into the cesspool of his undercover life.

Two weeks away from the street had done a lot to remove Diego from his mind. It was time to remove him from his appearance too. He could justify the change by telling himself the Diego cover was blown anyway, but in reality it had nothing to do with the assignment. Mac had lost so much of himself during this mission and he needed to find himself again. Strange feelings swirled around inside him and he didn't know what was real and what was a result of the situation.

And that scared the hell out of him.

Caitlyn hummed as she trimmed his hair. Her fingers caressed him with every cut. He could smell her familiar, arousing fragrance, and his body responded as if a switch had been thrown. Images of her in nothing but a towel burned in his head. Mac remembered the way her body felt against his, and how she tasted for that brief moment of insanity.

His groin jumped to complete attention and he was glad he had the towel covering his lap.

"Okay, I'm going to use the clippers on the back now. You're sure this is what you want."

"Positive." The quicker the better.

Cool air brushed against his neck as Caitlyn razed his hair close to his skull. He felt freer with each stroke of the clippers.

"Almost done, I just have to do the front and sides. You'll look ready for boot camp."

Caitlyn stepped in front of him, and he fought to keep his gaze averted. Her thin tank top left little to the imagination, and her breasts moved hypnotically underneath it. Looking down wasn't much better. Her miles and miles of legs were shapely and tan and he could imagine them wrapped around his waist.

He wiggled in the seat and put his hands under the towel to keep them from touching her.

"Hold still, I don't want to cut your ear by accident." She pushed his head down and pulled it close to her chest to hold it still while she trimmed around his ear.

Mac didn't dare breath. His lips were inches away from her breasts and her scent filled his brain. He wanted to move his mouth over and draw her nipple into it. Clenching his hands into fists, he fought the urge to run his fingers under her shirt and see if her skin was as soft as he remembered it.

"There. Almost done. And not even a little nick. That wasn't so bad, was it?" Caitlyn asked, stepping back and surveying her work.

"Not at all." It was worse than bad. It was torture.

"I'm going to try to do the top a little longer so you don't have Liam's cop haircut. If it doesn't work I can always cut it all off."

"Whatever you feel comfortable with." He was feeling decidedly *un*comfortable.

She tipped his head down again and hummed while she worked. Her legs straddled his, and he wasn't sure whether to curse the sweatpants that kept him from feeling her bare skin or thank the Lord for them.

"This is coming out great. Maybe I should try this on Liam next time." Caitlyn turned the clippers off with a flourish. "Want to see?" She grabbed a small mirror off the wall and brought it over.

A stranger stared back at him. It had been so long since he'd seen his face under all his hair, he almost didn't recognize his reflection. He had a few cuts from his shaving adventure but his face was free of the scruffy beard he'd sported for so long. Diego was gone.

Good riddance.

"What do you think?" Caitlyn asked anxiously, looking at him over the mirror.

"You do good work. Thanks. It's been so long since my hair was this short, I almost didn't recognize myself."

"Good. If you don't recognize yourself, maybe the people who are after you won't either." She spun around quickly and hung the mirror back on the wall.

Before he could stop her, she lifted the corners of the towel covering his chest and lap and pulled it away. The sweatpants did nothing to disguise the raging hard-on he still sported. Mac clamped his legs together, praying she wouldn't notice.

"Oh my." Her eyes widened and she licked her lips.

So much for hoping she didn't notice.

"It's morning. That happens to guys in the morning." It was only half a lie. Men did get erections in the morning. Just not ones the size of Texas.

"I know. I have slept with a man before. Plus I have three brothers." She shook her head slightly and moved behind him to brush the hair off the back of his neck with a washcloth.

Mac didn't want to think about her sleeping with another man when his body was on fire for her.

"I'm surprised your brothers let anyone get close enough for you to sleep with them." He meant it sound flippant but it came out sharper than he'd wanted.

"That's why I went to college out of state. They couldn't follow me around on dates in Florida."

She moved in front of him and tipped his head back. "Close your eyes, I need to brush off the hair on your forehead."

He closed his eyes, but that only increased his torment. Every brush of her fingers on his skin was intensified, her scent seemed magnified, and he could picture her naked much too easily for his peace of mind.

"Oh, one of your cuts is bleeding. Here, I'll get it." Caitlyn straddled his legs and pressed the washcloth to his face.

Her thighs brushed his and her breasts were inches from his mouth. The temptation was too much. Mac couldn't stop himself, and frankly, didn't want to. His body was still on fire from last night, and being this close to her was more than he could take and remain sane.

Consequences be damned. He had to taste her again.

Mac pulled her down onto his lap and captured her face in his hands. Looking right into her startled brown eyes, he drew her slowly forward, giving her plenty of time to stop him.

She didn't stop him.

Her eyes drifted closed and she let out a small sigh as her lips met his. Sweet. She was so sweet. Soft lips gave under the pressure of his mouth on hers. Mac released her face so he could explore her body instead.

He slipped his hands under her shirt and up her back. Silky smooth skin glided under his fingers as they roamed. Caitlyn gasped when his thumbs grazed her ribs and the underside of her breasts. Mac took advantage of her surprise and slipped his tongue inside the warm cavern of her mouth.

Caitlyn's hands dug into his chest as she responded to this new assault. Her tongue dueled with his, becoming more aggressive as he moved his hands higher on her body.

Blood pounded through his veins and his heart raced to keep up with it. Mac pulled her closer to him, her warmth cupping his hardness through their clothes. He could feel the pressure building as she rocked against him. Caitlyn's head fell back and he trailed kisses down her throat and collarbone.

Giving into the temptation that had been riding him for days, Mac drew her nipple through the shirt into his mouth. Caitlyn's hands clamped down on his head and she held him to her breast. Her hips thrust furiously against his, stoking the flames hotter and higher. He was ready to self-combust as it was, and they were still dressed.

A situation he could change with very little effort.

Mac released her nipple and lifted her tank top, revealing her breasts to his hungry gaze. Caitlyn lifted her arms to take the shirt off completely, but he stopped her, trapping her arms in the shirt.

He was about to feast on her bounty when the phone rang and they jumped apart like scalded cats.

Caitlyn fumbled with her shirt, trying to get her arms untangled. Before Caitlyn could answer it, the machine picked up.

Tom's recorded voice echoed in the kitchen. "You've reached the O'Toole residence, please leave a message."

"Hey, Cat just getting a head count. Are you doing dinner with us at the station tomorrow? Or are you too busy, again?" There was an emphasis on the last word and Mac felt his arousal die.

"I'm here, Jim." Caitlyn picked up the phone, cutting off the message. She held her shirt across her breasts and turned her back to Mac.

He wanted to leave, to give her some privacy, but he wasn't sure his legs would hold him yet. Her brother's voice might have cooled his ardor, but it would take a while for his blood pressure to come back to normal.

"I'll be there. Okay. Yes. I'm fine." Caitlyn looked over her shoulder at him. "Uh huh. Yup. Good-bye." She hung up the phone and slipped the shirt over her head.

"That was Jim, I take it?" he asked, more to break the silence than for any need for confirmation.

"Yeah, he wants to make sure I'm coming to dinner tomorrow night. I'd better go or they'll show up here in the fire trucks and barbeque on the front lawn."

"That wouldn't be good. You should go anyway, make things look as normal as possible." And give him a chance to pull himself together.

"I will. As long as you'll promise not to disappear while I'm gone." She looked him in the eye.

"Where would I go?" he asked, avoiding the promise.

"I don't know, but now that you're feeling better, you might get the insane idea you can go back out on the streets. It's only been two weeks since you had a gaping hole in your side."

"I know, but you're such a miracle worker I'm feeling almost as good as new." He certainly hadn't been thinking about any pain in his side a few minutes ago.

"That's what I'm afraid of. Now that you've shed your disguise and can move around without passing out, you think you can conquer the world."

"I'm going to have to leave eventually. I can't just hide away in your apartment reading Cosmo every day." He couldn't let her get attached to him. She'd only get hurt in the end. Nothing could keep him from finishing this job. Or at least nothing should.

Somehow, his dedication to the job had taken a back seat to Caitlyn and her safety since he'd woken up in her apartment.

Chapter Nine

"Earth to Caitlyn. Hello, anybody home?"

Caitlyn jumped as Jim clapped a hand on her shoulder. "Geez, Jimbo. You scared me half to death." She'd been lost in thought, remembering the steamy kiss Mac had planted on her yesterday. The tingle of awareness had stayed with her ever since.

"Well, wake up and pay attention. I called your name at least three times. Did you bring the potato salad?"

"Crap. I left it in the Jeep. Hold on, I'll get it." She started back out the bay door, hoping to steal a minute or two to gather her thoughts before facing the combined scrutiny of her brothers and the guys on the department. If she didn't get her head out of the clouds, they'd pick up on it and grill her all night long.

"Where'd you park?"

"I got a spot around the corner. I'll be right back." Caitlyn patted the pockets of her shorts looking for where she'd left her keys. She'd been a bit absent minded for the past two days.

"Wait up. Let me grab a radio and I'll go with you."

Before she could protest, Jimmy grabbed a portable walkie-talkie and caught up with her.

"I'm just going half a block away, not to Timbuktu." So much for having a few minutes to get her head on straight.

"I know, but I don't like you walking on the street alone. This isn't the most wonderful area of the city."

Caitlyn looked at him out of the corner of her eye. Something was wrong. She'd been so wrapped up in what was going on with Mac, she hadn't paid any attention to what was happening right under her nose.

"What's going on, Jim? You've got something on your mind."

"What do you mean? Just because I don't want you walking alone in the city at night, you think something is wrong?" He wouldn't look at her, though, and his hands were stuffed in his pants pockets.

"It's still light out and I've been walking around this city since Dad was on the department. Spill it, or I'll tell Maggie how you still eat cereal in your underwear."

At the mention of the redheaded nurse, Jim whipped his head around to her. "She already knows."

Caitlyn stopped dead in her tracks. Jim and Maggie? Already? "Hold the phone. Are you telling me you slept with her already? Didn't you just ask her out like two weeks ago?"

Jim had the grace to look embarrassed. "It happened kind of fast but yeah."

"Is that why you've been acting so strange? Are you worried about they guys finding out about Maggie, or that I would?" She hadn't worked with Maggie since the night her apartment got broken into. Apparently there was a reason Maggie hadn't called her in a while.

"I don't care what those bozos think. They'll bust my stones no matter what."

"But you're worried about what I'll think?" Caitlyn asked in surprise.

"Yeah. I mean, she's your friend and all." Jim looked even more uncomfortable.

"Well, I guess it depends on where you're going with this." She had to think on this for a minute. How did she feel about her brother sleeping with one of her friends? Caitlyn knew her brothers didn't lack for female companionship but they'd kept that part of their lives away from her in the past. With Jim sleeping with Maggie, that was no longer an option.

"Hell, if I knew that, I wouldn't be talking to you about it." He stopped walking and ran a hand through his hair. "If this was anyone else, I'd enjoy the time we spent together and move on."

"But—" Something was really bothering him.

"But this is all different. More...I don't know, just more intense than anything I've ever felt before."

"You're telling me you've never slept with a woman this soon before?"

"Hell, no. It's just with Maggie, it's different. I think about her all the time, in and out of bed. I like being with her even if we're not, you know, having sex."

"You're in love," Caitlyn said with amazement.

"Bullshit. I don't believe in that hearts and flower crap." But his eyes looked a little wild and he couldn't meet her gaze.

"You think about her all the time, you enjoy spending time with her when you're not having sex, and you've never felt this way before. If that's not love, I don't know what is."

"Infatuation. It's only been two weeks, for crying out loud."

"Yeah, right. Go ahead, keep lying to yourself if it makes you feel better, but don't take so long to admit it that you end up losing Maggie. She's a great person and I heartily approve, not that you're looking for my approval." Caitlyn resumed walking.

Her brother in love with her friend. Hard to believe it could happen so fast. *Wonder how long it's going to take him to admit it to himself.*

"Streets are quiet tonight," Jim said, closing the door on the subject.

"Yeah, the ER has been quiet lately too. Weird. Usually summer is the busiest time of the year."

"Now that you mention it, yeah, it has been quiet lately. Makes me nervous."

Caitlyn laughed. "You're never happy. If it's busy, then you bitch because you're running all night long. If it's quiet, then you're nervous. Make up your mind."

"It just feels like everyone is holding their breath or something. You know how right before a storm everything gets all quiet? That's what the city feels like to me, like a big storm is headed our way."

Caitlyn shivered at his words. She wished she could tell him about Mac and her fears, but she'd promised to keep silent.

A storm was coming and she feared Mac would be right in the middle of it. A chill chased its way down her spine despite the hot, humid air.

Reaching her Jeep, Caitlyn unlocked it and reached inside for the huge bowl of potato salad.

"Hey, what's this?" Jim squatted down next to the seat and scratched at spot on the carpet. "Looks like blood."

Blood? Oh no. She thought she'd gotten all of Mac's blood cleaned up. "Must be from that stray I picked up. I thought I managed to clean it all up, guess I missed a spot." She shoved the bowl in his hands and closed the door with her hip as soon as he got out of the way.

"How's he doing?"

"Ah, better. In fact, he's almost ready to go back out into the streets."

"You can't just send him back out into the streets. He'll only get beat up again."

No kidding. "Well, I can't keep him." But oh boy, would she like to.

"Not in that tiny apartment. Why don't you bring him to a shelter or put an ad in the paper or something? Give him a good home."

A bubble of nervous laughter rose up from her stomach and Caitlyn fought it down. Her brother would think she'd lost it completely if she laughed at his suggestion. "I'll figure something out. I just need to make sure he's healthy enough to move around before I let him go."

"Whatever. You're so softhearted, I hate to think of you spending all your time taking in strays only to send them back out again."

"I don't mind." That was an understatement. "It's very rewarding." More laughter threatened.

"You need to go out more. Maybe Maggie can set you up with someone and we can double date."

Not in this lifetime. There was no way she wanted to watch her brother and best friend make goo goo eyes at each other while she sat there with some poor sap they roped into coming along. "You're in love, so suddenly everyone else needs to be paired off too? Since when have you cared about my social life?"

"I am not 'in love' and I've always cared about your social life."

"Yeah, making sure I didn't have one. I'll take care of myself. You just worry about getting your head on straight before Maggie decides she doesn't need some hard-headed Irish man who can't admit his feelings in her life."

Jim paled in front of her and she almost felt bad for her words. Almost. At least he wasn't interested in her "stray" anymore.

Liam's car was parked illegally in front of the station when they got back. He must have just gotten there, because he was still in the driver's seat. As they got closer, he quickly clicked his cell phone closed and got out of the car.

Could Liam have someone in his life too? He'd been in bed with someone when he showed up at her place in the middle of the night. Man, everyone was hooking up except her.

"What took you so long? I'm starving." Liam gave her a one armed hug before trying to pick at the plastic wrap over the bowl Jim held.

"I think you'll survive." Caitlyn slapped his hands away from the bowl.

A call came from the back of the station. "Burgers are ready! Who wants cheese?"

"Come on, I want to get my burger before it's cooked to a hockey puck." Caitlyn wrapped an arm through each of her brothers' arms and herded them towards the picnic tables. With any luck at all, she'd get through the meal without letting something about Mac slip out. For the first time in her life, she actually wished for a fire call to interrupt dinner.

The alarms were amazingly silent.

Caitlyn laughed at the insults flying around the table but, for the most part, kept her mouth closed. There was enough good-natured bantering for her to get lost in the background. If anyone noticed she was quieter than usual, they didn't bring it up.

She was elbow deep in soapsuds when two hands grabbed her around the waist and spun her around. Water and bubbles flew as she was lifted off her feet.

"Hey. Is that any way to greet your long lost brother?" Tom's laughing brown eyes smiled down at her.

"Tom. When did you get into town?" She pulled him down for a drippy hug.

"About half an hour ago. I had some vacation time to use up, and since I was between assignments, I thought I'd come home for a while." A shadow crossed his face, but he quickly hid it behind a smile. "Had to check up on my little sis and make sure she wasn't shacked up with some guy."

"Like I could do that with the three of you around." She tried to make it sound teasing but it sounded weak. "Although, maybe you'd better check up on Liam. I'm pretty sure he was 'keeping company' the other night." Family loyalty be damned. If Tom was on Liam's case, he wouldn't be on hers.

"Really? Looks like my little brother's taken a page out of my book." He looked more pleased than annoyed by the thought.

"Oh, that's fair. Liam and Jim can sleep with whoever they want and you think it's great. If I so much as look at a guy, you're ready to break his kneecaps."

"You're a girl. It's different," he said as if that explained everything. "Is there any potato salad left? Louie is making me up a burger now but it's not the same without something on the side."

"There might be some but I'm stuck on dish duty tonight, so I can't get it for you." She turned back to the sink.

"You save me some salad and I'll finish up the dishes." He rolled up his sleeves, giving her a wink.

"It's a deal." She wasn't conning him, but at least she got out of doing the greasy pans.

Grabbing a paper plate, she loaded the last of the creamy salad on it and added some green salad and a few chips. Helping herself to one, she hopped up on the counter.

"So, where're you staying?" He usually stayed with Jim, since he had the only apartment with a guest room. If Jim was romancing Maggie though, he might not want the company.

"I don't know. You get a real bed yet?"

Panic rolled through her. If he wanted to stay with her,

there'd be no way she could dissuade him without telling him why.

"I have the futon in the living room. You could sleep on that." If she acted like she wanted him there, maybe he wouldn't be suspicious.

"That torture device disguised as a bed? No, thank you."

Time to throw her brothers to the wolves. "Oh come on, it'll be fun. Besides, Jim may not want you to stay with him. He's got a new girlfriend he's hot and heavy with now. You might cramp his style."

A devilish smile crossed Tom's face. "Oh really? Little brother has a girlfriend? Anyone I know?" He dried his hands off and scooped a handful of chips off his plate.

"I'm not sure. She's a friend of mine from work, Maggie."

"Redhead? Built like a—"

"Yup! That's her." Figured he'd remember her good-looking friends.

Before she could chide him for being a sexist pig, alarm bells filled the air. Firefighters rushed in organized chaos to the trucks and jumped into their gear. Louie and Jim ran through the kitchen on their way to their engine.

"Your burger's almost ready. Turn off the gas when you're done," Louie called.

"Jim! Give me your keys so I can drop my stuff at your place," Tom shouted to him.

A flash of panic crossed Jim's face, but he pulled the keys out of his pocket and tossed them across the room. "Don't touch the stereo, it took me a week to reprogram it after last time." He didn't have time to say more before hauling his gear on and hopping into the driver's seat.

Tom threw the keys up in the air and caught them with a chuckle. "Wonder if Maggie likes to surprise him by showing up in lingerie?"

"She might, but she's working tonight so you're out of luck."

"Too bad, it might have been interesting." Tom walked out back and returned with his burger. "It's been a long time since I've had something good and interesting pop into my life."

Another shadow filled his eyes.

"What's going on? Why are you really home?" Fear stabbed into her gut. Was something going on between Mac and him?

"I told you, I had some vacation time coming. Besides, I needed a change of pace." He looked at her briefly, then focused on eating.

"If you say so. Just remember, I'm here if you need me." She kissed him on top of his head.

"I know. You're always the sounding board. Must get old after a while."

"Not really. If you three didn't have me to talk to, you'd fester. If you're staying at Jim's, do you mind if I head home? I need to get some stuff done before work tomorrow."

"You still working nights?"

"Yup. I've got two twelves ahead of me, then four days off."

"Be careful at night, would you?"

"Oh, brother. Now you sound like Liam. I'm parking in the garage, there's nothing to worry about."

"Humor me and let me worry anyway. Just because the parking garage has a door and a guard doesn't mean it's safe."

No kidding. "I know. I'm being careful, but just to please you, I'll be even more careful, okay?"

"Okay. Oh, and one more thing."

"Yes?" *Please don't walk me to my car.*

"The potato salad needs more salt." Tom laughed as she threw a crumpled up napkin at him.

"Good night. I'll swing by Jim's later on and bring you some food."

If she went there maybe she could keep Tom from discovering Mac at her house.

&

Mac slipped into the house as quietly as he could. Caitlyn wasn't home yet, but he didn't want to alert her neighbors to his movements. His side was on fire and he felt like he'd run a marathon.

All for nothing.

He hadn't been able to find out a single thing about the Children's movements. The streets were quiet and no one was talking. A sick ball of nerves formed in the pit of his stomach.

From what he'd be able to pick up from Carlos' conversations, something big was coming. What it was, Mac didn't know. But with the number of weapons the Children had been flashing, it couldn't be good.

When the weapons first started appearing, Mac had thought the Children had been gearing up for a major turf battle. He'd suspected Carlos was trying for a hostile takeover of the other two big city gangs. But then the order had come down that no one was to be taking pot shots at the rival gang members.

It didn't make any sense. Carlos had consolidated his operations to just drug trafficking, letting his other interests go without a fight. Could he be getting ready to run? That didn't make sense. If he was trying to get out of the business, why accumulate so many guns?

No answers were forthcoming on the streets tonight. Not much had changed from when he left, except the tensions seemed to be that much higher. Every eye on the street watched everyone else warily. Mac hadn't dared go deep into Children territory for fear someone would recognize him.

Damn! He needed to do something, find out something, before the entire city exploded in gang warfare. And with the automatic weapons he'd seen flashed by Carlos' bodyguards, gang members wouldn't be the only ones getting shot.

Caitlyn would be home any minute and he was covered in sweat and grime from his adventures. She was already nervous about him leaving before he was ready. If she knew he was making forays out into the streets while she was gone, he'd never hear the end of it. He'd better grab a shower and clean up while he could.

Her scent lingered in the bathroom, making him painfully aware of his attraction to her. Mac didn't know how much longer he'd be able to survive without taking her to bed. The two kisses they shared had done more to whet his appetite for her than anything else. He thought about her constantly, dreamed of touching her nightly, and counted the hours until she got off work so he could talk to her again.

Man, he needed to get out of here soon. He was starting to lose his mind. Scrubbing a dab of shampoo over his bristly hair, Mac soaped and rinsed in record time. He might smell like flowers but at least he was clean.

No wonder he thought about her so much. He was seeped in her presence. And it made sense that he waited for her to come home from work. It was damn boring staring at the four walls for twelve hours. Now that he was healthier, he could actually get out of the house, but for a while he could barely get out of bed.

Still, he'd better be careful how often he hit the streets. He didn't want anyone following him back.

"Mac? I'm home." Caitlyn called out.

"I'm in the bathroom." Did he bring clean clothes in with him? No. Shit. His dirty sweats and T-shirt lay in a pile on the floor. Mac scooped them up and threw them in the laundry, then wrapped the towel around his waist.

"Oh, there you are." Caitlyn's eyes widened at his near naked state, and he could feel his body harden. One look, one gesture, that's all it took for him to respond to her.

"I was all sweaty, so I thought I'd take a shower before bed. How was dinner?" He wished she'd stop looking at him like she wanted to eat him whole.

"It was good. Interesting."

"Interesting, how?" Had she heard something?

"Jim cornered me to talk about Maggie, Liam was distant and left right after supper, and Tom showed up out of the blue."

"Tom's here?" Mac immediately perked up.

"Yeah, he said he had some vacation time to use up and since he was between assignments he thought he'd come home for a little while."

Suspicion reared its ugly head again. Things were building to a climax and Tom just happened to show up. Coincidence? Carlos definitely had a contact with the police, and the guns he was getting weren't coming from a local source. Could Tom be the government connection while Liam was the local one?

"How's he doing?" Mac asked to cover his surprise. He couldn't stand the thought of his partner being in cahoots with Carlos but he had to keep an open mind. Everyone was a suspect.

"Okay, I guess. Something's bothering him though, I could tell."

"Oh? How?"

"I can't explain it, he just wasn't his usual self. He tried to act normal and goofy, but every once in a while I'd see a look on his face. A sad look. There's something on his mind."

"If he just got off assignment, that isn't unusual. Especially when you've been in deep cover. It takes a little while to remember who you really are. Tom's been jumping from one mission to another. It's no wonder he has to take a break."

"Could be. I don't know. All I know is I almost wet my pants when he asked if he could bunk down here."

"What?"

"Relax, he doesn't want to sleep on the futon, and that's the only other bed I have. He's staying with Jim and plans on tormenting him mercilessly about having a new girlfriend."

"Sounds like Tom." The towel was slipping, so he snugged it tighter. The cloth brushed against his engorged penis and a shiver went through him. Almost as if an invisible cord connected them, Caitlyn shivered too. "So why do you think Liam was distant?" He needed to distract her and get some information but he was the one that was getting distracted.

"He barely said two words at dinner and kept looking at his cell phone. Then, as soon as he could, he bolted. Didn't even stay for dessert, and he loves pie."

"Did he know Tom was coming into town?"

"I don't think so, or he would have stayed." She shook her head as if to clear her thoughts. "Anyway, I made it through without slipping, and Tom isn't staying here so I consider it a successful night. I have to do a load of laundry, then I'm tucking it in."

Tucking it in. To her bed. That was less than ten yards away from his. Would she toss and turn as much as he did?

Could she ignore the fact that one thin wall separated them?

Her eyes were dilated and kept drifting to his torso. If she didn't move soon, his body would spontaneously combust from the looks she was giving him.

"Ah, if you give me a minute, I'll get dressed and you can have the bathroom to yourself."

"Good idea." She swallowed hard and spun around.

Mac had a lot to think about, but what kept his thoughts occupied had very little to do with the O'Toole brothers, and a great deal to do with their sister.

Chapter Ten

Screaming pain throbbed in Caitlyn's back and down her legs as her spine twisted in unnatural directions. She struggled to hold down the junkie so that Maggie could get his wrist restrained. For such a skinny man, he put up quite a fight.

"I know you've got drugs here. I need them, bitch! Now!" The junkie grabbed at the keys clipped to Maggie's belt.

Caitlyn locked his elbow and held on for dear life. Two security guards held his legs while a third secured them to the gurney. The patient weighed maybe one hundred and ten pounds soaking wet but the drugs in his system gave him inhuman strength.

"I need a hit."

"I'll give you a hit," Caitlyn mumbled under her breath as she struggled to hold him.

"Got it!" Maggie stepped back, rubbing her arm where she'd gotten hurt earlier.

"Are you okay?" Caitlyn waited to make sure the restraints would hold before she administered the shot that would calm the junkie down. It wasn't what he wanted but it would keep him from hurting himself until they could get him evaluated.

"I'm fine. I'll end up with a bruise but that's all. How about you? You were holding him."

"I might have pulled a muscle in my back but nothing serious." Caitlyn dismissed the pain. "A hot shower and some ibuprofen and I'll be good as new," she said, moving out into the hall.

"Baloney. I've pulled back muscles before. You'll be fine tonight because you're moving, but come tomorrow you'll barely be able to get out of bed." Maggie grabbed the schedule while Caitlyn filled out the chart on the junkie.

"I'm off tomorrow anyway. I'll take it easy for the next couple of days and be fine." Caitlyn hid a yawn behind her hand. She hadn't been sleeping well since she'd gotten a look at Mac wearing nothing but a towel that rode low on his hips. Sexual tension was better than coffee for keeping her awake at night.

"Darn right you will. In fact, you'll take the next week off." Maggie made some notes on the schedule and closed it with a decisive snap.

"What are you talking about? It's a stupid pulled muscle, nothing to get all upset about."

"It's not just that. You look stressed out and Jim thinks you're working too hard. He says you're so tired you aren't going out anymore."

"Oh." Caitlyn looked up at her friend. "So that's what this is all about. Jim is on your case about me working too hard, so you're going to give me a few extra days off." Her temper started to simmer. It was bad enough to have an interfering brother, but when he recruited her friend that was too much.

"It's not just that. Look at you. You've got circles under your eyes, you're crabby, and you've gotten so jumpy you're making me a nervous wreck. Just because Jim mentioned it doesn't mean that it's a bad thing. He really cares about you, and I do too."

Chagrin warred with temper. She *was* tired and she *was* cranky and she *could* use an extra day off to spend some time with Mac before he left. Why fight against something she wanted just because it came from her brother's interference?

"Okay, I give."

"That was easy." Maggie raised an eyebrow. "Too easy. Are you sure you didn't get hit in the head during that restraint?"

"Geez. If I argue then you call me crabby, and if I give in you call me crazy. A girl can't win around here."

"Then I guess it's a good thing you'll be on a mini vacation. Just think, six whole days without junkies screaming at you, drunks throwing up on you, and running your feet off."

"However will I survive?" Caitlyn laughed.

"I'm sure you'll find something to do." Maggie pulled her in for a quick hug before the intercom announced the arrival of another ambulance.

∞

"Darn it. I left my jacket in my locker." Maggie stopped two feet from the door to the parking garage.

"I doubt you'll need it, it's got to be eighty degrees still." Caitlyn fanned her face for emphasis.

"I know, but I have my dry cleaning ticket in there, and I need to pick up my dress tomorrow for the Appreciation Dinner. I have to go back and get it."

"I'll walk with you then. You shouldn't be walking the streets alone at midnight."

"Don't be silly. It makes no sense for both of us to be miserable just because I'm an airhead. I'll get Billy to walk me back. It's what he gets paid for."

"If you say so. My back is aching too much for me to argue." Caitlyn hurt with every step she took. It wouldn't break her heart to go straight home.

"See. I told you."

"Yeah, yeah, yeah. Just get Billy so I can leave with a clear conscience." Caitlyn waited for Maggie to get the security guard that manned the booth at the parking garage. Once she was sure Maggie wasn't going to risk going back alone, she headed for the garage entrance.

An arm wrapped around her throat, cutting off her air. Someone grabbed her hand, pulling it up behind her. Her shoulder burned from the strain.

"My money's in my purse. Go ahead and take it." Her pictures and credit cards weren't worth her life.

"I don't want your money. I want to know where Mac is." Hot, moist air that reeked of cigarettes wafted over her cheek.

"Mac?" Oh my God. They were after Mac and they knew she

was involved. "I don't know any Mac."

"Don't fuck with me!" The arm came off her neck and the click of a switchblade opening sounded in the air. Cold metal pressed against her throat, just behind her jaw. "Tell me where Mac is and I won't have to cut this pretty face of yours."

Caitlyn flinched as the tip of the knife pierced her skin. Her knees turned to water and she let out a small sob. She could feel a trickle of blood drip down her throat.

Think. She had to think instead of panicking.

What did Tom tell her to do in a situation like this? Her brain spun in circles and she couldn't focus. Fear made the blood pound in her ears and all she could hear was her rapid breathing.

"Tell me." He pulled her arm up higher, wrenching her shoulder painfully.

It all came back to her in a flood. Liam holding his arm across her throat and her hand pulled up behind her back. Without another thought, Caitlyn raked the sole of her shoe down her attacker's shin. While he was distracted from the pain, she grabbed his hand near the knife, digging her fingers in and holding tightly. Quickly, she turned and stepped back, pulling him with her.

Lashing out with a kick to his groin, Caitlyn dropped his hand and ran. She had a brief glimpse of a man with a jagged scar across his cheek before she fled into the parking garage and ran for the safety of her car.

Her hands shook so badly she could barely get the key into the lock. Tears streamed down her face as she fumbled with the door and got into the Jeep. As soon as she shut the door, she locked it and jammed the keys into the ignition.

Slow down. Slow down.

She had to calm down before she tried to drive home. They could be expecting her to run and try to follow her. The police. She'd go to the police station. They wouldn't follow her there.

But Mac didn't want anyone knowing about his involvement. If she went to the cop shop they'd ask questions that she couldn't answer. She had to keep Mac safe.

Throwing the Jeep into reverse, she backed out and worked her way out of the garage. No one followed her but she couldn't be sure. What to do, what to do? Adrenaline blurred her vision as she tried to see if the set of headlights in her mirror were the same ones as a minute ago.

Wait a minute. Just because she went to the police station didn't mean she had to tell them about it. If someone were following her, wouldn't they expect her to go to the cops? She could just say she was looking for Liam and leave.

Caitlyn dug around in her purse for a napkin or tissue or something to wipe the trickle of blood off her neck. Nothing. Not even a receipt. Her hand brushed the material of her windbreaker. That would smear the blood more than clean it.

But it would cover it up.

As she pulled into the police station, she wrestled the jacket over her head and made sure her hair stayed tucked under it to cover up her neck. Taking a deep breath to calm her shaking hands and even shakier nerves, she climbed out of the Jeep and walked up the stairs to the officer at the reception desk.

He didn't look familiar, thank God.

Caitlyn pasted a smile on her face and approached the window. "Hi, is Liam O'Toole working tonight?"

The officer looked her over quickly, then glanced at the duty sheet in front of him. "I'm sorry, Ma'am, he's not on tonight. Can I leave him a message?"

"No, that's okay. I'll catch up with him later. Thank you."

Caitlyn walked away from the reception window and squatted down as if tying her shoe. She wanted to give anyone who was watching her plenty of time to get nervous. Taking her time, she retied both shoes and walked slowly out of the station, searching for anything out of place.

The parking lot was deserted and the street empty of cars. If anyone suddenly pulled out behind her, they'd stand out like a sore thumb. Caitlyn walked to the car as calmly as she could, but inside, her heart beat furiously. She wanted to run to the Jeep and peel out of the lot.

Probably not a good idea in front of the police station.

Instead, she pulled out slowly and carefully, keeping a watchful eye on the rearview mirror. Using every back road and circuitous route she could think of, she wound her way home.

Just to be extra certain, Caitlyn drove around her block twice before pulling into the driveway and parking.

Cutting the engine, she laid her head on the steering wheel for a brief moment. She had to pull herself together before she faced Mac. The adrenaline had worn off and she felt exhausted. Every pain in her body was amplified, from the cut on her neck all the way to the muscle aches in her back and legs. Maybe she could just take a little nap in the Jeep.

A knock on the window brought her head up with a jolt and sent bolts of fear shooting through her body.

Mac peered in at her, a concerned look on his face.

Opening up the door, Caitlyn pushed him aside and got out. "For the love of God. Don't do that. I almost peed my pants." She grabbed his arm and hustled him towards the apartment.

"I heard you pull up, then when you didn't come in I got worried. I checked from the window and saw your head down. I didn't know what to think, so I came out to check on you."

"I thought you didn't want anyone to see you? Stay in the apartment before you get killed." Caitlyn's gaze darted around, searching for watchers.

"It's safe, I looked first."

"Yeah, sure." Once in the kitchen, Caitlyn shut the door and slid the lock home. "I need to talk to you, come on." Without waiting for him to follow her, she scurried to the living room to check the locks on the windows. It was stifling hot, but better sweaty and safe than cool and dead.

"What's going on? You're running around like a mouse on crack."

"We've got to make a plan. They know I know where you are." Caitlyn's back hurt with every step she took, but fear was a great motivator. She'd rest when she was sure all the windows and doors were secure.

"What do you mean?" Mac grabbed her arm and stopped her in her tracks. "What happened?"

"I was coming out of work and Maggie—you remember her? My friend who's dating Jim?" At Mac's nod, she continued. "We were walking to the parking garage when she realized she'd left her jacket in her locker. I waited to make sure she went back

with the security guard, then I went to step into the garage."
Caitlyn took a deep breath. Her legs started shaking as she
recalled the events of the night.

"Go on." Mac rubbed her arm.

"I was walking towards the door when someone grabbed me
and asked for Mac."

"Not Diego?"

"No. He said Mac. He wanted to know where Mac was."

"Damn it." He pounded his hand into his fist and spun
around.

His anger sent a shiver of fear through her, even though it
was directed elsewhere.

"How'd you get away?" He turned back to her, looking her
over for signs of injury.

Thank God she still had the jacket on. "I used some of the
tricks Tom and Liam taught me and ran for the Jeep."

"No wonder you were sitting in the car. What a night." Mac
took a step towards her but stopped before he reached her. He
shoved his hands into his pockets and stood stiffly away from
her.

Caitlyn shook off the desire to have him take her in his
arms. She could stand on her own two feet. Even if they were
shaking in their shoes. "You have no idea. Tonight was drug
night at the ER. We had so many junkies going through detox
that we almost ran out of restraints." As if the words called up
the pain, the muscles in her back throbbed in agony. "I'm going
to take a hot shower."

"Okay." Mac seemed lost in thought. He sat and turned
away from her.

Wincing in pain, Caitlyn pulled the windbreaker over her
head and crossed to the bathroom. After her shower she'd try
and talk Mac out of his funk but right now she didn't have the
energy.

"Son of a bitch!" Mac grabbed her again and pulled her to
him, sending new darts of pain through her back. "You're
bleeding!"

Her hand went to her neck and touched the sticky blood
there. "It's just a scratch. I'm sure it's stopped bleeding."

Caitlyn tried to keep up with Mac as he dragged her to the bathroom and flipped on the light.

"Bullshit, that's no scratch. That's a knife cut, and it's still seeping. Where's your first aid kit?"

"In the closet next to the washer and dryer. Just get me some peroxide and it'll be fine. Really, it hardly even hurts now."

Catching her first glimpse of the cut in the mirror, she had to admit it was pretty impressive looking. The trickle she'd felt sliding down her neck had stained her uniform shirt. Her hair was stuck to it, matted with blood in spots, and the wound leaked slowly.

"I can't believe you didn't tell me some punk pulled a knife on you. That's it, I'm out of here and you're moving in with Jim and Tom. Maybe between the two of them they can keep you safe. I'm sure as hell doing a crappy job."

"It's not up to you to keep me safe. And I'm not going into hiding." She winced away as he cleaned the blood off her neck with a washcloth.

"Yes, you are. This is the last straw. Call out of work, you're going to disappear for a while until I can be sure you're safe."

Caitlyn grabbed the cloth out of his hands and threw it in the sink. "I make my own decisions and you can just kiss my royal Irish ass if you think I'm going to let another man try to take over my life. I've had enough of that with my brothers." She stalked out of the bathroom.

"That's who I'm worried about." He stormed after her.

"My brothers? You're worried about them?"

"Yes. Tom made it clear in no uncertain terms that you were off limits. If they found out I not only have feelings for you but that I'm putting your life in danger—"

"You have feelings for me?" A warm fluttery feeling tried to make its way through the boiling anger in her belly. She conveniently ignored the rest of his sentence.

"Yes...I do. I didn't want to, but it just happened." He ran his hand over his chin, then let it drop to his side. "But that's beside the point. I still can't do anything about those feelings."

"Bullshit." She threw his words back at him. "That's the

only point." Caitlyn took a step closer to him. The flutters had taken over and were traveling through her entire body now.

"Either way, you still have to leave."

"No."

"No?" Mac looked incredulous.

"No. I'm not leaving you."

"But your neck. Your brothers—"

"Have got to realize that I'm an adult and I can make my own decisions. I'm not leaving you until all this is settled and I know you'll be safe." She was a step away from him now and sexual energy zipped between them on an invisible current.

"I might never be safe. In my line of work, I go from one dangerous assignment to another. That's no way to raise a family." His gaze blazed into hers, watching her every move.

"Who said anything about raising a family? We don't know what will happen tomorrow, forget next week. After losing my parents so young and having three brothers in dangerous jobs, I've learned to live for today."

"Every time I walk out the door, you'll have to wonder if I'll come back."

"So? I could step out that door and get run over by a bus or get into a car accident. You can't live your life worried about what could happen, you just have to enjoy what is happening."

"Can you tell me what's happening then? Cause I sure as hell can't figure it out." Mac drew her into his arms and lifted her chin with his callused hand.

"I can't either, but it'll be fun trying." Caitlyn went up on tiptoes and pulled his head down to meet hers.

Chapter Eleven

At the first touch of her lips, the last vestiges of fight went out of Mac's body. How could he continue to struggle against something that felt so right? Caitlyn's body fit perfectly against his, her softness a foil to the hard planes of his torso.

He had a desperate need to explore all of that softness.

Running his hands under her shirt, his fingers found the smooth texture of her belly. Her breathing grew rapid as he pushed her shirt higher.

"You're sure about this? I'm not going to ask again."

"Good. I've been sure for a long time. I've just been waiting for you." She shrugged out of her shirt and dropped it on the floor.

With her hand on his, she pulled him towards the door to her room, tossing a come hither smile over her shoulder. Mac's mouth watered at the thought of spending the night stretched out on her bed next to her. He had a lot of fantasies that took place on this bed, and he was going to act out as many of them as he could tonight.

"I should shower first," Caitlyn said, untying her pants. "I'm a little sweaty."

"Later. I'll wash your back." His pulse jumped three notches as she stood in only a pair of lacy white panties and a matching bra. "I'll only get you sweatier anyway.

He yanked off his shirt and pulled her close, reveling in the feel of her nearly naked skin against his chest. Tunneling his fingers into her beautiful hair, he drew her face up for another kiss. Caitlyn's arms wrapped around his neck and she responded to him by sliding her tongue along his lips in a tantalizing caress.

With a groan, he opened his mouth to duel with her tongue. One hand moved down until he reached her bra. He unfastened the clasp and pulled the interfering garment from her body.

His erection pulsed painfully between his legs. "You're so beautiful."

Caitlyn blushed and looked down briefly. "You're none too shabby yourself." Reaching out, she drew him to the bed and knelt on it.

Mac pulled his pants off before he joined her. Her eyes widened at the sight of his naked penis standing at attention. For a minute, he was afraid he might have scared her, but then she licked her lips and reached out to touch his length.

"Not yet. My control is hanging on by a thread right now." To ease her disappointment, Mac laid her down gently amongst the pillows. Lying on his uninjured side, he ran his fingers lightly over her collarbone and between the valley of her breasts.

Her nipples pebbled up and seemed to beg for his kiss. Leaning over, he drew one of the pink peaks into his mouth and rolled it over his tongue. His other hand kneaded her breast and he marveled at the creamy texture.

Caitlyn's hands held his head to her breast and her hips lifted in supplication. Mac moved to her other luscious globe and let his fingers drift down her abdomen until they rested slightly above her waistband.

"You're killing me," she gasped as he slid a finger just under the elastic, but no lower.

"This is only the beginning." Mac trailed nibbling kisses down the lower slope of her breast, then followed the path his hand had taken.

Her scent filled his senses, seducing him as he caressed her body. He rolled until he could kneel between her legs. Taking his finger out from under her panties, Mac let his hand feather lightly over her quivering thighs.

"I've wanted to touch you like this for so long. Every time you gave me a good night kiss, I thought about doing this."

"What took you so long?" She gasped and arched up as his hand grazed the very center of her pleasure through the silk of her underwear.

"Patience, my sweet Caitlyn, patience."

Caitlyn was ready to tell him what he could do with his patience. Her body was on fire for him and she didn't want to wait a second longer. The sight of a naked and aroused Mac was breathtaking. He had muscles on top of muscles and she wanted to touch every one of them. Her fingers itched to feel his steely hardness, but he wouldn't let her. Instead, she dug her hands into the comforter beneath her and held on for dear life.

He was driving her mad. Calloused fingertips brushed over her skin and wakened every nerve ending in her body. And they all wanted more. Her entire being cried out for him to touch her *there* and end her torment. Never had she been so on fire for a man.

"Mac, hurry." She didn't care if it came out like a demand, she couldn't take much more.

"Where's the fun in that? There are so many things I've dreamed of doing to you. I'm not going to rush through them when I finally have the chance."

Heat pooled in her core and spread through her body, making her legs weak and her head spin. Caitlyn felt worshipped, treasured. His lips teased the inside of her thigh, sending shivers of anticipation to her center. Lord. She was ready to explode and he hadn't even taken off her underwear yet.

As if reading her mind, Mac slipped his fingers under the elastic of her panties and slowly dragged them down her legs. She was free and open to his gaze.

And gaze he did.

Caitlyn tried to close her legs in embarrassment, but he wouldn't let her.

"Don't hide from me. I've wanted to see you like this for so long, wet and willing for me, don't deny me now."

"Denying you is the last thing on my mind." Caitlyn reared

up and pulled him to her, capturing his mouth in a kiss.

All the pent up need she had went into that kiss. His weight felt so solid, so right, on top of her. But she wanted more. Much more.

"Ah, do you have any—"

"Hold on." Caitlyn reached for the box she'd recently purchased, just in case.

She handed him the box and Mac fumbled for the condom. Caitlyn almost whimpered at the delay. Finally, she heard the package tear and felt him probing her entrance.

"Look at me. I want to watch you as I make you mine." Mac stared down at her intently.

The pull was overwhelming, and Caitlyn got lost in his eyes. She tried to relax her body as he slipped inside but it was still a tight fit.

"Am I hurting you?" Mac asked, concern and desire coloring his words.

"No, just, ah, stretching. It's been a while for me." He slid in a few more inches, igniting every nerve ending along the way.

"Good." Mac threw his head back as he slammed home, burying himself to the hilt.

Caitlyn's world tipped on its axis. Waves of pleasure carried her higher and higher as Mac moved inside of her. Colors danced behind her eyes as she rode this strange and wonderful tidal wave.

Mac's hands grasped her hips and lifted them higher, giving him better access and hitting pleasure spots she didn't even know she had. Caitlyn clutched his shoulders, needing an anchor to keep her from flying into space.

"Let go. Don't hold back from me," Mac demanded, driving into her.

She didn't know what he wanted from her, wasn't sure how to let go, but when he caressed the nub between her legs, it didn't matter.

"Mac!" Anchor or no, Caitlyn took off to the stars and exploded into a million pieces.

❧

Caitlyn snuggled against Mac's broad back. He was snoring softly, and instead of annoying her, she found it endearing. She didn't want anything to break this mood. She wished she could just freeze time and stay like this forever. Last night had been more amazing than she could ever imagine and she never wanted this feeling to end.

They'd made love through the night, stopping only to shower, and if Caitlyn's back hadn't been aching they probably would have made love there too. The massage Mac gave her to ease the soreness had lead to another hot and sweaty bout, so she couldn't complain too much.

Who would've thought such a crappy shift at work would lead to such bliss when she came home? Maybe she should thank the thug who nicked her throat since it made Mac admit his feelings for her.

"What are you smiling about?" Mac rolled over and pulled her close, wrapping an arm around her.

"I thought you were sleeping. How did you know I was smiling?" Caitlyn ran her fingers through the hair on his chest.

"I was, but I felt you pressed against me and the insatiable monster between my legs woke me up. Then I caught your reflection in the mirror over the dresser. Does this mean you have no regrets?"

"Regrets? The only regret I have is it took you so long to give in." Caitlyn pushed up on her elbow to look down at him and winced in pain.

"What's wrong? Your back again?" Mac laid her down gently.

"Yeah. It must have stiffened up while I slept. It sure didn't bother me last night."

"I'll say. Hold on, I'll get you some ibuprofen."

"It'll be okay in a few minutes, I just need to get moving." Caitlyn tried to get up again, but pain shot from her back straight down her legs.

"Why don't you let me play nurse for a change? You can get up and moving after the medicine has a chance to work."

"I think you just want to get even for me keeping you in bed when you were hurt." Caitlyn settled down among the pillows. If he wanted to pamper her, who was she to complain?

"Yup. But I also have a vested interest in making sure you aren't hurting later." He shot her a devilish wink and climbed out of bed. "I'll put some coffee on too."

Mac stretched and ran his hand over his stubble before pulling on his boxers. My, oh my, coffee in bed and a view of killer buns. Was there any better way to wake up? She could get used to this.

Caitlyn closed her eyes and breathed a deep sigh of contentment. She could still smell him on the sheets, mingled with the smells of their amorous activities. Having sex with Mac involved every single sense. The sounds of running water and off key humming were homey and comforting. It was a beautiful day and she hadn't even been outside yet.

"You look like the cat who ate the canary," Mac said a few minutes later as he handed her a mug of steaming coffee and two little capsules.

"If it had been a canary, I wouldn't be this happy," Caitlyn shot back, letting the sheet slip to her waist as she sat up to accept the coffee.

Mac looked shocked at her bawdy words for a second, then laughed. "I can't believe you just said that."

"Hey, you don't grow up around a fire department and not talk like that. You either beat 'em or join 'em. I was such a tom boy as a kid none of my brothers' friends even thought to censor their words until I hit my teens, and by that time it was too late."

Climbing into bed, Mac joined her under the sheet and sipped his own coffee. "It's just you look like such an innocent, I don't think of you as 'one of the guys'."

"A fact for which I'm eternally grateful." Caitlyn ran her hand down his muscular thigh.

"Keep that up, and you'll be more grateful."

"Is that a promise?" Caitlyn put down her coffee, willing to ignore the pain in her back for a little fun.

"I should have known better," Mac said, putting down his coffee and tickling her.

117

"Stop! I'm too hurt to be tickled," Caitlyn squealed as he continued his assault on her ribs and sides.

"Now I've got you." Mac renewed his barrage, making Caitlyn scream with laughter.

Caitlyn was trying to defend her most sensitive spots when her bedroom door crashed open.

"Get your hands off her, dirt bag!"

Mac threw his body over Caitlyn's, shielding her from the attacker.

"Tom?" Caitlyn pushed him away and lifted the sheet up to cover her breasts.

"Mac?" Tom stood in the doorway, gun in hand and a bemused expression on his face. "What are you doing here? In Connecticut? In bed with my sister?"

His expression hardened and Mac had to do some quick thinking. If Tom had blown his cover, he wouldn't be so surprised to see him in Connecticut. But could he still be involved? Mac wanted to trust his partner but there were still too many questions for him to risk it.

"It's a long story. Mind if we get dressed first? Then we can talk."

"You're damn right we'll talk." Tom put the gun away and walked towards the kitchen.

Caitlyn's eyes were wide and she still clutched the sheet to her chest. "I didn't know he was coming over today. He has a key to the apartment, I'm sorry."

"It's not your fault." He stroked a finger down her cheek. Their time together was over. Whether because of Tom or because of his work, it didn't matter. He'd been able to forget the danger he'd put her in but Tom's arrival brought him back to down to earth with a thud. "Come on, let's get dressed before he blows a gasket."

He was going to need to do some quick talking to keep Tom from finding out about the assignment and his suspicions.

Mac warmed his coffee and Caitlyn's before sitting down at the kitchen table. Tom leaned against the counter, tapping his fingers on the scratched surface.

"Well? I'm waiting for an explanation." He eyed them both impatiently.

Before Mac could open his mouth Caitlyn went on the offensive. "I don't see where we owe you any explanation. I'm a grown woman. Mac was in my room, in my *bed*, because I wanted him there. That's all you need to know."

"I thought I told you Caitlyn was off limits to you?" Tom shot at Mac. "She's not going to be another notch on your belt."

"It's none of your business if I'm a notch or not." Caitlyn stood and glared defiantly. "And how dare you declare me off limits to anyone. If I want to have sex with the entire Northeast branch of the FBI then I will."

"Like hell."

They were toe-to-toe, fists clenched and ready to fight.

"Ah, if I could interrupt this little display of family unity," Mac interjected.

"No!" Two furious brown gazes shot his way.

Mac leaned back in his chair and watched the show. There was nothing he could do until they calmed down, and this would give him some time to make up a plausible story until he was sure about Tom's presence in Connecticut.

"I don't care how 'mature' you think you are, you're still an innocent compared to most men, especially him." Tom pointed his thumb at Mac.

"I'm no worse than you." Hell, Tom was making him out to be a gigolo. Mac wasn't a saint, but he wasn't that bad either.

Neither sibling paid attention to his comment.

"How do you know how experienced I am? You don't know what I did or didn't do in college. That's why I went so far away! For all you know, I could have slept with the entire football team."

Tom's face was so red it was almost purple. A muscle ticked in his jaw and the veins on the side of his throat stood out. "I'm trying to look out for your best interests, and you're pushing my buttons."

Caitlyn took a deep breath and backed down a bit. "I didn't sleep around in college and I have no intention of starting now.

But that doesn't mean I can't take care of myself. Mac and I understand that this isn't a permanent thing. His job is too risky for us to consider a future, so right now we're living for today."

Mac got a sick feeling in his gut at her words. She was right. They didn't have any plans for the future. But when she said it that way, it sounded cheap.

"So you're just having an affair? Is that what you're telling me?" Tom's jaw was still clenched.

"We're enjoying one another's company for as long as it lasts." For the first time, Caitlyn shot a glance in his direction.

"And how long will that be, partner?" Tom glared at Mac.

"As long as I can make it," Mac answered. Considering the need for Caitlyn to go into hiding and him to disappear, their time together could probably be counted in minutes.

Tom slapped his hand against his leg. "I don't like it, but like you said, you're all grown up now. There's not much I can do about it. Just as long as we understand each other." Tom stared him down.

Oh yeah, Mac understood. He understood that if he hurt Caitlyn he was a dead man.

"I understand you." Loud and clear.

"Good. Now what the hell are you doing up here? Last I heard you were tapped for deep cover on some super secret mission."

"I was, I am. I just ran into a little snag."

"What sort of snag?" Tom pulled out a chair and straddled it.

"He got shot and almost bled to death under my car," Caitlyn said wryly.

"Christ!" Tom jumped and looked closely at him. "Where were you shot?"

Concern? Or a guilty conscience?

"In the back. I wasn't sure if it was random gang violence or if my cover was blown but I couldn't go to the hospital."

"That could be a bit hard to explain. How'd you find Cat?"

Mac snorted and spun his mug around. "Dumb luck."

"Good thing it wasn't someone who would've called the police first and asked questions later." Tom relaxed a bit. "You stash your badge in your shoe?"

Mac nodded. Getting caught with a badge when deep undercover was a risk but if he got killed he wanted to be identified. Most cops knew to look at the thick soles of sneakers for weapons or drugs. If they did, they'd find his badge.

"You must not have got hit too bad. You were acting pretty healthy a few minutes ago."

Caitlyn hid a laugh behind her hand and Mac nudged her under the table. They didn't need to goad Tom when he was finally calming down.

"I was shot almost three weeks ago. Low caliber bullet, straight through. The worst part was healing the exit wound."

"Bet it still hurt like a bitch." Tom nodded in sympathy.

"Yup."

Tom looked Mac dead in the eye. "How much can you tell me about what you're doing up here?"

A tiny bit of tension slipped from Mac's shoulders. Tom wasn't grilling him for information about the mission. If he'd been involved he'd want to know more, wouldn't he?

"Not much, only that I'm solo and my cover is blown."

"You're sure?" He raised an eyebrow.

"They asked for Mac when they grabbed me last night, not Diego—" Caitlyn clapped her hands over her mouth as if she could take back the words, but it was too late.

"Who grabbed you last night?" Tom's voice shook the rafters.

"One guy, and I got out of it." Caitlyn wouldn't look her brother in the eye.

Mac saw his opening and took it. "You got away after he sliced you on the neck."

"What?" Tom jumped up, knocking the chair in his haste. "You were hurt? Where? Show me!"

Caitlyn shot Mac a deadly look. "He nicked me to make a point. I've bled more from shaving my legs."

"This time. But what about the next time someone grabs

you? Or maybe they won't even bother grabbing you, maybe they'll just shoot you from a distance," Mac said to throw a scare into her, but his plan backfired. He was the one who felt the shiver of fear chase down his spine at the thought of someone gunning for her.

"There won't be a next time."

"Damn straight there won't be. You need to go into hiding until we can take care of this." Tom crossed his arms over his chest.

"We? I don't recall inviting you to the party." Mac shot a glance at his partner.

"I don't need an invitation. They took a swipe at my sister, that's invitation enough." Tom's eyes hardened.

"Back off. This is my fight and I can't involve you or your family any further." Was Tom angling in so that he could get insider information?

"It's no longer just your fight." Caitlyn stood next to her brother.

Mac faced down the two determined O'Tooles. "The safety of this assignment is at stake. I can't trust anyone with the information I have."

Comprehension dawned slowly over Tom's face. "Shit. You think I'm involved, don't you?" He looked shocked, then angry.

"Of course not. Tell him, Mac. You don't think Tom has anything to do with this." Caitlyn's eyes were wide and her hands fluttered nervously with her necklace. "Tell him."

Mac remained silent.

"He can't deny it. He's worried that I've turned. My own partner. That's probably why he hooked up with you, to see if we were all involved. What is it, pal, drugs? Weapons? Did you think I was peddling that crap?"

"Stop it! Just stop it!" Caitlyn put her hands over her ears. A look of horror crossed her face. "You can't believe that."

"I don't want to believe your family has anything to do with this. Tom is like a brother to me."

"That's not saying you don't believe it." Her voice choked up and her eyes grew glassy with tears. "How could you? How could you stay with me for weeks, sleep with me and think my brother had anything to do with the people who shot you?"

"Caitlyn—" Mac put his hand out to touch her, but she slapped it away and ran from the room.

He started after her but Tom held him back. "Let her go."

Mac shook off the restraining hand and took a step towards the living room. Two steps later he was thrown to the floor, hitting the wood with a crash that rattled his teeth. He tried to fight Tom off his back, struggling with the heavier man.

"Stop fighting me! Look! Tracking beam up there—"

No sooner had the words come out of his mouth then the air above them exploded. Bullets sprayed around the kitchen and glass went flying. The coffee pot got hit and hot coffee splashed on the floor.

"Go, go! Get Caitlyn, I'll cover you back." Tom pulled a 9mm handgun out of the waistband of his jeans and crawled to the window.

More shots sounded from the living room, and Caitlyn screamed. Crouching down, Mac worked his way to Caitlyn's room. She was on the floor, huddled behind the nightstand opposite the window.

"What's going on? I was lying on the bed and bullets started flying." Her face was tear stained but her voice was steady.

"I don't know, Tom's got the kitchen. I need to get your gun from the living room. Do you have more ammo?" He cursed himself for not being more careful. If he'd been paying attention to Caitlyn's safety instead of her body, they wouldn't be in this mess.

"In the fire box under my bed. The key is in the nightstand." She moved to get it and Mac held her back.

"I'll get it, you stay low. I've got to think of a way out of this mess, and I can't do it worrying about you."

"What? Afraid I'll stab you in the back?" Caitlyn snapped out.

Mac didn't bother to defend himself. He was just doing his job, and if she couldn't understand that, too bad. "Stay here."

A barrage of shots came from the kitchen. Tom was drawing their fire so Mac could save Caitlyn. He'd better get to it before Tom ran out of ammo.

Reaching around, Mac fumbled to open the drawer to the nightstand. Key in hand, he rolled across the floor to the bed. Sheets that still carried their mingled scents were covered in broken glass and splinters of wood.

Focus!

He could think about their one night together later. Right now he needed to get them out of here alive. The firebox was heavy and full of junk. Buried beneath papers and bankbooks was a box of ammo for Caitlyn's Walther. A quick check showed only a handful of bullets was missing. Good.

"We're going to the living room. Stay low, and when we get there, I want at least one piece of furniture between you and the windows at all times."

"What are you going to be doing?"

"Backing up Tom." More shots flew overhead.

"I thought you suspected him?"

"He's still my partner."

Caitlyn mumbled something incoherent under her breath, but Mac didn't have time to figure out what it was. Herding her to the living room, he made sure she was as protected as possible by the recliner before he grabbed the gun.

Tom was reloading a clip when Mac crawled into the kitchen.

"You always carry a gun and a spare clip when you visit your sister?" Mac took the other side of the window and fired at a flash of red behind a garbage can. Thank God, it was late morning or the neighbors would be around.

"You always flap your gums when you're getting shot at?"

Ignoring the jibe, Mac searched for more telltale flashes of red. "How many?"

"At least three, maybe four. I think I took one out while you were pussy-footing around."

"There!" Mac spotted thug wearing a red bandana running for cover. Aiming carefully, he nailed him twice in the thigh.

"One more down."

"Make that two, I got the one by the garbage can."

Silence filled the air, broken only by the sound of sirens in the distance.

"Whatdaya think? One or two left? And are they waiting for a shot or running?"

Tires squealed and horns blared.

"Running," they said in unison.

"I can't be here when the cops come." Mac looked at Tom, trying to read his eyes. Could he trust him? He'd just saved his life. Hell, Tom had saved his life more than once. His gut said Tom was clean, and right about now his gut was all he had going for him.

"Take my car. I'll cover for you." Tom tossed him the keys, no questions asked.

Mac caught the keys in one hand. Where he'd go, he had no idea.

Chapter Twelve

Caitlyn paced the confines of Jim's apartment. Although bigger than her own, it was still too small to contain her restless energy. Where was Mac? Did he really think Tom was involved with his case?

"If you wear a hole in Jim's rug, he isn't going to be happy with you." Tom clicked off the TV and dropped the remote on the beaten up coffee table under his feet.

"How can you sit still at a time like this? Your partner accused you of being a traitor, we've been shot at, and now Mac is off God knows where in your car. And you're watching crappy talk shows."

"All in a day's work, kiddo."

"Don't you dare 'kiddo' me. And maybe it's all in your day's work but not in mine." Caitlyn flopped down into an armchair.

"Which is why I want you out of it. You're not cut out for thugs carrying guns."

"I didn't ask to have a bleeding man roll under my car, you know." She stood and crossed to the window to peek out. "I was just trying to help my brother's partner stay alive."

"Oh, so was that CPR you were giving Mac this morning?"

"Ha, ha. Very funny. What do you have against him anyway? I thought you liked him as your partner."

"I do like him as my partner. He's a great guy and I trust him with my life. Have trusted him with my life many times. That's why him thinking I have something to do with this pisses me off so much."

A glimmer of sympathy broke through her self-pity and worry. "I'm sorry, Tom. I wasn't even thinking about how all of this might be hurting you too."

"Hey, don't worry about me. I'm fine."

Caitlyn sat next to him on the couch. "Why would he suspect you? It doesn't make sense."

"Well, it depends on the case. If it involves the local municipalities, I have connections with both fire and police. If there's something going on where they suspect one or both of being dirty, then it makes sense to question me."

"But...but he's your partner!" Caitlyn sputtered indignantly. How could Tom defend him?

"It happens all the time. You'd like to think that everyone you work with has the same ideals and morals that you do but the truth is some of them turn. It's a tough job with very little thanks or recognition. We're always the tough guys and a lot of what we do goes unnoticed by the general public. That gets to you after a while."

"I can't believe I'm hearing this. You sound like you agree with him."

"I'm just trying to explain. Yeah, it bugs me that Mac thinks I'd turn, but he has to keep an open mind. If you're blinded by emotion, you can't do your job."

"Would you ever suspect him?" Caitlyn asked.

"Depends on the situation. Mac doesn't have the family connections I do, but if I caught him in a situation that was questionable, I might be suspicious. I'd have to be."

There was no way she could live like that. Her family was her foundation. She knew no matter what happened, no matter what she did, her brothers would be there for her. If she didn't have that bone-deep support in her life, she'd never have survived their parents' deaths and stayed sane.

Caitlyn leaned over and kissed Tom on the cheek.

"What was that for? Do you forgive me for barging in on you?"

"No. But I'm grateful that you do the job you do."

"It's a tough job but someone has to do it," he joked.

"Exactly. And I, for one, do appreciate all you do so I can

sleep safely at night."

Tom gave her an odd look, but didn't say anything.

"I'm going to take a shower. When Jim gets home I think we should call a family meeting. I have a feeling we haven't heard the last of Mac."

"We'd better not have. He still has my car."

∞

What a freaking day. Mac eyed the comings and goings of his former "brothers" as they went about their business. Drug traffic seemed to be up since the last time he was out. The corner where the Children set up shop was busy with junkies begging for just one hit. Cars rolled up to the curb and furtive transactions took place through tinted windows.

Carlos must have gotten a new supplier or something. There was more crap on the street than he'd seen in all the months he'd been working undercover. What was going on?

A pimped out car with its radio blasting a thumping bass line rounded the corner and several heads turned. Hands reached for weapons and junkies scurried for cover like rats sensing a storm. The car cruised by slowly and Mac caught a glimpse of a blue bandana wrapped around a dark head.

Shit! What were the 525s doing here? Mac had seen little kids shot at just for wearing the wrong colors and this guy was cruising down the street announcing his affiliations?

Blood pounded in his veins and he reached for his gun. This could be a blood bath if someone moved too fast.

"Hey Miguel, you up for a trade?" The driver called out to the oldest of the Children standing on the corner.

"Maybe. Whatcha got?" Miguel walked cautiously towards the car, his hand hovering near the gun Mac knew was stashed in the back of his pants.

"How about we trade a blow for some blow?" He laughed at his own wit.

"Show me the girl. And it better be a girl. I don't want one of your nasty-ass fags."

Mac could see Miguel's nostrils flare from his hiding place. Could this be for real? Was one of Satan's Children going to make a deal with one of the 525s? What the hell was going on?

Apparently the girl met his standards, because Miguel motioned for one of his boys to bring him something, which he handed over to the driver. The passenger door opened and Miguel rounded the hood and climbed in.

Could this be happening? Before Mac had left, a cease-fire had been declared. But tensions still ran high. No 525 would have dared to come to this corner without heavy firepower backing him up. How had so much changed in less than a month?

The driver stepped out of the car and Mac caught a glimpse of a skinny girl on her knees in front of Miguel. The car rocked a little bit and a nervous twitter went through the crowd of youths watching. As the driver snorted his lines off a sliver of a mirror, hands moved away from hidden guns. This was a business transaction, not a set up.

Before he could wrap his mind around this new partnership, Miguel stepped out of the car, hitching his pants up.

"Nice doing business with you, man." The driver wiped off his nose and climbed back into the car.

Mac crouched in his hiding spot, stunned. Were the Children and the 525s working together? Could they be planning a war on the Black Hands? That wasn't beyond the realm of believability. Still, old hatreds ran deep amongst all three gangs. It was hard to believe they could bury the hatchet and not in each other's backs.

A youth, no older than eleven or twelve, came running up to Miguel. "Five-oh! Cops are coming!"

"Move!" Miguel shouted.

There was a flurry of activity as blankets were packed up and junkies scattered. The formerly bustling street corner was deserted except for some empty vials strewn on the sidewalk. Miguel stood in a doorway mere feet away from Mac. Sweat dripped down his neck as he waited for his "brother" to glance down at the window well where he hid. It wouldn't take more than a stray breeze to move the newspapers he had covering him and he'd be visible.

Luckily, Miguel's attention was focused on the unmarked police car driving slowly through the street. As the car slowed down, the passenger window opened and Miguel visibly relaxed. With a quick look around, Miguel slipped into the passenger's seat and rolled up the window.

Not willing to push his luck any more, Mac waited for the car to pull away, then hightailed it out of the neighborhood while everyone was still in hiding. He had a lot of thinking to do, and crouching in a window well covered in newspaper wasn't the place for it.

Mac used every ounce of training he had to slip out of the neighborhood unseen. He'd taken courses in jungle training. This was only another form of jungle. The wildlife might be punks and drug addicts, but they were just as dangerous as snakes and panthers.

Using the shadows as cover, he blended from one building to another, walking silently in the night-darkened streets. His stomach muscles ached and his stamina wasn't what it used to be, but all things considered, he wasn't in as bad shape as he could have been.

And Caitlyn had been worried about him. Ha!

Well, that wouldn't be a problem any more. After he admitted to suspecting Tom of being involved with the case, she wouldn't be concerned about his welfare now. Hell, she probably hoped he would get hit.

No, she wasn't that type. She might be pissed off, but she wouldn't wish him harm. Mac had a minute to regret how things shook down. It wasn't like he *wanted* to suspect his best friend of being in cahoots with scumbags like Carlos. But it was his job, damn it.

A covered bus stop stood empty at this time of night and Mac risked sitting down. The bus would be there soon and he could take it back to the commuter lot where he'd ditched Tom's car. He'd have to return it sooner or later, but he might very well end up sleeping in it for the rest of tonight.

The nearly empty bus pulled up and Mac got on. Good thing he'd taken that handful of change from Tom's ashtray. He slouched down near a window and pulled his baseball cap low over his eyes. With his face shaved and his hair shorn, he probably wouldn't be recognized, but why take chances?

What the hell was going on in the city? Mac had been brought undercover because the FBI and the Bureau of Alcohol, Tobacco and Firearms were worried about the number of weapons intercepted in this little city. The numbers didn't add up, and that made folks nervous. He knew going in he'd have no local backup because the locals were the ones under suspicion.

But how far up did the corruption go? The police car that Miguel had gotten into wasn't from a beat cop. Could someone in Mac's department be involved?

Tom?

Mac shook his head against the thought. It was one thing to have an open mind, it was another to ignore his gut. His instincts screamed at him, telling him that Tom and the rest of the O'Tooles weren't involved. Tom had saved his life just this morning.

But he could have done that just to save his sister. Was he just making excuses to believe in Tom because he wanted to see Caitlyn again?

No. Mac shook his head as if to dislodge the niggling thought. Whether or not he believed in Tom's innocence, he still couldn't see Caitlyn again. Some things were better left alone.

It was for the best anyway, he thought, denying the surge of regret tightening his chest. What kind of life could he offer her? He was in deep cover for months at a time, he never knew when he'd be home or even what he'd look like on any given assignment.

Sure, she was used to that in some respects because of her brother, but having a lover in the FBI was a little different. Mac knew there were guys who had wives and families and were able to keep their jobs separate, but he didn't think he was up to that balancing act. There was a reason the divorce rate was so high in his field.

Christ, he was getting maudlin. Last night had been the most amazing experience of his entire life. He should be grateful that he'd had a taste of heaven, instead of moaning about losing it. Caitlyn was probably counting her blessings that it ended quickly before her heart got involved.

The bus stopped with a hiss of air brakes. Mac got off and watched the other passengers until they all stumbled to their cars and left the lot. When he was sure no one was around, he slipped up to Tom's sedan and peered under it. Checking the car for explosives might be a bit paranoid, but better paranoid than dead.

Nothing seemed out of order. He was probably over anxious but lately it felt like his life was one disaster after another. The only calm he'd had was the time he spent at Caitlyn's.

Slipping into the car, he locked the door and slid low in the driver's seat. He had some heavy thinking to do and it didn't involve Caitlyn. It was time he admitted it, he needed help. Big time. If the 525s and the Children were cooperating, he had to assume the Hands were cooperating too. If all three of the city's gangs were working together instead of at cross-purposes, they'd have an army of gigantic proportions.

Who was directing that army though?

Mac dug around in the glove box, looking for something to either prove or disprove Tom's innocence. There was a wad of napkins from a fast food place, some maps of metro D.C. and a pack of matches. Not much to go on there.

In the back seat was Tom's briefcase. If he had any incriminating evidence, he wouldn't keep it in there. Still, there might be something Mac could work with in there. Plus, he was nosy. It went with the job.

Unzipping the pockets one by one, Mac rifled around, finding a PDA, a calculator, some pens and a tangle of wires that probably belonged to the laptop in the main compartment. He might have some information on there, but Mac didn't have time to figure out his password. In frustration, Mac dropped the case onto the passenger seat where it tipped over. A little blue booklet fell to the floor.

Tom's passport.

Mac picked it up and flipped it open. It was a smudgy picture of Tom but it had his undercover name on it. He flipped through the pages looking for where Tom had been last.

Nicaragua. And he'd only just returned to the states. Mac flipped through looking to see how long he'd been down there.

Shit. No wonder he was carrying a gun and extra clips. Tom had been in that hell since they split up over six months ago. That would explain why he was taking a vacation.

And would clear him from any involvement with the gangs. He couldn't have blown Mac's cover if he was in the jungle up till a week or so ago.

Relief flooded Mac's body. It had killed him to think of his partner being dirty, but he had to keep his options open. He needed Tom's help badly and now he could use it without watching his back.

And he could see Caitlyn again.

He had to stop thinking about her. It was enough to make him question his sanity. She was just a woman, like any other.

Okay, not like any other but still just a woman.

A woman with laughing eyes and creamy skin. One who responded to his touch like she was on fire.

Mac's body hardened at the memories from last night. No, Caitlyn wasn't just any woman. Too bad if he tried to touch her again, she'd bite his hand off.

Or would she?

Chapter Thirteen

A hand clamped over her mouth startling Caitlyn out of a fitful sleep.

"What are you doing in here? I thought Tom was sleeping at Jim's?" Mac's voice whispered in her ear, sending tingles through her body.

Caitlyn tried to mumble out an answer but Mac's hand still covered her mouth.

"If I let you go, will you promise not to scream?"

The darkness covered the rolling of her eyes but she nodded her head yes.

"Now, why are you in the guest room?" Mac knelt on the bed and his weight made her roll towards him.

"Because I'm the girl, that's why. Tom's on the couch and Liam's on the floor in Jim's room. My place is a mess so I'm staying here until it gets fixed up. I'll never get my security deposit back at this rate."

"Oh great, all the O'Toole's are here to pound me into dust at the same time."

"Then why did you come back?" Caitlyn's heart rose in her chest. Did he miss her as much as she missed him? Even though she'd fought against it all day, her hurt and sadness smothered the anger she felt towards him.

"I have to talk to Tom. I know he's not involved with this."

"What? Did you get proof? Is that where you've been?" She tried to ignore the heat coming off his body. The T-shirt she'd worn to bed was bunched up around her waist and the only thing covering her lower body was a thin, crumpled sheet.

"I don't have time to explain. I'm in way over my head and I need to talk to him."

"Oh." Her heart sunk with disappointment. He wasn't there to see her, he was there to see Tom. "He's in the living room, on the couch." Her gaze dropped.

"Good. Thanks." He shifted his weight, but didn't get off the bed. "Listen, I'm sorry I didn't tell you of my suspicions earlier. I've been undercover for so long I don't trust anybody."

"Yeah, Tom explained it to me. I get it." And, Lord above, how it hurt.

"All right then, I'll just go get Tom," he whispered, leaning closer.

"Okay," she whispered back, anticipation churning low in her belly.

"We shouldn't be doing this."

"I know, I'm still mad at you."

"Uh huh." His lips brushed against hers, softly at first, then more insistently.

Desire spread like wild fire through her body. Caitlyn's limbs got looser and her breasts grew full and heavy. She wrapped her arms around his neck and pulled him closer. It felt like forever since she'd touched him, kissed him.

The overhead light came on with a snap. "'Bout time you got here. Coffee's on in the kitchen." Tom turned around and padded down the hallway without waiting for a response.

"Go. I'll be there in a minute," Caitlyn said, blinking blindly from the light. She needed some time to gather her out of control thoughts before she faced her brothers and Mac.

"Caitlyn, this doesn't change anything." He brushed a finger down her cheek.

Her rapidly beating heart hitched at his words. "I know. So much for having feelings for me."

"I do have feelings for you but that doesn't change who, or what, I am. I'm no good for you, just ask Tom."

"Don't give me that 'you're too good for me' bullshit. You either want me or you don't, the rest is semantics." She yanked the sheet up to her chest. The anger felt better than the hollow empty feeling his words gave her.

"Caitlyn—"

"Go, they're waiting for you." Crossing her arms over her chest she turned her head away from him. This was what she got for giving into her baser urges. Stupid, insufferable man.

The soft snick of the door closing sounded like a gunshot to her straining ears. Damn it, she wasn't sure if she was madder at him for kissing her or for stopping. No matter how angry she was at him for his lack of trust, there was no denying her body's reaction to Mac.

"Well, it'll just have to get over it." Caitlyn threw off the sheet and slipped on a pair of shorts. She'd pull herself together then head to the kitchen. There was no way she was going to miss the summit meeting the men were having.

The smell of coffee teased her as she made her way down the hall. Not that she needed much more stimulation, but the caffeine couldn't hurt. All conversation died as Caitlyn stepped into the room.

"Am I interrupting?" Caitlyn shot a challenging look at her brothers and Mac. If they thought she was going to bow out of this gracefully, they had another think coming.

"No, not at all. Mac was just catching us up on how he ended up in your bed—ah, apartment." Tom helped himself to more coffee and neither Liam nor Jim would look her in the eye.

"I think we can move on from there, don't you?" She did *not* need the three of them playing big brother on her and threatening Mac with bodily harm. If he was going to get pummeled for sleeping with her under false pretenses, she'd be the one doing the pummeling.

"Sure, sure." Liam tipped back in his chair and tossed a crumpled napkin on the table.

"Here, have a seat. I was getting ready to fill your brothers in on what I know." Mac stood and pulled a worn kitchen chair out for her.

"Really? That's a switch. You mean we don't have to pry the information out of you with bamboo shoots under your fingernails?" A shiver of awareness chased down her spine as she sat in the chair he held out for her. Caitlyn hunched over a bit to keep her hardened nipples from showing through her shirt. She wished she'd thought to put a bra on before she came out.

"Cut him some slack, Cat. He's just doing his job." Tom handed her a mug of coffee and some creamer.

"Yeah, yeah, I know. Who made the coffee?"

"I did," Liam said, letting his chair drop back on all four legs.

Caitlyn added a generous dollop of cream. Liam made police station coffee. It was strong enough to peel the paint off the walls.

Mac cleared his throat and moved to the counter. "Here's what I have so far. I was brought into the city to go deep into the gang politics.

"What was your cover?" Tom asked.

"Drug dealer. I started out as a new supplier after we busted one of their old ones and made an opening. After a few months I started working my way into the ranks of Satan's Children. I was living in an apartment with them and going through the initiation rites."

Liam let out a low whistle. "I've heard about those. The Children are tough to get into. We haven't been able to get a single guy in. They've all ended up beaten up or dead."

"I know. That's why I was sent in. A record number of high grade weapons had made their way into Hartford, yet nothing was being done by local authorities."

Liam stood and faced Mac. "Hold it just a minute there, buddy. We're busting our asses on the streets every day trying to take these guys down. We don't need some stinking fed to come in and tell us we're not doing our job."

"Did you know about the weapons?" Mac asked calmly.

Caitlyn watched Liam's face closely. She knew the minute the realization hit that this was bigger than he could ever imagine.

"There's someone on the inside." Liam clenched his jaw and turned away. "That's why you're here. Someone in the P.D. is dirty. Shit. Someone ran Caitlyn's plates. That's how they knew where she lived." His face paled. "One of the guys in my department is involved with the guy who grabbed my sister."

"More than one, I think," Mac said softly. "I watched one of the Children's lieutenants get into an unmarked car today. The entire time I was with them, no one spent more than one night in jail for routine drug busts. And the ones that did get caught never went to trial."

"Let me guess, they were released on a technicality?" Liam snorted.

"That, or the paperwork went missing. Very few Children have gone away since I started my investigation. Not only that but a cease fire was called early in the summer."

"A cease fire?" Jim asked.

"Yup. Word came down from Carlos that we were to hold our fire on other gangs. And none of them took pot shots at us either, so it was city wide."

"That doesn't make sense. The gangs never work together. They're always fighting for territory." Liam ran his hand over his closely cropped hair. "Who's strong enough to unite the gangs and make it stick?"

"That's what I mean to find out."

Mac watched Caitlyn out of the corner of his eye. He was trying to pay attention to Liam's facial expressions, to try to read him, but he kept getting distracted by Caitlyn's presence. She'd remained quiet once she stared down her brothers but he could tell she was focusing on every word.

"So, what did you find out?" Tom rested his hand on Liam's shoulder, but the younger man shrugged it off.

"Not a hell of a lot before my cover was blown. I know enough to put most of the Children away on drug trafficking charges but I don't know squat about the weapons."

"Could Carlos be the one uniting the gangs?" Jim asked.

Mac shook his head. "I don't think so. He's not smart enough. Someone is directing him but I haven't been able to find out who it is."

Caitlyn stood and crossed to the refrigerator. Going on tiptoes, she grabbed a yellow legal pad off the top. Mac's pulse bumped up a few notches as the muscles in her legs were displayed to perfection. Getting a boner in front of her brothers probably wouldn't go over very well.

"What're you doing?" Tom asked.

"Taking notes. I think better when I see things on paper." She dug through a pile of papers on the counter until she came up with a pen. "So far we know that the Children are getting guns from somewhere, the local police either don't know about it or are looking the other way—"

"Hey!" Liam looked at her sharply.

"Present company excluded. Liam, we have to face facts. I know it hurts, but you can't stick your head in the sand." Caitlyn's face softened as she looked at her brother.

"All we have is his word for it. A couple hours ago, you were ready to string him up by his nuts and now you think he knows everything? He must be pretty good in the sack for you to give up your family like that."

"That's enough." Tom slapped his hand down on the counter. "I know you're pissed, I'm pissed too. You don't have to believe Mac just look at the facts and draw your own conclusions. How many drug busts have you heard about? How many gang fights have come through? How many Children have slipped through the cracks?"

"How the hell should I know? I work traffic." Liam's jaw was set in a stubborn line and a muscle ticked in the side of it.

"We've had a lot of overdoses but not many gunshot wounds in the ER," Caitlyn said softly.

Mac could see the hurt on her face. She really loved her brothers, and Liam's words must have hit her hard. He ached for causing such a rift but he pushed that aside. His emotions had got her in the middle in the first place. She didn't need him butting in now.

"There's been an eerie quiet in the streets. Even Friday nights have been relatively dull." Jim ran a hand over Caitlyn's hair.

This was the touchiest family Mac had ever seen. Earlier Tom had tried to console Liam, and now Jim was trying to comfort Caitlyn. Their unity was something Mac had never experienced before. His heart ached to be part of such a close group of people.

"Isn't it better to assume the worst and work out a plan, than to blindly defend something and hope you're right?" Caitlyn tried again.

Liam looked at the faces around the room. Even Mac could read the concern on them. "All right, for the sake of argument, I'll go along with this. For now. I refuse to believe my whole department is dirty." He crossed his arms over his chest.

"Okay. Hypothetically then, we have the city's gangs no longer fighting amongst themselves, guns coming into the city at a rapid rate, and questionable circumstances keeping the Children out of jail. Are members of the other gangs getting out of jail too?"

"I don't know. I'm working solo on this. I don't have any local contacts at all," Mac said.

"I can find out. I know enough of the names to look at the logs discreetly," Liam offered.

Mac focused on him. "Very discreetly. I don't want anything to tip them off."

"You do your job, I'll do mine," Liam shot back.

"Tame the testosterone and let's get back to the facts. Is there anything else you can add to what we already have, Mac?" Caitlyn asked him.

"Yeah, one more thing. Right before I was shot, Carlos got rid of his prostitutes and shut down his loan sharking operation. The only thing the Children were doing was running drugs."

"That doesn't make any sense," Jim said.

"That depends. Who's picking up those areas?" Tom looked at Mac.

"While I was scoping things out today, I saw one of the 525's pull in and make a trade. Drugs for...ah..." he shot a glance at Caitlyn. "Services. Not a shot was fired."

"A 525 pulled into Children territory and wasn't riddled with bullets?" Liam asked, his eyebrows raised in disbelief.

"Yup."

"So if the 525s needed to get drugs from the Children and traded sex for it, does that mean they're specializing now?" Caitlyn tapped the pen on the pad and bit her lower lip. "If they each had their own area, they wouldn't be fighting each other. So why the guns?"

"Why would any of them give up any area? It doesn't make

sense for the 525s to just give up their drug trade. That's a lot of money we're talking about." Jim got up and grabbed a half empty bag of chips. "And why would the Children give up their prostitutes? There's not as much money there, but the convenience factor alone would be worth keeping them around."

"And we have no idea what's going on with the Black Hands. They're at the other end of the city, so we don't get as many of them in the ER." Caitlyn helped herself to a handful of chips.

"If we continue with what we know, we can hazard a guess that they're specializing now too. So, theoretically, we have the city's gang population amassing guns and working together." Tom looked sick at the thought.

"Shit."

"And," Mac looked at Liam. "There's someone on the inside who knows what is going on and is keeping the gangs on the streets."

"But why?" Caitlyn's brown eyes were filled with anxiety as she turned them on him.

Oh how he wished he could replace that worry with the laughter that normally shone out of those whiskey colored depths.

Tom broke the connection between them. "Money? Power? Who knows? This is all a guessing game. We need to get more facts before we can find out who's behind all this and figure out their reasoning."

"Easier said than done. My cover is shot, literally. I can do surveillance work but I can't get back into Carlos' stronghold. He has every eye on the street looking for me."

"And Caitlyn," Jim added.

Four sets of eyes turned to her.

"What? Don't look at me like that." She stood and crossed her arms over her chest.

"We just want you safe, kiddo." Tom said.

"I'm not your 'kiddo'. I'm an adult and I won't be shuffled off to East Bumfuck just to ease all your minds. I've been part of this from the start, and I'll see it through to the end."

"Hasn't being cut and shot at taught you anything? These

141

guys mean business!" Liam shouted.

"So do I. I can get information through the hospital records that none of you can. You need me."

"I can get that if we need it so badly. You can go visit Uncle Jamie in New Hampshire."

"No. I'm staying right here. Get used to it."

Mac stepped in to prevent another O'Toole family feud. "She stays. We can take turns keeping an eye on her. She's probably safer with us watching out for her than if she was packed up somewhere we couldn't see what she was doing."

"We? She's our sister, we'll watch over her." Liam's tone begged for a fight.

Mac grunted, but didn't say anything. He wasn't going to get into a pissing contest with Liam now. As long as Caitlyn was safe, that's all that mattered to him.

"So what's the POA?" Tom asked.

"POA?" Caitlyn looked at him.

"Plan of Action. We need to decide what we're going to do, and figure out how we're going to accomplish that with little information and no backup."

Tom looked at Mac.

"I think the biggest thing is that we need to discover who is behind the gang's cooperative bent. Then we need to figure out how deep the corruption is. And lastly, we need to find out what their objective is and stop it before the city goes up in flames." Mac leaned against the counter.

"Hell, is that all?" Jim asked.

"And we need to stay alive," Caitlyn said quietly.

Chapter Fourteen

Jim's apartment had become Command Headquarters. Caitlyn felt like all she did was make sandwiches and coffee, then clean up after meals. It irritated her that she couldn't help out more, but there wasn't a whole lot she could do in her area of expertise.

At least she hoped not. If she had to use her medical skills it would be because one of the men she cared for was hurt, and that was not a scenario she wanted to consider.

That Mac was lumped in with that group of men wasn't something she wanted to think too much about either.

They'd declared an unspoken truce and hadn't discussed much more than whether he wanted mustard or mayo on his ham sandwich. The tension between them tied her up in knots, but there wasn't much she could do about it. It wasn't like her brothers gave her a minute alone with Mac anyway.

There always seemed to be someone around whenever Mac came in the door. Not that she minded. She wasn't going to sleep with Mac again, even though he'd smartened up and took her brothers off his suspect list. Nope, she wasn't an idiot, she knew better than to court heartache in a six-foot-three package.

Even if that package was so sexy it made her teeth itch.

She'd done a lot of thinking since their one night together. There was plenty of time for introspection when she was stuck in Jim's apartment with nothing to do until she went back to work. Sleeping with Mac had been a mind-bending experience, but just because it was awesome didn't mean it was good for her.

It was a narrow miss, but she'd escaped with her heart intact. When Mac got on his horse and rode off into the sunset, she'd be able to wave goodbye without a tear.

Okay, maybe just one.

There was something about him that called to a part deep inside her. She knew where he was in the apartment without even looking. It was like a current ran between them and she drew energy from his presence. At times, she could feel his gaze on her and knew he felt it too.

But he never acted on it.

That was a good thing, right?

Caitlyn snorted at herself and finished washing the latest set of lunch dishes. Who was she kidding? If Mac crooked his finger at her, she'd jump him on the spot. It was only his control that kept her from making a fool of herself. She wanted Mac and the need grew every day.

It wasn't just his looks—though those were enough to take her breath away. With his hair cut short and his jaw free of whiskers, the strong lines of his face stood out clearly. His sky blue eyes drew her attention time and time again. During their daily meetings, she'd catch him staring at her and a surge of pure lust would shoot through her. All it took was one look from those blazing orbs of his and she was toast.

God, what was wrong with her? Mac and her brothers were scouring the city looking for clues to what was going on and she was lusting after a man who made it clear she'd only been a temporary convenience.

A notch on his belt. If it wasn't so painful, it would be funny. She'd told Tom she didn't care if she was just another woman in a long line of Mac's conquests, but the truth was she did care. A lot. Was it naïve to want to be someone special?

No. But it was naïve to think that Mac would change because of her. She should just take the experience for what it was—good sex between two consenting adults—and go on with her life. Eventually she'd forget about him and find someone else to fall in love with and have a family with.

Mac was definitely not the family man. And nothing she could do would change that.

"Why the long face?"

Caitlyn jumped and spilled water on the floor. Mac had come up behind her so quietly she hadn't even heard him.

"Just thinking. I didn't know you were here. Where's Liam? Isn't it his turn to baby-sit me?" Caitlyn covered the shaking of her hands by wiping up the water on the floor.

"I don't know. Tom and I split up a few hours ago and agreed to meet back here and compare notes."

"Oh. Are you hungry? I could make you a sandwich?" she asked, for something to say.

"No, I'm fine. I grabbed something earlier. Where's Jim?"

"He just left for work." They were all alone.

"Ah, well. I'm going to grab a shower while I can." He rubbed a hand over his jaw.

A shower. You had to be naked to take a shower. Caitlyn's heart skipped a beat. She knew exactly what Mac looked like naked. Heat pooled between her legs.

"Okay. I'll... I'll be in here. Cleaning." Tension was so thick she could practically see it flow between them. One look, one gesture and she'd be on him like white on rice. She spun around and started wiping the counter like her life depended on it.

Mac's image reflected back at her from the window above the sink. He raised his hand, but dropped it before leaving the room.

As soon as she was sure the coast was clear, Caitlyn sank down to sit on the floor. Dear God. How could she want him this badly? Her heart raced and blood pounded in her veins. Her skin felt too tight to contain the pent up need inside her.

Before she got swept up in memories from their one night together the phone rang.

"Hello?"

"Cat?" Liam's voice was almost drowned out by the sound of rushing traffic in the background.

"Yeah." Who'd he expect?

"We've got a tractor trailer accident. I'm going to be stuck here for a while. Is Jim there?"

"No, he's working twelve to twelve tonight. Mac is here though."

"Alone?"

Caitlyn sighed. "Yes, alone. I'm sure Tom will come rushing to protect my virtue any minute though, so you don't have to worry."

"You don't have to get all snotty about it. I don't want to see you hurt, you know."

"I know—"

"Hey, I've gotta go, things are getting hairy here. Take care and stay inside."

"Okay," she said to empty air. Liam had already disconnected.

He didn't want to see her hurt. Mac thought she was too good for him. Didn't anybody care what she thought or wanted?

Did she even know what she wanted?

Oh yeah, she knew. She just wasn't sure it was good for her to get what she wanted. Tossing the cordless phone on the table, Caitlyn tidied up the papers and things in the kitchen. Jim's apartment was big, but having five people crammed into it made for a lot of junk. Correction, having four men crammed into it made for a lot of junk.

She made her way into the living room, picking up discarded socks and shoes along the way.

"I feel like their mother, not their sister," she muttered.

Grabbing a shirt off the back of a chair, she folded it and laid it on the table. Mac's scent drifted from the shirt and the surge of lust flared again.

"Here, I'll take that," Mac said from behind her.

Wearing nothing but slightly faded jeans.

Caitlyn's mouth watered. His hair was still damp and he smelled like soap.

"Sure." Her voice was thick with desire. She cleared her throat and handed the T-shirt over. Their fingers brushed and the contact was electric. Caitlyn was afraid to look down because she was sure her nipples were poking through her thin shirt.

"Who was that on the phone?" Mac pushed his arms through the sleeves and pulled the soft cotton over his head.

She had to shake her head to clear it. Her powers of concentration were deserting her by the minute. "Liam. He's stuck in the middle of a tractor trailer accident and doesn't know when he'll be home."

"Oh." Laser-like gaze burned into her.

"I'm sure Tom will be home any minute." Caitlyn fiddled with the orphaned socks in her hand. "Ah, I think I'll do a load of laundry. Do you have anything that needs to be done?"

"Considering most of what I'm wearing belongs to your brothers, I'm sure I can come up with something."

Those jeans and that white T-shirt didn't look nearly as good on Jim. "I'll just get going...and do the laundry." *Get out of here before you make an ass of yourself.*

Caitlyn escaped to the bathroom and started a load of clothes. She'd have to lock herself in the guest room. It should be humiliating to want someone who didn't want you back, but obviously her body didn't care about her pride. Nope. Her body could care less if she sunk so low that she threw herself at Mac. All it cared about was scratching the itch he gave her.

Well I do care! I won't throw myself at anyone. If he doesn't want me, so be it. Caitlyn crossed to her room and flopped on the bed. The spare bedroom doubled as an office. A twin bed was nestled in between a computer desk and bookshelves with all sorts of huge binders jammed in.

She could always brush up on her emergency medical care if she wanted to keep busy. Maybe she'd check her email and kill some time that way. Tom would be home soon to break the tension. It was hard to get hot and heavy over Mac with her older brother watching her every move.

Her email was somewhat less than inspiring. Mostly junk mail or spam. And right now she did not want to see anything about enlarging her male member or lasting all night. She was biblically certain Mac didn't need any chemical enhancements to perform.

Was there anything that didn't remind her of sex? When had she become this desperate? Solitaire. She'd play the mind-numbing card game until Tom came home or her eyeballs dried out.

She was down three hundred dollars to the computer when

there was a soft knock on the door.

"Do you mind if I use the computer? I'd like to check up a couple of websites." Mac leaned against the doorway.

"Sure, I'm just checking my email." She quickly clicked off the card game and got out of the chair. "I'll leave you alone so you can work in peace."

Mac held her hand and stopped her from leaving. "Actually, I could use your help. I'm going to go through the government officials in the city. If you could help me keep track of who I checked out and who I haven't, I'd appreciate it."

"Okay. If you think I can help." There was only one chair and Caitlyn let Mac have it, kneeling on the floor instead. The position put her much too close to him, but she had little choice if she wanted to see what was on the monitor.

"You've been a big help so far."

"Me? Please. All I've done is make sandwiches and coffee and clean up after everyone."

"And you've taken notes and organized the information so we're not reinventing the wheel. Just because you're not on the street digging through trashcans doesn't mean you aren't helping out just as much as Tom or I."

"Do you really do that? Dig through trashcans? I thought that was just something on TV."

"Oh yeah, dig through them, hide behind them, you name it. TV doesn't get half of what we do right, but a lot can be found out by looking through someone's trash."

Mac's fingers flew over the keyboard as he brought up the city's website. As Caitlyn reached across the desk for a pad and a pen, her breasts brushed against Mac's leg and shot fire through her body.

"So what do you want me to do?" *Please don't read into that.*

"I'm going to go through all the city officials looking for ties to the gang members I know. I just need you to keep track of who I think has potential connections." His warm breath brushed down over her face. He smelled of mint toothpaste and Caitlyn remembered the taste of his mouth on hers too well.

"Okay."

Caitlyn tried to get her breathing under control as Mac scrolled through the web pages in front of him at a furious rate. His feet were bare and for the first time she noticed he had a sprinkling of black hair on his toes. It figured, he even had cute feet. Couldn't she find anything on him that wasn't sexy?

"Ah-ha!"

"What? Did you find something?"

"The Chief of Police, see this picture of him at the Grand Opening celebration? He's standing right next to Miguel."

"Miguel?"

"Yeah, he was one of my roommates in the hellhole I lived in. He was itching to take over for Carlos, but hadn't worked up the courage to make a bid yet."

"So that's a connection?"

"It could be. Mark it down, I'll do some more digging on that angle later."

Caitlyn stood and stretched her back and legs. Kneeling on the ground made her knees ache.

"Is your back still bothering you?" Mac turned towards her.

"No, I'm just stiff from kneeling on the floor. Give me a second and I'll be fine."

"Go ahead and sit on the bed, I'll let you know if I find anything."

Oh no. She wasn't going anywhere near the bed. "No worries. I'm fine, see?" Caitlyn stretched her arms over her head.

Mac let out a groan low in his throat. She looked closer at him. His hands were clenched in fists and sweat dotted his brow. He wasn't as unaffected by her as she had thought.

Now. What should she do about it?

Before she could make a decision, Mac stood, putting him within touching distance. Kissing distance.

"I should go check on a few things. I'll be right back." He stepped towards the door.

"Coward," she muttered.

"What?" Mac spun around. His pupils were dilated with desire and she could see his pulse beating in his neck. "What did you say?"

"Nothing, nothing at all." Her blood pounded furiously in her veins as Mac stepped into her personal space.

"I *know* you didn't just call me a coward."

"And what if I did?" she challenged. Come on, take the decision out of her hands.

"Then I'd just have to prove to you how wrong you are." His body hovered over hers, pushing her back until her legs hit the bed and she couldn't retreat any farther.

"I don't know, that might be hard to do. It looked like you were running away just now." Heat zipped through her, fast and furious.

"Me? Running away? I don't think so. It's you who's been running scared for the last couple days."

"Ha! What do I have to be afraid of?"

"This." Mac's hands pulled her head up to meet his and he captured her lips in a fiery kiss.

Caitlyn wrapped her arms around his neck and fell back onto the bed. He landed on her with a thud. His weight felt so good on her so right. She could feel his erection pressing through his jeans and her fingers itched to stroke it.

"I've wanted to do this forever," Mac mumbled against her neck as he kissed his way down her neck to the V of her shirt.

"What took you so long?" Caitlyn ripped his shirt over his head so she could explore the muscles of his chest and abs. She wanted to touch him everywhere at once, but his mouth on hers grabbed her attention instead.

Mac's tongue dipped between her lips, tempting her to open up and play. She needed no further urging to join him. He sucked her lower lip lightly, sending bolts of pleasure straight to her core. She thrust her hips against his, trying to ease the ache.

The need only intensified when Mac ran his hands along her legs over her hip and up her rib cage to her breast. He lightly squeezed her tender globes before stripping off her shirt and bra. When his hot mouth sucked in her pebbled nipple and rolled it over his tongue, she thought she'd come right there.

"So sweet," Mac whispered, blowing cool air over the

moistened tip.

She wasn't feeling at all sweet. She was feeling hot! Caitlyn pulled Mac up to her and rolled on top of him. The feel of his naked skin against hers was a sensual bonfire, heating her blood to the boiling point. Leaning over, she rubbed her breasts against his chest. The action sent arrows of lust shooting straight between her legs.

"God! I love the feel of you."

Mac's fingers slipped through her hair and held her head still for his exploration. She felt his muscles tense and ripple under her as he held himself in check. Another surge of heat headed south. There was something oh so very seductive about having all that leashed power under her fingertips.

Her body ached for more. Caitlyn rubbed against his denim-clad erection and shivered in pleasure at the contact.

"You're killing me," Mac groaned. His hands slipped to the waistband of her shorts and gently eased them over her hips.

Caitlyn wiggled to help him rid her of the clothes as quickly as possible. Cool air blew across her behind and added another caress to her already over-stimulated body. Mac ran his hands up the backs of her thighs, then back down again.

"I think you're a little overdressed for the party." Caitlyn smiled, then kissed her way down his chest until she reached one flat, brown nipple. Drawing it between her teeth, she teased him as he had done to her.

"If you'd stop turning my mind to mush, I might be able to remember how to unzip my fly." His hands moved to her breasts as she scooched lower.

"Don't worry, I'll take care of it." Caitlyn licked and nipped the delicious expanse of skin covering the bulging muscles of his abdomen. "Although, there is something very sexy about a studly male in a pair of jeans and nothing else."

She leaned back to take in the sight. Her breath caught in her throat as she traced the curve of his hipbone above the waistband of his jeans. Oh yeah, very sexy.

"It can't be any better than the view from here." Mac reached up and cupped her breasts, using his thumbs to tease her nipples.

The friction of his denim-covered legs between her bare

things was beginning to drive her to distraction. Almost against her will, her fingers unsnapped his jeans and slowly drew down the zipper. He was naked underneath and his penis sprung out into her hand as she peeled the jeans back.

Caitlyn's hands shook as she reached out to stroke his length. The texture was so soft, yet underneath was so hard. The contrast was fascinating. She slid down a little more, pulling his pants off as she went until he was as naked as she. Kneeling between his legs, she let her fingers drift up his inner thighs until she reached his erection again.

"If you keep playing with me, this will be over before it begins." Mac's hands were clenched into fists by his side and sweat dotted his forehead.

"But it's so much fun."

"I can think of something a little more fun." Mac pulled her to him and snared her mouth in a blazing kiss that held all the hunger and need he had for her. His mouth devoured hers, dragging her down into a storm of passion she had no intention of escaping.

The tip of Mac's penis probed her entrance, tempting her with its nearness.

"I hope Jim has some protection in here." Caitlyn lunged for the nightstand by the narrow bed and fumbled around inside. Please have something. She did not want to go rifling through his room looking for a condom right now.

A glimmer of foil caught her eye and she pounced on it. "Thank God!" Caitlyn ripped the package open with shaking hands.

"Slow down there a minute. I haven't had a chance to play yet." Mac rolled her to her side, trapping her hands between them.

Fire burned through her as his fingers trailed over her hip and thigh. With a little nudge, he spread her legs and caressed her inner thigh, going higher and higher, an inch at a time. Every nerve ending in her body clamored for more, but he took his own sweet time reaching the core of her that ached for him.

"You're so hot, so wet for me." His finger feathered lightly over her nubbin and she arched her hips for more.

One finger slipped inside her stretching her. His thumb

rubbed against her pleasure spot and fire spread through her whole body. When Mac leaned over and drew her nipple into his mouth, she had to hold back a moan of ecstasy.

His finger pumped in and out of her and the pleasure grew to unimaginable heights until she couldn't take it any more. Caitlyn's hips bucked as waves of release coursed through her body, shooting her into the stars.

She was still coming down to earth when Mac gently took the condom from her listless hands. "I'll take that now, thanks."

"Sure," she said vaguely. After that explosion, he could do whatever he wanted. Caitlyn opened her eyes slightly to see him stretch out over her. Her heart rate picked up speed again at the sight of those muscles above her. Maybe she wasn't too tired after all.

"Do you know how badly I've wanted to touch you? Taste you?" Mac's gaze blazed into her own. His jaw clenched as he entered her slowly. When he was in to the hilt, he threw his head back in obvious pleasure.

"Oh yeah, I know." If he wanted her nearly as bad as she wanted him, she knew exactly what he was going through. "Let's not waste another second of it." Caitlyn wrapped her legs around his waist and thrust her hips up to meet his.

Mac grabbed her hips and controlled their pace. Each slide of his body in hers brought them higher and higher. Caitlyn held onto his shoulders for dear life, not sure she could survive another mind-blowing orgasm, but willing to try.

"Come for me," he whispered against her lips, reaching between their bodies to stroke her nub again.

"I don't think that'll be a problem." Lights danced behind her eyes as pleasure exploded inside her. Mac's breathing was ragged in her ear, and she knew he was close too.

"I love how you feel around me. You're so tight, so hot." His voice was gruff, low and sexy. It added to the total sensory overload taking over her body, sending her closer to the edge.

Giving in to the tidal waves of lust swamping her, Caitlyn let go and convulsed in rapture.

"Yes!" Mac shouted, driving harder into her until he too shivered to completion.

Chapter Fifteen

Sweat cooled on his back as his breathing slowed to normal. Reality could wait for a few more minutes, couldn't it? For just a moment, he wanted to enjoy the bone-melting feeling of satisfaction that drifted through him. Caitlyn's silky skin surrounded him and he could think of no heaven greater than feeling those legs around his waist.

Her hand lightly drifted up and down his back. "I suppose we should get up and get back to work," she said, although she didn't seem too eager to move either.

"Yeah, I guess. If Tom catches us in bed again, he'll probably have a heart attack." As soon as the words were out of his mouth, he wished he could call them back. Caitlyn stiffened beneath him and her hand dropped to her side.

"You're right. This doesn't solve anything."

"No, but it felt good." Mac looked down at her and stroked the hair off her face. She wouldn't meet his gaze.

"It sure did. But it's time to get back to business. We have to figure out who's after your ass, besides me." She smiled at him, but it didn't reach her eyes.

"Are you okay?" Something was going on behind those brown eyes of hers. Whatever it was troubled her deeply.

"Nothing I can't handle." She tried to move again, but he held her still.

"Tell me." His finger drifted over her lower lip.

"It's nothing, really. It just bothers me to think of someone trying to kill you. I—I think my feelings are more involved than

I'd planned on." She shook her head, dislodging his finger. "Look, it's my issue, okay? It doesn't have to change anything."

Mac let out a deep breath. Was she trying to tell him her feelings went deep? A cold shiver of fear chased down his spine and he rolled off her.

"It's not that I don't care about you too, but I'm not really the 'happily ever after' type of guy." Shit. The last thing he'd wanted to do was hurt her more.

"I know. Believe me, I can read between the lines." She sat up and reached for her shirt. "I told you, it's my problem and I'll deal with it. When it's time for you to leave, you can do so with a clear conscience."

"It's not that. It's just—"

"It's just that you have a job to do. An important job and a relationship isn't part of that." She stepped into her shorts and faced him. "I told you, it's my problem and I'll deal with it. I know how important this job is to you." She twisted her hair back behind her head. "I'm going to change the laundry over. Let me know if you need any more help on the computer."

Mac watched her go and felt a stab of regret that their brief moment of connection was gone. He had to do his job. It was all he had in his life. He'd worked too hard for too long to just give it up. Right?

Of course he wasn't going to give up his job. Mac pulled his jeans on roughly. He lived for the danger, the challenge, the adrenaline rush of working undercover. There was no way he could just give it up and work behind some desk somewhere. Yanking his shirt over his head, he pushed those thoughts away. He was a fed and a damn good one. Caitlyn might be the best thing to step into his life in a long time, but that didn't mean he had to get all crazy about it.

A little voice in the back of his head snickered, *Too late.*

Tom's voice came from the kitchen. "Where's Mac?"

Caitlyn's voice was louder than necessary. "I think he's in the office on the computer. He said something about checking out the government websites."

Mac tucked in the T-shirt and slid into the chair seconds before he heard Tom's footfalls outside the room. He jiggled the mouse and cleared off the screen saver a breath before Tom walked in.

"Find anything good?" Tom asked from the doorway.

"Maybe." Mac glanced around to see if they'd left any telltale signs of their activities. Shit. The condom wrapper was half under the bed.

"Whatcha got?" Tom asked as he moved into the room.

Mac got out of the chair and held it out for Tom, stepping between him and the wrapper. "Here, take a look. That's the Chief of Police next to Miguel."

"So it is. Coincidence or collusion?"

"At this point I think we go with collusion. One of us needs to follow the Chief and the other needs to keep an eye on Miguel." Mac eased back and stepped on the foil wrapper.

"I'll follow Miguel. He's not familiar with what I look like and the Chief is."

"But you don't know the territory like I do."

Tom looked at him incredulously. "Are you kidding me? I grew up in this city. I know it better than half the punks in that gang. You worry about staying out of sight with the Chief, I'll take care of Miguel."

"When do we start?"

"As soon as Liam gets back and can watch Caitlyn."

"Caitlyn can watch herself," she called from the doorway. "I promise not to go out of the apartment or talk to strangers, but I refuse to be baby-sat any longer. The mission is more important than my safety."

"Nothing is more important than your safety," Mac said. "A few more hours either way won't make a difference."

Tom looked at him curiously, but Mac ignored him.

"It will to me. I need some privacy, and if I can't leave here to get it, the least you can do is get out of my hair for a little while."

He looked at Tom. It was his call. Mac had given up any right to offer protection when he told her he wasn't around for the long haul.

Tom slapped his hand against his thigh. "I don't like it."

"What else is new? Do you think I love being stuck in a

house with four men constantly underfoot? I'm used to living on my own and I need time for—girl things."

Oh boy, she was pulling out the big guns. The mere mention of mysterious "girl things" was sure to make Tom uncomfortable. Bravo. Tom shifted his weight.

"You won't go out of the apartment? And you won't open the door at all?"

"Scout's honor." She held up her hand, palm outward.

"You were never a Girl Scout."

"Tom, don't be difficult. It's only for a few hours and I promise not to even stand near the window, okay?"

"I still don't like it."

"You don't have to like it. You just have to do it. Please. I'm going crazy here. I've never looked forward to going to work so much in my life, just to get out of the house."

Tom muttered something under his breath, but didn't continue to fight. "All right, but I'm calling Liam and telling him to get his ass home as soon as possible."

"I'd expect nothing less. Now grab something to eat before you go." She stepped out of the way so Tom could leave.

"If my presence here is going to cause you problems, I can find somewhere else to stay," Mac said to her when Tom left the room.

"I know you might find this hard to believe, but surprisingly enough, my entire being isn't focused on you. I don't care if you stay here or not. Right now I just want some peace and quiet—without testosterone." She wouldn't look at him, but instead glanced down at her fingernails. "You need to be out there chasing down the connections between the gangs and the chief, not baby-sitting me. I'll be fine for the few hours Liam will be gone."

"Will you?" Just because he didn't want the picket fence with her didn't mean he didn't care about her. Couldn't she see that?

"Yes. I'm tough. Now go on before Tom gets antsy."

"I heard that," Tom called from the hallway.

ॐ

Caitlyn locked the door behind her brother and Mac and put the chain lock on for good measure. Alone at last. Good, now no one would see her cry.

No. She wouldn't shed a single tear over her own stupidity. It was her choice to give into her hormones. So she only had herself to blame if her dumb feelings got hurt. What did she expect? That just because she and Mac had great sex he would declare his undying love for her and vow to leave the undercover life he'd chosen?

Yeah, right. Idiot. Why couldn't she look at things the same way a guy did? She had a need and he filled it. Quite well. Why did she have to let her feelings get involved?

Could she be mistaking infatuation and lust for deeper feelings?

No, she'd been infatuated before and had been in lust before too. This was different. Mac was different. She'd never felt this intensity of emotion before and it scared and thrilled her at once.

Just thinking about him gave her a flutter in her tummy. Remembering his taste and his touch sent waves of excitement through her. But it was more than that. And it was that "more" that she needed to think about without Mac and her brothers around.

Pulling clothes out of the dryer, she absently paired up the socks and folded them. Too bad it wasn't as easy to organize her thoughts. The way she saw it, she had two choices. She could keep her feelings to herself and put up a brave front when Mac left. That had been her original plan.

Except she didn't suffer in silence very well.

The other choice was she could fight for what she wanted and try to make Mac see that he was throwing out the best thing that ever happened to him. That was more her style, but took moxie she didn't know if she had. She'd have to convince her brothers *and* Mac that they could work things out with his job and still have a life together.

Because she wasn't settling for anything less.

Her heart suddenly felt lighter. Now she had to develop a plan of action to nab her man. Hopefully it would be less dangerous than the one the guys were involved in. Mac would get his man and she'd get him.

Still chuckling over her own wit, she almost jumped out of her skin when there was a banging on the door.

Caitlyn's heart pounded in her chest. The guys had left half an hour ago and Liam had a key. Who could be at the door? The hammering continued. What should she do? She didn't have a weapon and she couldn't call the police. Crap. Why had she told them she didn't need anyone watching over her?

"Damn it, Jim. I know you're in there, open up!"

Maggie?

Caitlyn scurried to the door and peered through the peephole. The redhead stared back at her with a furious expression on her face and hands on her hips. "I don't care if your brother knows about us, I'm talking to you even if I have to shout through this damn door."

"Cripes Maggie, hold on." Caitlyn undid the locks and opened the door. Quickly looking up and down the hallway, she didn't see anyone so she pulled Maggie inside.

"Caitlyn? What are you doing here? Where's Jim?"

"He's working twelve to twelve today. What's going on?"

"You tell me." She stepped into the apartment and dropped her purse on the table. "Everything was going great, then your brother shows up out of the blue and suddenly Jim doesn't have time for me. The occasional phone call is it. What? Am I not good enough for the high and mighty Thomas O'Toole or something? I'm good enough to screw, but not to meet the whole family?" She stormed furiously into the kitchen and helped herself to a can of soda.

"If he doesn't want me, than he should have the balls to cut me loose instead of stringing me along." Her furious face began to crumple and tears fell from her eyes.

"Oh, Mags, don't cry. Jim's crazy about you."

"He...has...a...funny...way...of...showing...it," she sobbed.

"Come here." Caitlyn pulled her friend into her arms and hugged her tightly until the storm of weeping slowed somewhat.

"Sit down and I'll try to explain things a bit."

Maggie grabbed a napkin and blew her nose. "I don't know what's wrong with me. I've never been a cryer. I don't do it well you know. My face gets all blotchy and my eyes get red and puffy. I'm too vain to cry in public." She offered a watery smile and took a sip of soda. "But lately, I can't seem to help myself. I thought what Jim and I had was real, you know?"

"I think it is. I know Jim is head over heels for you."

"Then why cut me off? Why hasn't he introduced me to his brother? The way he talks about Tom, it seems like he values his opinion an awful lot. Is he worried that I won't cut the mustard?"

"Don't be ridiculous. It's just—complicated." How much to tell? "Let me see if I can make you understand without breaking confidences."

Caitlyn took a deep breath to gather her thoughts.

"Okay, you know Tom works for the FBI, right?" At Maggie's nod, she continued. "Tom is involved with a case up here and needs all our help to solve it. It, ah, it's gotten a little dicier than we ever expected. I'm sure when it's all over, Jim will be knocking on your door and apologizing profusely." She'd make sure he did it with roses and jewelry too.

"But why couldn't he just come out and tell me that instead of blowing me off? I would have understood if he had things he had to do instead of hanging out at my place watching movies."

"I don't know. He's a man, why do they do anything?" Caitlyn stood and grabbed a quart of ice cream out of the fridge and two spoons.

"Men, you can't live with them and you can't shoot them."

"Tell me about it." Caitlyn scooped out a big glob of chocolate and popped it in her mouth.

"Oh really?" A sly grin crossed Maggie's face. "And what man are you contemplating shooting? Jim never mentioned anything about a man in your life."

"He didn't know about him," Caitlyn said around a mouthful of ice cream.

"Do tell. At least I can count on you to fill me in on all the juicy details."

Caitlyn hesitated a minute. How much should she reveal? Screw it, she needed to talk to someone, a girl someone.

"He's Tom's partner and he's involved in the case too. I've known him, sort of, for a while, but only recently has it gotten more intense."

"How intense?" Maggie leaned forward, anticipation lighting her eyes.

Caitlyn's breath hitched. "Real intense. Like, keep you up at night tossing and turning intense."

"Oh my God! I know just what you mean." Maggie put her hand over her heart then dug into the rapidly dwindling ice cream.

"The only problem is, he doesn't want a relationship."

"Bastard. He just wants sex?"

"No. I mean, yes. Well, not really."

"It's a yes or no question, you can't pick all of the above."

"Yes, we had sex, and it was incredible. But no, he's the one warning me off. I'm the one trying to get him in bed."

"So you're just after him for sex?" Maggie looked at her in surprise.

"No. Although that's what I told myself in the beginning. I was going to just live for the moment and enjoy whatever pleasure he could give me."

"Then your feelings got involved."

"Yup." The spoon dipped again.

"But his didn't?"

"I don't know. He says he's not the 'happily ever after' type, and his job certainly doesn't lend itself to dinner at five every night, but I can't help but think there's something there."

Maggie sat back in her chair. "Aren't we a pair? You've got it as bad as I do."

Caitlyn didn't even have to ask what. "That's what I'm afraid of. And I don't know what to do about it. Part of me feels like I should just suck it up and when he goes, I'll smile bravely and wave goodbye."

"And the other part?"

"Wants to fight like hell for him, so if he leaves anyway he's miserable about it for the rest of his life." Caitlyn stood and put the spoons in the sink.

"I'd go with Plan B myself, but I'm a fighter."

"I was leaning that way when you pounded on the door."

"You just have to be prepared for the worst. He might not feel the same way you do." Maggie looked at her in sympathy.

"I know, but if I don't try and find out, I'll always wonder if it could have worked out."

"True. Either way you stand the chance of getting hurt. I'd rather go down swinging." Maggie wiped her mouth with a napkin and stood. "Well, since Jim isn't coming back any time soon, I think I'll head home. I only stopped by because I was on my way home from the mall and had worked up a good case of mad."

"I hear you. I'd be pissed too." Caitlyn walked her to the door. "What'd ya get at the mall? Anything good?"

"The bath store was having a sale, so I picked up a bunch of stuff there. Then I hit the candy store and bought a pound of fudge. I figured I'd hit the liquor store on the way home and buy a bottle of wine, take a bubble bath, then eat myself into a chocolate coma."

"Oh man, I'm jealous. I'd love a bubble bath. Something frilly and totally girlie." She let out a wistful sigh. "Thank God you came over when you did. I've been surrounded by men all week. I'm going into testosterone overload."

"If Tom looks anything like Liam or Jim then I'd say you were living every woman's dream."

"Ha! Not when you're related to them and they treat you like either a maid or a baby."

"You're right, that sucks. You deserve the bath more than I do. I'll even split the fudge."

Caitlyn's eyes lit up at the thought of such a luxury. "Really? You'd do that?"

"Sure. I bought more bath gel than I'll ever use. Besides, now that I know Jim's just an idiot and not dumping me, I can afford to be generous." She laughed and slung her purse over her shoulder.

"Good, then I don't feel guilty for taking it. Thank you." She hugged Maggie.

"No, thank you. I'm glad you were here instead of Jim. I'd have felt like a fool if I barged in here screaming with his brothers looking on. I guess I wasn't thinking. I swear these men suck your brain cells out of your head."

"You and me both, sister."

Chapter Sixteen

Mac waited outside a seedy looking apartment building for the Chief of Police to emerge. He was on the outskirts of Children's territory and his neck prickled with the danger of it. Now he had to worry about getting spotted by the chief and any random passer-by. The relaxed, satisfied feeling he'd had with Caitlyn seemed years ago instead of only hours.

His pulse jumped as he remembered the feel of Caitlyn surrounding him. She was a confusing mixture of tough girl and sexy vixen and he couldn't get a handle on her. First she told him her feelings ran deep, then she told him to get out, that her world didn't revolve around him.

Hell, he knew he wasn't the center of her universe, but she could've given him a chance to recover before tossing him out of the house.

"Mac, come in." Tom's voice came through the earpiece of the two-way radios he had scored for them.

"Go ahead." He barely had to whisper for the microphone to pick up his words.

"What's your location?"

"I'm outside an apartment on the corner of Washington and Lincoln. Where're you?"

"About half a block away. Is this where you lived?"

"Nope, we were closer to the park. The chief went in about ten minutes ago. I wonder if Miguel is headed this way?"

"I'll let you know in a few. Man, this kid's good at checking for tails. He managed to shake me once, but I caught up with him." Tom's voice held a bit of admiration.

"Makes you wonder if he knows he's being watched."

"Don't insult me."

It didn't take long for Mac to pick up Miguel slipping onto the fire escape on the side of the building. If he hadn't been hiding in the alley, he'd have missed him completely.

"I'm on the B side of the building, behind the dumpster. Miguel just shimmied up the fire escape like a squirrel."

"I got you in my sights, make some room for me."

Tom slipped silently next to Mac. It was a good thing Tom had warned him of his approach or Mac never would have recognized him. A black skullcap was pulled low over his head, almost hiding his eyes. Baggy jeans and a loose shirt disguised his shape and he'd done something to darken the skin of his hands and face. He blended in as well or better than Mac did, and Mac had lived there the last six months.

"This puts a bit of confirmation on things, doesn't it?" Tom crouched down behind the dumpster and pulled a candy bar out of a deep pocket.

"Got any more of those?"

Tom handed a second one over. Mac blocked out the smells of rotting food and urine that were prevalent in the alley and focused on the sweet chocolate instead. He'd eaten in worse places.

"We need some surveillance equipment so we can find out what they're saying and get some evidence."

"Can't do that without a warrant."

"No shit, but how are we going to get a warrant for surveillance equipment unless we can take something to the judge? I'm not going through the locals, that's for sure. Could Liam help?"

Tom looked thoughtful. "Maybe, but I hate to involve him if we don't have to. He's already risking his career by searching the records illegally."

"Might I remind you that hundreds of automatic weapons are flooding the streets? If we don't find out what's going down, losing his job is going to be the least of his worries."

"I'll talk to him tonight. Did you see the apartment Miguel went into?"

Mac let the subject die. Tom would come around eventually. "Third floor, two windows from the left."

Mac lifted his binoculars carefully. A stray glint of light off the lenses could give him away.

"Can you see anything?" Tom asked.

"No, the shades are down. I can't even get a silhouette to tell how many people are in there."

"Then we wait."

A plan began to form in Mac's mind, but it all hinged on getting Liam's help. If they could snag at least a listening and recording device, they could get enough evidence to set up a full-blown sting. If nothing else, they'd know what was going on.

"Should we put a tail on Carlos too?" Tom asked, interrupting his thoughts.

"Not yet. We don't have the manpower, and I think Miguel is making a play to take Carlos out. Let's keep an eye on him and the chief, see if we can get some more information and take it from there. I want to know when all of this is going down as much as I want to know who the players are."

"Here comes Miguel." Tom pointed to the fire escape.

Mac froze in place. If Miguel looked down, he'd be able to spot them around the dumpster. The youth slid down the rusty ladder and landed in a crouch. Looking furtively in both directions before getting up, Miguel's gaze passed their hiding place and moved on. With one last look, he scurried to the end of the alley and slipped out into the street.

Less than ten minutes later, the chief slipped out the back door and climbed into a beat up Chevy that waited on the street.

"Guess that answers that question," Tom said.

"We've got to tell Liam."

"I know," Tom said with a resigned sigh. "Come on, he should be home by now. Where'd you leave my car?" Mac had used Tom's car to follow the chief's activities. Since Miguel stayed pretty close to home, usually, Tom didn't need it.

"Commuter lot. You got bus fare?"

"Great. We smell like dumpster and now we have to take the bus."

"Could be worse, we could smell like outhouse, again."

"Don't remind me."

౪

"I'll get you the equipment on one condition. I get to be in on it." A muscle twitched in Liam's jaw as he faced down Tom and Mac.

Caitlyn's heart ached for him. Liam had respected the chief a great deal, so this must be killing him. It was one thing to think there was a dirty officer in the department. Hearing that it went all the way to the top must be devastating.

Tom looked to Mac who shrugged as if to say, "it's your call".

"Okay. We could use some extra manpower anyway. Will you be able to take this to a judge to get a warrant?"

"I'll do it. Just because my chief's dirty doesn't mean I am too."

"Li, no one thinks you're dirty. We just don't want you in the middle anymore than you have to be," Tom said.

"Like I have a choice? If I don't do something, who will? You can't trust anyone else. I'll do my job." Liam stalked out of the room.

Tom went to follow him, but Mac held him back. "Let him go. He needs to work this out for himself."

"I'll go," Caitlyn got up from the table and searched for Liam.

She found him in her room, playing solitaire.

"Do you need something? I can go—somewhere."

"Nope, just thought I'd watch and see if you're a better card player than I am. Doesn't look like it."

Liam gave her a weak smile and clicked off the game. "Did Tom send you in here to talk to me?"

"No, he wanted to come in, but I figured you two would get into a fist fight and break something and then I'd have no place to sleep, so I came instead."

"Ha, ha. Very funny. Look, I'm fine, I don't need a shoulder to cry on just because my department is dirtier than the river."

"I didn't think you'd need a shoulder to cry on, but I thought you might like to talk about it a bit."

"What's there to talk about? I became a cop to help others, and my Chief of Police is using that pledge to run guns and drugs that will be used on other cops. Serve and protect, yeah, right." He tipped back in his chair and looked out the window.

"We don't know the whole story, maybe there's more to it than meets the eye."

"Yeah, maybe he's just running guns to pay for his sick mother's operation. Wake up! He turned his back on all of us on the streets. And I'm going to make sure he gets nailed for it."

"Why don't we prove it first? Then you can worry about nailing him." Caitlyn didn't like the look on his face.

"Oh, I'll make sure we get proof. I have a friend in the equipment room, I can get us anything we need."

Caitlyn didn't know what else to say. Liam was obviously feeling betrayed, and nothing could change that. Only time could lessen the pain, but that wasn't what he wanted to hear right now.

"Just don't do anything stupid. Who knows what's going to happen when everything shakes down? I don't want to see you get killed. Who else would I be able to pick on?"

Liam smiled and dodged her mock punch. "Come on, let's go in the kitchen and work out a plan with your boyfriend."

"He's not my boyfriend," Caitlyn said quickly.

"Oh really? Then I guess you use condoms for decorations these days?" He pointed to the blue foil wrapper on the floor.

"Ah, I, ah." She didn't know what to say. It was one thing to discuss her sex life in general, it was another to have evidence of it right there in front of her brother.

"Don't panic. I'll keep my mouth shut about it."

"Until you need to use it against me." Caitlyn picked up the wrapper and buried it in the garbage under some tissues.

"Of course. What do you see in him anyway? He's arrogant as hell, and even more annoying than Tom. Or is that it? Sleeping with him pisses Tom off, so that's why you do it."

"Not by a long shot." Caitlyn sat on the bed. "I didn't plan on sleeping with him. It started out I was just trying to keep him alive, then we spent more time together and got to know each other. He can be really funny, and he's so smart. He really isn't arrogant, you know."

"Yeah, right."

"Honestly. He's just dedicated to his job and focused on it. He wants to solve this case and nothing is going to stand in his way. Even when he could barely stand because of the pain, he insisted I keep his cover."

"You don't have to get all mushy about it."

"I'm not getting mushy, it's just, well...I like him."

"Does that mean I'm going to have to look at his ugly mug across the dinner table every holiday?"

Caitlyn's heart lurched. She wanted that more than anything else, but didn't see it happening. "Probably not. He's not interested in long term."

"Then what the hell is he doing—"

"Never mind." Caitlyn stood and kissed Liam on the cheek. "I'll worry about my future, you just make sure you stay safe while you're playing cops and robbers."

"I'm not playing a cop, I am a cop."

"Are you sure?" She poked him in the side. "I bet you went to one of those internet police academies and got your badge in two weeks," she teased, poking him again.

"Cut it out." He batted her hands away.

"Whatcha gonna do, tough guy? Arrest me?" Caitlyn continued to tickle him, hoping her teasing would distract him from her love life and his bad mood.

"I don't need to arrest you when I can kick your ass." He stood and tried to grab her hands.

"You and what army?" She jabbed him in the ribs.

"Ouch! Your nails are sharp." Feinting to the right, he dodged left and grabbed her arm. With a quick heave, he had her over his shoulder.

"Put me down!" she shrieked, breathless with laughter.

"Not so tough now are you?" Liam spun around in the tiny

room.

"I'll throw up all over you," she laughed, getting dizzy.

"You'd better not!"

Before Caitlyn could catch her breath, Liam stepped on something and lost his balance, dropping her on the bed with a thud. Her head hit the headboard with a resounding thunk and the frame collapsed beneath her.

Tom and Mac came racing into the room to find Liam sprawled on top of her.

"What the hell is going on here?" Mac stormed into the room and hauled Liam off her. "Are you okay? What happened?"

Caitlyn stood slowly, rubbing her head. "Nothing, Liam and I were just horsing around."

"Are you hurt? Let me see." He pulled her close to look at her head. "Jesus, you could have killed her! You outweigh her by seventy-five pounds, man. You should be more careful," Mac shot at Liam.

"I don't need you telling me how to treat my sister. At least I'm not fucking her and leaving her high and dry." Liam accused.

"Liam, shut up." Caitlyn moved between the two of them.

"I'm not leaving her high and dry, and I'm not 'fucking' her." Mac faced him down.

"Enough!" Caitlyn put a hand on either chest. "Mac, Liam and I horse around like that all the time, there was no harm done, so back off."

He stepped back, but his face was still thunderous.

"Liam, what Mac and I do is my business. Mine. So butt out."

"It's not right. He has no business..."

"I said enough. Why don't you go back to your place for a bit and take a break. We can't do anything today anyway."

Liam gave one last furious glare to Mac before pushing past Tom and stomping out.

"That was real helpful, Mac, thanks," she snarled at him. "I almost had him out of the grumps and you had to bust in here like some rescuing hero." Caitlyn squatted down to check out the damage to the bed. Thank God their earlier activities hadn't broken it. Of course, that was probably what weakened it in the first place.

"How bad is it?" Mac bent down next to her. His scent invaded her senses and her mind spun with images of him moving over her.

"Not that bad, the frame just came out of the slot. If you pick it up, I should be able to get it back in." *Don't think about putting tabs into slots!*

Mac tried not to think about the last time he'd been this close to Caitlyn and a bed at the same time. He could feel Tom staring a hole in his back and knew he had some explaining to do. Great. That would be loads of fun.

The frame slid into the headboard without much fuss and Caitlyn hurried away from him. What had she told Liam before the two of them started wrestling?

"Come on, Mac. I want to get an early start tomorrow, so let's get the game plan straight tonight."

"Don't forget I need a ride into work tomorrow," Caitlyn said from the hallway.

"Out of the question," Mac said before Tom could open his mouth. There was no way she was going to work unless he could post a guard on her.

"I don't believe I asked your permission. I have a job to do."

"Cat, the hospital is smack dab in the middle of the Children's territory. Don't you think you could call out until we know what's going on?" Tom asked.

"No. I've already had extra days off because of my back, I can't leave them short-handed again. Besides, if all hell breaks loose, the hospital needs to be prepared. Lives could depend on it."

She had a point there, but Mac hated the idea of her being vulnerable.

"If one of you drops me off and another picks me up, I don't see how there could be a problem. No one's going to come into the ER with guns a-blazing and take a shot at me."

"How do you know?" Mac met her gaze over the bed.

"Because we have security guards and I'm behind locked doors."

A cold knot of fear formed in his gut. He'd felt a measure of comfort knowing she was safe in the apartment with one of the O'Tooles always handy. The thought of her being in the middle of everything scared the hell out of him.

"We can't keep her prisoner here. Jim can take her in and we'll pick her up," Tom said.

If her overprotective brother wasn't worried about it, Mac couldn't very well keep pushing the issue. But it still made him feel uneasy. Someone had taken a stab at her—literally—at work already, what would stop them from doing it again?

Chapter Seventeen

The Man waited for the cop to leave his office, then closed the door. The last shipment of guns had arrived and everything was in place. He'd contact the three gang leaders and get them ready to move. The timing had to be perfect.

Months of preparation had gone into this operation and nothing was going to ruin it for him. Not even one hard to kill federal agent. How much did he know? That idiot Carlos assured him that "Diego" hadn't been involved in any of the gun runs, but he could just be covering his ass.

Diego must know more. But how much? Enough for the Man to abandon his operation? His fist clenched around a pencil. Not when he was so close. Summer was ending and the media was hungry for a story. Just as he'd planned. When the gangs started rioting and looting, he'd sweep in and look like a hero on the ten o'clock news.

A slow smile spread over his face at the thought. Once he got rid of Carlos and the others of his ilk, he'd have total control over the gangs' activities. He wouldn't be greedy about it, oh no. A ten percent cut of the profits was a fair exchange for protection from the cops. Money would trickle into a secured account in the Caymans, and after his retirement, he'd have something to supplement his government pension.

And the city would thank him for it.

All he had to do was dispose of McDougal. And thanks to his informants, he knew just the right way to do so.

∽

Caitlyn had never looked forward to work so much in her life. She was showered and dressed a good hour before her shift started and nagged at Jim until he got out of bed to take her in early.

"Come on, lazy bones. I want to get in and make some phone calls before I go on duty." She whipped the covers off Jim's slumbering form.

"Hey!" He yanked the sheet up to cover his boxers. "Can't you make your phone calls here? I didn't get home until after three."

"It's not my fault you had some heavy sucking up to do with Maggie. You should have called her and told her what was going on."

"How did you know…"

"I'm a woman, I have my ways. Now get up. I already made coffee and poured you some cereal." He didn't need to know Maggie had stopped over yesterday. She'd promised to not let anyone in and even though Maggie was safe enough, she didn't want a lecture.

"Christ, can't a guy get some privacy around here? I'll be glad when this is all over and you all go away," Jim grumbled, reaching for his jeans on the floor.

Caitlyn's heart sunk at the thought of Mac going away, but she shook it off. She still hadn't figured out how to make him miserable without her, but she would. After work.

"Poor baby. Is your family wreaking havoc on your love life?" Now he knew how she felt.

"Shut up and get me some coffee. The least you could do is pour me a cup since you're making me get up after only six hours sleep."

Once Caitlyn was sure he was really up and moving, she skipped out of the room and into the kitchen. She'd happily pour him coffee if it got him moving.

Jim was still in a fog when he stumbled into the kitchen a few minutes later, but at least he was dressed.

"Yum. I'll miss your coffee when you go. But that's the only thing." He blew cautiously on the steaming brew.

"I love you too. You know, if you drink that on the way to

the hospital, you can come back to bed sooner." She tapped her feet anxiously.

"What's the rush? Why can't you make your damn phone calls from here?"

"I can't make them here because I need to look up the schedule. I want to put a few folks on guard to come in early if we need them. I have a feeling we're going to need extra help sooner, rather than later."

Jim focused on her words. "That's not a bad idea. You could tell them you heard through the grapevine there was going to be another disaster drill and you wanted to be ready. Liam and I could do the same thing."

Caitlyn thought about it for a moment. "That could work. I'll say I heard it from Liam, he can say he heard it from you, and you could say you heard it from me. No one wants another clusterfuck like the last one, so they'd be on their guards."

Since 9/11, the various municipalities had begun working together to plan for future attacks. Disaster drills were designed for the police, fire, and emergency medical services to prepare for mass casualty incidents. They were invariably mass confusion, with a few people doing all the work and the rest of the folks standing around getting in the way. The media had a field day with the poor performance after the last one.

"You know, for a girl, you're pretty smart." Jim smiled evilly at her.

Caitlyn rolled her eyes. "You're not so shabby yourself, for a brother. Now come on."

Jim groused all the way to the hospital, but she didn't care. She felt like a prisoner on a one-day pass. Freedom! She was finally out of the apartment and out from under four pairs of watchful eyes.

"Just drop me off at the emergency entrance," Caitlyn said, reaching for the door.

"Not on your life. I'll walk you into the hospital and have a little talk with the security guards while I'm at it."

Caitlyn rolled her eyes but didn't bother to argue. What good would it do her? Besides, if it made him feel more comfortable leaving her alone, she'd put up with the escort. For now anyway.

"Hey, Caitlyn. How's your back?" Nancy, the emergency room secretary asked as Caitlyn walked in.

"Good as new. A little stretching and some rest and I'm back in fighting form."

"Just in time too. City hall put out an alert. They're noticing an increase in gang activity. We could be in for a busy night."

"Really?"

"That's what the fax said." Nancy pulled the memo out of a pile on her desk and handed it over.

Caitlyn skimmed the carefully worded memo. Things had been quiet for a while. Why would city hall think that there was an increase in gang activity coming? The return number on the fax form looked familiar. Could it be from the police station? Could this have been sent out by the chief?

"Has the phone tree been activated for this? I mean, do we have backups ready in case we get inundated with gunshot patients?"

"Not really. The word from the higher ups is that we'll take it under advisement." She rolled her eyes. It was easy for the administration to say they'd take it under advisement. They weren't the ones who'd be flooded with patients and not enough staff.

Great. Back to her original plan. "Listen, between you and me, I heard from my brother that another disaster drill was in the works. The fire departments are putting everyone on call and planning for it. Do you think you and I could make a few phone calls and get our teams in place?"

"Well, we can't make it official, but we could call some of our off duty friends and let them know about a pending drill. In a friendly way of course." The secretary pulled a binder down and opened it up. "Here's A through M, I'll take N through Z."

"You're too good. I'll take this to the staff lounge and pass the word."

"Thanks. And I'm only doing this because I'm not letting those hip wagon kings make us look bad. I know your brother's a paramedic, but some of his buddies are real jerks. If they start flying in here with mass casualties, we'll be ready for them."

Caitlyn smiled and took her list to the relative quiet of the staff lounge. Word would spread like wildfire through the hospital and phone lines would be buzzing on every floor. No one wanted a repeat of the media flogging they'd gotten last time. The hospital would be ready for whatever was coming, she just wished she knew what it was.

80

Tom clicked off his cell phone with a laugh as Mac climbed into the passenger seat of his car with two cups of steaming coffee.

"What's so funny?"

"My little brother is smarter than I thought. Listen to this. Jim had this idea to get the municipalities ready without making a brouhaha."

"I've gotta hear this. Nothing happens with the munies without at least ten memos and five action committees." Mac took a cautious sip of his coffee.

"I guess the city had a mass casualty drill a few months back and it was a disaster."

"No pun intended?"

"Ha, ha. Anyway, as usual, they all blamed each other for the mess and the papers and nightly news ripped them up one side and down the other." Tom pulled out into traffic, careful not to spill his coffee.

"I can see it now. The big story on the ten o'clock news, 'Is Hartford ready for another 9/11?'"

"Exactly. Anyway, Caitlyn went into work and told some folks there that she heard from Jim that they were planning another drill. Then Jim called some of his buddies and said he heard from Liam that there was another drill in the works."

"And let me guess, Liam called his buddies and said he heard from Caitlyn that they were preparing for a drill?"

"You got it. None of them want to be caught with their pants down this time and word is spreading faster than lightning."

"That could backfire on us," Mac said working through the consequences aloud. "If the chief is involved, he'll hear about it. And since he knows there's no drill planned, he might smell a rat."

"Maybe. Either way, it doesn't hurt to be prepared, and if nothing comes of it they can always blame it on a rumor."

"True, but it will put him on his guard." Mac felt a stirring in his gut. Something was wrong, but he couldn't put his finger on it.

"Like he's not already? He knows you're out and about. I figure he's either going to cut and run or move his operation up to get the most money if it all blows up." Tom slowed down and turned into the commuter lot.

"I don't know. My instincts are screaming that something is going to happen soon, but for the life of me I can't figure out what it is."

"There's nothing more we can do about it than what we're already doing. Now, do you want to follow the chief again and I'll take Miguel?"

"No, they won't meet again so soon. If yesterday's meeting was to put everything in place, then the action will come from the streets."

"Then that's where we're headed." Tom reached around and hauled a bulging backpack out from the back seat.

Both men pulled on baggy jeans and loose shirts. Mac added a pair of headphones and an MP3 player to the disguise. Slipping into "Diego" mode, he let a bitterness creep into his face before he stuffed his gun into the back of his pants and slipped out of the car.

"You take the corner and I'll scout out Carlos' place. If something big is going down, he'll be right in the thick of it," Mac said.

"Here, take the radio. Click it twice if you need something. I've got it on vibrate so no one should hear it on the street."

Mac took the radio and slipped it in one of the deep pants pockets. "I'll take the first bus, you take the second."

"Got it. Watch your back." Tom put his fist out.

"You too." Mac thumped his fist on top of Tom's and

slipped on some sunglasses before gliding towards the bus stop.

The little booth was almost empty, just one elderly Hispanic woman who clutched her purse to her chest and scotched closer to the other end of the bench at Mac's approach. He ignored her and turned the MP3 player on until the bass line made his teeth ache. After this assignment ended, he was never listening to rap again.

It didn't take long for the bus to roll in. Mac paid his fare and slouched low in a window seat. The dark glasses he wore hid his light eyes and let him take in his surroundings unobserved. There was a definite tension in the air. Fewer people than normal were on the bus. As Mac gazed out at the passing neighborhoods, it appeared that folks were holding up inside.

Oh yeah, something was going down today. He checked his reflection in the grimy bus window. If someone looked closely they might be able to tell that he and Diego were the same person, but unless they were looking for the connection, his disguise should hold. He looked like any number of restless thugs that prowled the streets.

Mac picked a stop a few blocks from Carlos' headquarters. He wanted to get a feel for the neighborhood before he found a spot to hide. His neck prickled with awareness as he slipped through the streets. Curtains twitched as he passed quiet buildings, but no one came out. The atmosphere reminded him of an old Western movie, just before the two gunslingers met at high noon. Any second he expected to hear eerie music in the background.

Good Lord, he was losing it.

A clatter behind him had Mac jumping for cover. A skinny dog trotted down the street, nosing a can scavenged from someone's trash. Mac laughed weakly at himself. His heart pounded in his throat and his pulse raced. He was getting too old for this when a stray dog could scare ten years off his life.

Mac waited for the dog to pass him. He didn't need to call attention to himself by having a flea-bitten mutt dogging his heels. Caitlyn probably would have scooped him up and taken him home. She had such a soft heart for strays of all types.

Including him.

He pushed thoughts of her out of his head. There was no room for error in this mission, and getting caught in the emotional knots she tied him in would only trip him up. He had to focus his attention on finding out what Carlos was up to.

For the hundredth time, he wished there had been time for Liam to get them that surveillance equipment. Being able to hear what was said behind closed doors would give them a much-needed edge. No sense crying over what they didn't have. He'd use what tools he had and pray they were enough. Stealth and instinct had gotten him through many a hairy situation. This time would be no different.

He hoped.

Dodging the lookouts Mac knew were hiding around Carlos' apartment, he crept behind a dumpster and pulled some of the overflow around him. Reeking garbage bags provided the cover he needed to keep all but the most determined searchers away. No bag lady or bum would go dumpster hopping in this neighborhood. At least not if they wanted to keep any treasures they picked up along the way.

Mac settled in and kept an eye on the main entrance and the corner fire escape. There was a chance that visitors could come through the back door, but that was a chance he'd have to take. As it was, he could only see the front door if he craned his neck precariously around the dumpster.

The midday heat made the garbage that much more fragrant, and Mac had to fight off biting flies that thought he made a great snack. Sitting in piles of refuse was starting to get old. There had to be a better way to make a living and still help others. Bile rose in his throat as he caught another whiff of stale urine and rotting food.

He bet Accounts never had to sit for hours behind dumpsters. Maybe when this was all over, he'd put in a transfer. Yeah, accounting was looking pretty good right about now. Nice neat rows of numbers, coffee breaks, a corner office. And coming home to Caitlyn at five thirty every night.

Wait a minute there, buddy. Where did that come from? He wasn't thinking seriously about getting out of fieldwork, was he? Yeah, he had feelings for Caitlyn, but that didn't mean he was going to change his entire life around for her.

But would it only be for her? Hadn't he been feeling more

and more disillusioned as this case wore on? Long before he met Caitlyn, he'd felt disgust at what he'd had to do to maintain his cover. He'd told himself it was for the greater good, a means to an end, but the stains on his soul grew every day.

Being around the O'Tooles had shown him what he was missing, always on the outside looking in. Working undercover didn't lend itself to close relationships, or so he'd always told himself. But didn't Tom maintain a relationship with his family? He didn't isolate himself from the rest of the world just because he went deep underground for months at a time.

It might be nice to have someone worrying about him for a change. To have someone to come home to. To love.

Hello? Get your head out of the clouds, buddy. Mac shook himself. This was not the time to contemplate major life decisions. He had a job to do, and when it was all over he'd take a vacation and think about his future then. On a beach somewhere, with a cold beer in one hand and a leggy babe in the other.

Unbidden, a picture of Caitlyn in a bikini flashed into his brain. Now that would be a vacation. To have her all to himself without worrying about older brothers walking in on them or gang members trying to kill him. Vacation nothing, that would be heaven.

For the first time that day, Mac wished whatever was going to happen would happen soon so he could make his daydream a reality. Oh brother, he needed to get his head on straight before it got blown off while he was fantasizing about Caitlyn in a bikini.

Mac shifted his weight to a more comfortable position. His wound hardly bothered him at all anymore, as long as he didn't try to stretch his arms over his head. Good thing too, since he'd been crawling all over the city for the last week. He still couldn't believe his luck in landing under Caitlyn's Jeep. It must have been fate.

Now he knew he'd been out in the sun too long. The combination of his odiferous surrounds and heat must have fried his brains. He made his own destiny and fate had nothing to do with it.

On the other hand, he'd take any good luck that happened to come his way.

"And look at that. Patience and good luck strikes again," Mac muttered to himself as shiny black sedan pulled in front of the building and parked illegally.

This wasn't Carlos' car, and he was sure he'd never seen it around the neighborhood before. Mac's heart rate picked up, and adrenaline zipped through his system. He reached into his pocket and clicked the radio twice before snagging the disposable camera he'd bought at the gas station that morning. It didn't have a zoom lens or anything, but it could take a picture without the tell tale flash of Jim's automatic camera.

Mac waited with baited breath to see who would emerge from the black car. He took a picture of the license plate while he was waiting. If he couldn't get a look at the passengers, at least he could have Liam run the plates.

"Come on, come on." Mac urged the riders to get out so he could get a shot at them. The doors remained firmly closed. He couldn't see squat through the darkly tinted windows, no matter how hard he squinted to get a hint of the occupants of the vehicle.

The door to the apartment building burst open and two of Carlos' bodyguards strutted out and flanked the door. Carlos followed slowly after them, searching the street for any onlookers. Mac held still behind his shield of garbage and cardboard boxes. Any movement would draw the eye to his hiding place.

When Carlos deemed it safe, he stepped to the back door of the sedan and opened it. Mac clicked the camera, getting a good shot of Carlos opening the door. He waited with his finger poised over the button for his next shot. Mac was laying odds that it was the Chief of Police. A picture of Carlos with the chief should be proof enough to take to any judge.

Good thing he wasn't a gambling man, cause he would have been wrong. Dead wrong.

Chapter Eighteen

Mac was so stunned he almost forgot to snap the picture. The mayor? The mayor of the city was shaking hands with Carlos and following him into the building. He took two more pictures in quick succession. They might not come out clearly, but the mayor's face would be recognizable even to the blindest of judges.

The mayor? What could he get out of it? Mac was stunned. He'd met with Mayor Nadowny once when the mayor gave a talk to the Northeast division about Hartford's unique dichotomy. Tom had been there too. Shit. He knew Mac and Tom were partners.

If he knew that, then he could easily figure out who was hiding him. Fear slammed him in the gut. Mac didn't dare leave his hiding spot or the driver of the car would spot him. Where the hell was Tom? They had to call Liam and Jim. And Caitlyn. She still thought it was the chief.

Calm down! Mac forced himself to think rationally. If the mayor was here, he couldn't be after Caitlyn. Once he left, he would meet up with Tom and they'd gather the troops and reevaluate this latest revelation. There was nothing to worry about.

Even so, Mac felt the knot of fear in his stomach get bigger and bigger.

It wasn't long before the apartment door opened again. The same two bodyguards flanked the doors and Carlos came out, leading the mayor. Mac snapped another picture for good measure, this one with Carlos' arm around Nadowny. Didn't they look chummy?

Time crawled by as Mac waited for the mayor to get into his car and pull away. Stinging sweat dripped into his eyes and more slid down the back of his shirt. Finally, the car started with a low rumble and eased away from the curb. Mac froze and waited for the car to pass his spot in the alley.

He couldn't blow it now. He had to be patient and wait until the coast was clear. Carlos had retreated to the safety of his lair, but still Mac waited. Just as he was about to slip from his hiding spot, the fire escape ladder creaked. Mac's heart jumped into his throat. Was he nailed?

Slowly, he sunk lower in his piles and looked out of the corner of his eye. A lone man was furtively climbing down the fire escape. Miguel!

And he looked scared.

Without thinking, Mac crawled along the alley floor. His hands splashed in puddles better left uninvestigated. Just as Miguel reached the last rung of the ladder and prepared to jump the rest of the way down, Mac leapt up and grabbed the slender youth around the waist.

"Scream and we're both dead." Mac waited for him to drop his weight and held his grip on Miguel even as his side screamed in pain.

"We got to get outta here, man." Miguel's voice held a thread of panic. "If they see me, I'll be six feet under before you can say 'Amen'."

"Don't worry, I have the perfect place to go. Come on, my brother, we're catching the next bus out of town." Mac let Miguel slide down his body until he could lock his arm up behind him.

"Diego? That you, man?"

"Yup, and you've got some explaining to do."

Mac held Miguel's arm in a death grip all the way out of the Children's territory and onto the bus. Using his body as a shield, he showed Miguel the gun as soon as they sat to prevent any last minute runs for freedom.

The radio vibrated in his pocket and Mac pulled it out without letting go of the gun. Miguel didn't seem too eager to jump off a moving bus and slouched low under the window.

"Where the hell are you?" Tom growled through the tinny

connection.

"On the A bus heading back to the commuter lot. Meet me there, I've got some company with me."

"Who?"

"I'll show you as soon as you get your ass back here. Call in the troops, there's been a new development in the case."

"I hate this guessing game shit." Tom hung up.

Miguel remained silent, even when they got off the bus and Mac pushed him into the back seat of Tom's car. He slid down low again and kept a wary eye out every time a bus rolled into the lot. Mac wanted to shout questions at the young lieutenant, but kept his curiosity in check. He'd wait until Tom was there to help him and listen to Miguel's first responses.

After twenty minutes and three buses, Tom finally made his way to the car. He raised an eyebrow at Miguel's presence as he slid into the driver's seat, but didn't say anything until they pulled out of the lot.

"Now this is a surprise. You want to fill me in?" Tom asked, looking at Mac through the rear view mirror to the back seat where he sat with the gun still trained on Miguel.

"I was watching Carlos' place when he got a visitor, the honorable Mayor Nadowny. No sooner had Nadowny pulled away than I caught—literally—Miguel coming down the fire escape."

"The mayor? You've got to be kidding me? Not the chief?"

"Nope. And I've got the meeting on film. I hope."

"So, where does that leave us?" Tom accelerated onto the highway.

"That depends on what our friend Miguel here has to say." Mac jabbed him in the ribs with the barrel of the gun.

"Who are you? I know you're five-oh, but who's this cracker?" Miguel nodded belligerently in Tom's direction.

"My partner in the FBI." Mac watched his reaction. Miguel's eyes widened and his hands shook slightly.

"I want to make a phone call." Sweat dotted his upper lip.

"You're not under arrest, my friend. We don't have to let you make a phone call. Hell, we don't have to let you take a wiz if we don't want to," Tom said from the front seat.

Guess Tom was going to play "bad cop" this time around. That was usually Mac's job, with his light blue eyes he tended to strike fear in the hearts of most of their suspects.

"Come on Miguel, tell us what's going down. We've seen you with the chief several times. I also spotted your exchange with the 525s. Fill me in on what's been going on since someone shot me in the back."

"Man, I had nothing to do with that. You gotta believe me. That was all Carlos."

"Sure, sure it was."

"I ain't lyin!" The whites of Miguel's eyes stood out starkly from his darkly tanned face.

"Why don't you tell me everything and let me decide who to believe?"

"Look, this is how it went down. Carlos gets paranoid all the time. He has connections with the cops, so he took the can of soda you drank from at his place and sent it somewhere. A few weeks later your prints come back and you're busted."

"Your prints should've been on file as Diego." Tom's eyes looked worried in the rear view mirror.

"I don't know, man. Maybe it was something else. All I know is word went out that you was to be popped and whoever got you got five Gs."

"That's all I was worth? Five thousand? How insulting."

"You're worth twice that in Columbia. Maybe you should go back down there if your ego's feeling bruised," Tom shot out sarcastically.

"So where does the chief figure into this? Is he Carlos' connection?"

"No." Miguel clammed up.

"I have a full tank of gas, I can drive around all day until I find a place to dump your body."

"Come on Miguel, the game's over. I've got proof that the mayor is involved with Carlos and that you're involved with the chief. Save yourself."

"I don't know nothing."

Mac waited. They were at a stalemate and time was wasting. "Tom, why don't you call Caitlyn and tell her what we found out and tell her to keep her eyes open."

"You think they're going after her?"

"I don't know anything for sure, but something tells me they aren't just going to let her get away scot-free. The mayor knows both of us, and someone ran her plates. Chances are he's put two and two together."

Tom tossed his cell phone back to Mac and pulled an illegal U-turn. "You call her and tell her to stay put, I'll be there in ten minutes."

༄

Why had she missed being at work again? Caitlyn stretched her aching back and tried to work a kink out of her neck. She'd never seen so many psychiatric evaluations in one shift in her entire career. The only other time she'd ever had this many at once was before a bad storm and that was probably to have someplace warm to spend the night.

"Caitlyn, go grab some supper while you can," Caitlyn's head nurse directed her.

It was barely five o'clock, but if she didn't go now, chances were she wouldn't get another opportunity.

"I'll be back as soon as I can choke down a sandwich or something."

"Take your time. If we need you we'll page you."

Caitlyn didn't doubt they would.

The cafeteria was busy with other hospital personal trying to grab a bite to eat before rushing back to work. Everyone looked frazzled, more so than usual. That memo from city hall must have everyone anxious.

Well, she wasn't going to let a stupid memo keep her from eating. It might be the only time she'd get to sit down until midnight. The grilled cheese sandwich and fries she'd ordered didn't seem all that appetizing, but they'd fill her up for a while.

She'd no sooner taken a bite of gooey cheese and soggy bread then she saw the Chief of Police walk through the door.

Holy crap. Caitlyn slid to a chair behind a potted plant and hoped he wouldn't see her. Apparently he wasn't looking for her, because after a quick glance around the crowded room, he headed straight for one of the maintenance people sitting by herself.

Caitlyn didn't recognize the woman. She must work on another floor. Carefully keeping her back to the two of them, she walked over to the condiment station and pretended to get some ketchup. With straining ears, she tried to catch part of their conversation. The cafeteria was so noisy, she couldn't pick up much. She waited for a lull in conversation.

"You have to tell me where he is! Miguel left me a strange message about tonight, and now he's not answering his phone."

Caitlyn looked out of the corner of her eye and saw the woman shaking her head and gesturing with her hands. The chief leaned over the table and looked around. She had to call Tom! If the chief wanted Miguel, maybe something was happening now.

Walking casually back to the table, Caitlyn grabbed her purse and picked up her lunch tray. She couldn't use her cell phone in the hospital, so she'd have to go to the parking lot to call Tom. Dumping her mostly uneaten dinner, Caitlyn took the stairs as fast as she could. As she hustled through the lobby doors, she heard her name being paged.

Damn, she'd have to make this quick so she could get back to the ER Her hands shook as she dug through her purse for her phone. She walked away from the smokers who congregated outside the main doors and dialed Tom's number.

It seemed to take forever for the signal to connect. She tapped her foot impatiently as it rang and rang with no answer.

"What's the point of having one of these things if you're not going to answer it?" At least he'd see her number on the phone if he bothered to check his messages. She snapped the phone closed with a little more energy than was necessary.

As she turned to go back into the hospital, a car pulled up to the curb and stopped in front of her. Maybe they needed directions? The hospital complex was a maze if you didn't know where to park. She could take a minute to give directions before she went back to work.

The car door opened and a gentleman in a suit got out of

the back seat. He looked at her name badge and a smile crept across his face.

"Can I help you?" Caitlyn asked. The hair at the back of her neck prickled. She took a step backwards. He looked like a businessman, but something about that smile bothered her.

"Are you Tom O'Toole's sister?"

"Yes I am. Why?" Was he hurt? Could this be someone from his office? Wouldn't they have called her if there were a problem?

"I need to talk to you, there's been an...incident."

Fear immediately lodged in her throat. Not Tom! She took a step forward then stopped.

"What kind of incident?" Something wasn't right here. "Wait a minute. Aren't you Mayor Nadowny? What do you know about my brother?" Caitlyn turned and waved to the guard on duty in the lobby. She didn't know what the mayor wanted, but he was giving her the willies and she wanted someone there.

"Get her!"

A hand clapped over her mouth. A strong arm wrapped around her waist and picked her up off the ground. She fought back with every dirty trick she could think of, biting at the hand that held her and kicking back with her heels. A grunt of pain sounded, but the arm stayed wrapped around her.

She was dumped in the back seat of the car and Nadowny climbed in after her. Caitlyn scrambled for the other door, hoping to get out before they knew what she was doing, but Nadowny grabbed her braid and yanked her back.

"Go! Go!"

Caitlyn was thrown back as the car sped off. The last thing she saw was Nadowny's face before pain slammed through her head and the world went dark.

ॐ

"She's not answering the page." Mac's gut was screaming at him that something was wrong. "It shouldn't take her this long to get to a phone."

"We're almost there, just hold on. Maybe she's in the bathroom or something." Tom's face was pinched with fear, but his hands remained steady on the wheel. They were doing sixty miles an hour on the city streets, so it was a good thing he wasn't shaking.

Mac turned to Miguel. "So help me God, if one hair on her head is disturbed your life won't be worth spit."

"Dude, I had nothing to do with any chick. You have to believe me."

"I don't have to do shit." Mac silently urged Tom to go faster.

Tom rounded the corner and Mac would have sworn they were on two wheels. As they screeched to a halt in front of the hospital, Mac saw a black sedan pulling away.

"That's him. Follow him!"

"What? That's who?"

"The mayor, the mayor. That's his car."

Tom didn't ask any more questions but followed the black car. He hadn't gone a hundred feet when an ambulance came by with lights flashing and sirens wailing, cutting him off.

Mac and Miguel were thrown forward as Tom slammed on the breaks.

"Shit!" Tom pounded his fist on the steering wheel.

Before Mac could form a new plan, Miguel shoved open the door and jumped out. Mac scrambled after him, throwing all his pent up anger and frustration into his stride. Miguel looked over his shoulder and put on an extra burst of speed, charging right for the Emergency Room doors.

Mac gained on him with every step. If he made it to the hospital, one of the guards would grab him for sure, but Mac wanted to be the one to catch him. Miguel was headed straight for the sliding glass doors. At the rate of speed he was moving, he'd slam into them before they opened.

Just as Mac slowed down to keep from charging head long into plate glass, the door opened and Miguel smashed into the person walking out.

Who happened to be none other than the Chief of Police.

Chapter Nineteen

Mac paced up and down the hall of Jim's apartment. Miguel, the chief, and the O'Tooles were in the kitchen, but he couldn't sit still. They had Caitlyn. And it was his fault.

"Would you sit down? I don't want to have to repeat all of this." Tom stopped him as he was preparing to make another turn.

"I can't sit."

"Then stand, but pay attention. We need to know who the players are so we can get her back. Pacing isn't going to do her any good."

"How can you be so calm? She's your sister, for God's sake."

"No kidding. I'm not calm, I'm pissed as hell, but there's nothing we can do about it yet."

Mac grunted and moved into the kitchen. Miguel had babbled incoherently to the chief in a mixture of Spanish and English when Mac caught up to him. The chief took one look at Mac's face and the badge Tom flashed and hustled them all aside. He had agreed to meet at Jim's apartment when Mac threatened to call his supervisor at the FBI.

Now, both sides were staring each other down, waiting for the other side to break. Jim looked at Mac and Tom, then at the chief and Miguel and threw his hands up in the air.

"This is ridiculous! You're all sitting here with information that can help the other ones out, but instead of cooperating, you're playing power games. Fine, I'll be the weak one and speak first. Chief, we saw you meeting with Miguel. Miguel, we saw you having relations with the 525s. You all know Mac, also known as Diego, is a federal agent, and Tom is his partner. Now stop the stupid cop games and fill in the blanks." Jim sat back in his chair and crossed his arms over his chest.

"A lot like your sister, isn't he?" Mac said to Tom. "Okay, I'll go first. My supervisor who'd heard about guns being run through Hartford from the ATF tagged me for this assignment. I went deep undercover and was accepted for the most part." He shot a glance at Miguel. "Until one night, I got shot in the back. At that time the gangs had just declared a cease-fire. I saw cases of automatic rifles transferred from Carlos' apartment to a warehouse somewhere in the city."

The chief looked at Miguel, who nodded, then back at Mac. "Miguel is my sister's stepson. He got into some trouble with the gangs. As a way of easing his sentence, he agreed to work with the police as an undercover agent."

"Oh? And who else knew about this assignment?" Mac leaned back against the counter and tapped his fingers on the surface.

"No one. There's a leak in the department."

Tom scoffed. "No? Really?"

The chief went on, ignoring Tom. "And I couldn't risk someone finding out. My sister still lives in that neighborhood. The whole family would get killed if word ever got out."

"They might still," Mac interjected. "Something is going on and I want to know what. Miguel, how much did you overhear when the mayor came calling?"

Miguel looked to the chief again, who nodded slightly. He wiped his hands on his baggy jeans and then clasped them together on the table. The heavy gold bracelet he wore clattered against the wood, betraying his nervousness.

"You sure he ain't gonna bust me? Diego saw a lot of shit."

"I'm not after you. I want Carlos and his boss. I'll let the chief worry about your drug deals." Mac wasn't so sure Miguel was on the up and up with the chief, which would explain his nervousness.

"I followed Carlos, just like you said." He looked at the chief again. "He had his bodyguards chase everyone off for a while, so I knew something was up. I hid in his apartment while he went to get the dude he was meeting. From what he told his posse, this was the first time he was meeting him in person. 'Till now it's been 'the Man' this and 'the Man' that. Guess the Man didn't want anyone knowing who he was."

"Can't imagine why." Tom bent a paper clip in unnatural directions.

"So I waited on the fire escape until the Man came in and I listened at the bedroom door."

"Cut to the chase. What did you hear?" Mac was ready to pull the information out of his mouth with hot tongs.

"The Man says tonight's the night. He's going to take care of the last piece of the puzzle, then he'll call Carlos. When Carlos gets the call, everyone's supposed to go wild."

"What do you mean?" Mac wanted to be sure he knew exactly what was happening.

"We're supposed to get the guns and start breaking into stores, stealing stuff and setting fires. The Hands and the 525s are going to go postal too. This city's going to go up in flames."

Miguel didn't look all too upset about the prospect either. The chief was going to have his hands full keeping this one out of trouble.

"I don't get it. What could the mayor get out of having his city looted and burned? It's only three months until election, why would he want to cause so much destruction?" Tom asked.

"To get re-elected. He'll blame it all on the police department and call in the National Guard. They'll come in and clean up the streets. Meanwhile, he'll wipe out any of his enemies during the looting and come out smelling like a rose." The chief swore a blue streak.

"That seems awful extreme just to get re-elected." Jim didn't look convinced.

"Look at what happened after 9/11," Mac said, pushing his chair back. "They were ready to canonize their mayor for how he responded in a crisis. Nadowny will jump in and be part of the clean up, he'll make some quick decisions and fight to get the National Guard out there. Hell, they'll be ready to elect him president." Mac wanted to punch something. It was disgustingly clever. He didn't know why he didn't figure it out before.

"Bastard. Hundreds of lives will be ruined, all so he can get re-elected."

"It's not going to happen." Liam stood.

"How are we going to stop it? We've got no proof and no time, plus he has Caitlyn." Mac wasn't going to let the hotheaded O'Toole put Caitlyn at risk. He'd let the whole city burn down before he let her get hurt.

"I don't know, but we're going to do something. I grew up in this city and I protect it for a living. I'm not going to let this asshole tear it down."

"Think, Liam. We can't go tearing off half-cocked. We need a plan." Tom clapped a hand on his brother's shoulder.

Liam slapped his hands on the table in frustration. He opened his mouth to say something more, but was stopped by Tom's phone ringing.

"O'Toole," he said, putting it on speakerphone and motioning for silence.

"If you want your sister back, you'll follow these directions."

"Who is this?" Tom asked.

"Doesn't matter. Just listen and do what I say or you'll get your sister back in pieces."

Anger burned through Mac's veins. He clenched his fist to keep from swearing in fury. He had to remain silent, but a scream of rage built inside.

"I'm listening."

"Good boy. Bring Diego and all the evidence he has to the warehouse on the corner of White and Broad. When we have him, you can get the girl."

"How do we know you haven't already killed her?" Tom's face held no expression, but his hands gripped the table so hard his knuckles were white.

"Hold on, I'll put her on the phone."

There was a muffled rustling, as if someone put their hand over the receiver, then it cleared.

"Don't do it! Take the evidence and run!" Caitlyn screamed.

The slap of skin meeting skin echoed through the phone and her voice stopped mid scream.

"Be there at nine tonight or she's dead. Don't bring in anyone else. I'll know if you do." The phone clicked off with an ominous buzz.

"Son-of-a-bitch!" Mac swore and kicked a nearby chair.

"What are we going to do? We can't let them hurt her—more." Jim's voice held a hint of fear.

"We do what he says and exchange me for her." Mac had been a hostage before. He never thought he'd do it again. Only this time, they couldn't afford to let him live.

"No fucking way. We've got enough evidence combined to at least bring it to a judge for a search warrant." The chief stood and faced down Mac.

"Except if we do that, they'll kill my sister. I don't give a shit about the mayor at this point." Jim rapped his hands sharply on the table.

"She's not worth an entire city of people!" the chief shouted back.

The room descended into a screaming match as tempers flared. Mac waited for a pause and stepped between the warring parties. "I didn't say I was going in like a lamb to the slaughter. They can't let me live, and now that Caitlyn has seen the mayor, they can't let her live either. I'll go in wired. I'm sure they'll want to find out exactly what I know before they try to kill me."

"You're talking about your death, man." The chief sat with a thud.

Mac knew the chief cared more for his value as a witness than for his safety. "Not if I have backup, I'm not. While they're interrogating me, you'll mobilize our forces to storm the warehouse." Mac looked at Miguel. "Do you know the warehouse he's talking about? You're much higher up than I was."

Miguel nodded. "Yeah, it's an old run down place, lots of little rooms up top, but all open at street level. It's where we stored the guns."

"Okay. I go in and insist on seeing Caitlyn first, keeping up a running commentary so you know where I'm headed. When I make sure Caitlyn is safe and I can keep her that way, I'll give the signal and you'll storm the place."

"How? We've got two hours to pull an army out of nowhere. How the hell do you expect to do that?" The chief threw his hands up in the air.

"Jim, Liam, I believe you might be able to help us with this," Mac said, raising an eyebrow.

Liam looked uncomfortably at his chief. "Ah, I put out a word or two about a possible disaster drill happening today. I only have to make two calls to get every off duty police officer in the city mobilized."

"Where did you get the authorization to do that?"

"Who gives a shit?" Tom said to the chief. "All that matters is, we have manpower at the ready. I'm betting we'd have every firefighter in the tri-city area on hand too."

Jim nodded in agreement. "If I tell them it's for Caitlyn, they'll call in more folks than you can count. She grew up around that department. There isn't a man there who wouldn't walk through fire for her."

Mac hoped it wouldn't come to that. Visions of a junkie waving an automatic rifle around in a nursery filled with newborns flashed into his brain. His thigh ached where he had picked up a bullet.

Could he do it again? Could he put himself in a situation where a cold-blooded killer waited for him? The junkie had only been after drugs. Carlos and the mayor were after his blood.

It didn't matter. He'd put his life on the line time and time again for the good of the company and the country. This time it'd be to save Caitlyn, and if that meant dying in the process, so be it. Hell, if it weren't for her he'd have died from blood loss the night he got shot. He'd already cheated death by a month. If he had his way, he'd cheat death for a whole lot longer. And so would Caitlyn.

"I can't wear a regular wire, they're sure to be looking for that. Do you have access to any quick taps?"

A quick tap was a transmitting device small enough to be concealed in the sole of a shoe. It had a limited battery life and couldn't record on it's own, but if the receiver was paired up with a tape recorder, anything said in a five foot vicinity of the transmitter would get taped. The feds had used them for a few years now, but Mac wasn't sure if they'd made their way to local police forces yet.

"Ah," Liam shot a glance at the chief. "I have one, and a receiver, but it's just a prototype a buddy of mine got his hands on. It hasn't been used yet."

"Can you get it and get back here in less than an hour?" Tom asked.

"Sure. It's in my car."

Tom and Mac looked at him in surprise. "You told me you wanted surveillance equipment, so I got some."

"I was talking about long range listening devices, not quick taps." Tom planted his hands on his hips.

"Do you want to bitch about what I got or do you want me to go and get it?"

Mac stepped in before another family battle could ensue. "Thanks, Liam. Having that on hand gives us more time to plan. Can you make those calls when you get back? I want as many bodies backing me up as I can get."

"You get my sister out alive, and I'll throw every body I've got behind you."

An unspoken agreement passed between the two of them. For the first time, Mac felt accepted. Too bad he might not live long enough to enjoy the experience.

"Let's make those phone calls, boys. We've got a lot to do and not much time to do it in."

॥ ॥

The coppery taste of blood filled Caitlyn's mouth. Her head felt like a troupe of Irish step dancers pounded away inside it. Opening gritty eyes, she tried to remember where she was. What the hell had happened to her? Her whole body ached.

She took in her surroundings, straining to recall why she felt like she'd been hit by a truck. The room was dim. Fading sunlight slipped through dirty windows high over head. It smelled musty from disuse and dust danced liberally in the dying rays of sun. A desk was the only furniture in the room and huge wooden boxes were stacked to the ceiling in every other available inch. Caitlyn gingerly sat up, wincing as the dancers pounded harder on her brain. Her cheek throbbed too and felt tender to the touch.

The memory of a fist coming straight towards her flashed into her brain. She wasn't positive, but the guy that hit her this time looked an awful lot like the guy who grabbed her outside of work. He had the same scar on his cheek and he smelled the same. He also punched damn hard. So hard she'd blacked out.

And not for the first time.

She remembered getting thrown into the mayor's car and getting hit on the head with something. She'd never passed out in her life and here she'd done it twice in a matter of hours.

It wasn't an experience she wanted to repeat anytime soon.

The memories flipped through her mind like a movie. Coming back to consciousness while she was thrown over some thug's shoulder. Being sat up in a chair while the guy with the scar on his face held a gun to her head. Her purse being searched and her phone taken.

Had she really told Tom to forget about her and not turn the evidence over? It had seemed like the right thing to do at the time. The heroic thing to do.

Too bad she wasn't a hero.

She really, really wanted someone to come riding to the rescue right about now. Fear chased through her body and her knees grew weak with it. The taste of blood in her mouth and the throbbing of her cheekbone only reminded her that these guys meant business. Even if Mac turned himself in, she'd still be dead. They couldn't afford to let her live.

Tom and Mac would know that. They wouldn't let Mac throw his life away when the mayor had no intention of letting her live. Would they? Panic tried to strangle her. She didn't want to die. But she didn't want Mac killed either.

What could she do? She wasn't a fed or even a cop. She was a nurse, for God's sake. Her training had to do with saving people, not single-handedly saving the city from a madman.

"You think they'll go for it?"

Caitlyn jumped at the voice so close to her ear. Looking around, she couldn't see anyone else in the room.

"Yeah, they'll have to. Feds always play by the rules. They'll try something, though."

The voices drifted up to her from a heating vent on the

floor. Caitlyn peered through the slats and saw two young men with red bandanas tied over their heads sitting at a table beneath her. Way beneath her. She squinted down and tried to get an idea of what was below her. It looked like a great big room.

Boxes, windows high up, she could be in a factory or some type of warehouse. Gingerly getting to her feet, she crept to the wooden crates piled high around her. They were sealed tight. Crap. Without a crow bar, she wouldn't be able to figure out what was inside. Even if she had a crow bar, it wasn't worth investigating. She wanted them thinking she was sleeping for as long as possible.

Caitlyn climbed on the desk and used that to help her get on top some boxes until she could look out the filthy window. All she could see was the roof of another building right next door. If she could get out the skinny window, she'd be able to jump to the roof and get away.

Except she wasn't a size two.

Well, she wasn't getting out that way. What next? She refused to contemplate giving up. Just because she couldn't fight these guys didn't mean she had to sit here and just take whatever they dished out.

Think, damn it. If this were a game, what would she do? Caitlyn tried to pretend it was just Jim and Liam playing spy again, not a panic inducing matter of life and death. What would she do if they locked her up?

It had happened more than once, until the time she hid behind the playroom couch and fell asleep. Tom had been babysitting and was furious because they couldn't find her. After an hour, she'd woken up from her nap and gone to the kitchen for a snack. Tom had called the neighbors and they had scoured the neighborhood for her.

That was it. If she couldn't escape, she just had to hide and make them think she'd escaped. But how? The boxes were too heavy to move. If she slipped behind one of them, she'd never be able to get out, and they'd be able to find her too quickly. She looked at the desk. Nah, that's the first place they'd look.

The ceiling was out, nothing but wires and duct work, no false panels to hide behind there. A single ventilation grill stuck down from one of the ducts with a big sign warning against blocking the vent.

Caitlyn measured the distance from the box to the grill. Could she reach it from the next stack of boxes? And if she could, how the hell was she going to get in? She really didn't like heights. If she fell, it was a good twelve feet to the ground.

"Yo, Cheech! It's time to go! Carlos gave the word." An excited shout came clearly through the heating vent below.

"Yeah, man. I want a new stereo. Let's hit Radio Shack first."

"Then come on. Let's get there before the Hands do. Grab a bar, man, this place is going up in flames. The city's ours tonight!" A theatrically evil laugh echoed through the building.

The laugh sent shivers down her spine. Whatever was going on, it was starting now. Which meant there wasn't long before they'd come for her. She could sit there and wait for them or she could get her ass in the ventilation duct. Well, try to get in the duct anyway.

Taking a deep breath, Caitlyn clattered to the stack of boxes closest to the grille. The stack wobbled underneath her, and her knees turned to water. Man, she hated heights.

"Just don't look down and you'll be fine." Yeah, right. Her head ached and her face still throbbed, but she climbed steadily higher despite the fear and the pain.

On shaking legs, she balanced on the top of the pile of boxes. Her perch was unsteady at best, but she was closer to the vent than she thought. Using an overhead beam for balance, Caitlyn stretched her fingers to the grille to see if she could wiggle it off. She was going to have to use two hands at some point, but her fingers felt glued to the I-beam above her.

The grille didn't want to budge, damn. What now? The screw holding the side closest to her was a little loose, but not loose enough for her fingers to twist it. She had a nifty gadget in her purse that came complete with a screwdriver. Fat lot of good that did her here. Her uniform didn't come equipped with a tool belt.

But, she did have her ID badge. The metal clip might be able to grasp the screw. It was worth a try at least. Caitlyn unclipped the badge from her shirt and fumbled to attach it to the screw.

It wasn't as easy as she thought. The clip kept slipping every time she turned the screw, but eventually it came out far enough for her to grab it with her fingers. Flecks of rust blew into her eyes and she had to blink rapidly to clear them.

No more noise drifted up from the floor below and Caitlyn wondered what was going on. Surely they wouldn't have left her all alone while they went out and looted the city? Someone had to be there to "exchange" her for Mac, right?

Sweat dripped down her back as she worked the screw loose. How long was this freaking thing anyway? Her hand was beginning to cramp from holding onto the I-beam and her legs shook from the strain of balancing on the boxes.

Finally the stupid screw wobbled out. The grille creaked as she swung it out on the remaining screw. Thank God she didn't have to undo that one too.

Caitlyn took a deep breath for courage. And then another, just in case. Praying to anyone who would listen, she felt around inside the vent for a ledge or something she could use to get a grip. Her nail caught on something and tore and sharp pain shot through her finger.

"Come on, O'Toole, that's the least of your worries right now."

There had to be something there for her to grab onto. How did they clean these suckers unless they could climb in them? Caitlyn had no idea if it had ever been cleaned, but it made sense that there had to be some way in.

Creeping her other hand closer to the duct, Caitlyn leaned out a little more to explore higher up in shaft. Was that a ledge? She reached farther up. Yes! There was a little shelf there, if she could—What? Hang there with her feet dangling over open space? If there were no other handholds, she was sunk.

Resting most of her body weight on the outside of the duct, she stretched out as far as she dared and felt around blindly for another hold. There was something there! If she could just reach a little higher...

Caitlyn's feet slipped out from under her, pushing the box she was standing on precariously close to the edge. The arm inside the duct screamed in pain and she held onto the duct for dear life while the other arm lost its grip completely.

"Oh God, oh God, oh God." Caitlyn bit her lip to keep from crying out in pain and fear. She didn't know how much longer she could hold on. Using her free hand, she reached inside the shaft to feel for another handhold, anything to take the weight off her one arm.

Sweaty palms didn't make for great gripping and Caitlyn started to panic. What if she slipped? How long could she possibly hold on?

Suck it up. She was not going to die right here, right now. Gritting her teeth with the effort, Caitlyn reached with her left hand for the second handhold she prayed was there. Her numb fingers brushed over what felt like a handle. She grabbed onto it desperately and used her right hand to find another.

Yes! Her arms ached with the strain, but she fought on. She worked out, damn it, she could do this. Another six inches and her head disappeared inside the shaft. It was dark and smelled of dust and mold. For a moment she was blinded, but her eyes quickly adjusted to the dim interior and she could see where the shaft bent and went horizontal.

Horizontal was looking pretty damn good right about now. Every inch was grueling torture as her muscles shook with the effort of climbing higher in the shaft. If she could just get high enough to draw her legs up, she could use them to take some of the pressure off her arms.

"Just a little higher. I can do this. I *will* do this." It was only one body length from the opening to the bend, she could get there.

The last handhold was inches from the turn in the shaft. One more good heave and she could grab it. From there she could draw her legs up and angle her way inside. She strained for the handle, grunting with the effort. It was within her grasp, just one more millimeter.

Her hand slipped.

Caitlyn clutched with her remaining hand and tried to regain her lost inches. Her heart raced in her chest and spots danced before her eyes. Oh yeah, she needed to breathe. She had to reach that handle *now*. Her muscles spasmed from this unaccustomed exercise.

She would not give up. What choice did she have? She'd

either reach the handle and pull herself up, or she'd let go and die right there. Her brothers' faces flashed in front of her eyes. Mac's sky blue eyes filled her brain, telling her things without words, giving her promises if only she could hold on long enough to hear them.

Damn it, she would not give up. With every last ounce of stubborn will in her body, Caitlyn reached for the last handle. And got it!

Her head thumped the top of the duct as she pulled herself higher, but the pain didn't register. With frantic strength, she pulled her knees to her chest one at a time until she could find purchase on the lip of the shaft. Caitlyn pushed her way onto the length of duct in front of her and collapsed.

Dust billowed up around her face making her sneeze repeatedly, but she didn't care. Her fingers were bloody and swollen from her efforts, but by God she was alive. And she meant to stay that way.

It was tempting, oh so tempting, to just lay in the filthy duct for an hour or so while her body recovered, but she knew she had to cover her tracks. Worming her way further into the shaft, Caitlyn wiggled and squirmed around until she could face the opening again.

With one hand braced on the handholds she'd just fought her way up, she carefully inched the other hand down until she could reach the grille. Or at least she tried too. She was short by less than an inch.

There was no way she was pushing out any farther. Her heart lurched at the very thought of falling head first out of the shaft. There had to be a way...

Her ID badge! What had she done with it? Pushing back up to safety, Caitlyn patted herself down looking for the badge. Unconsciously, she must have clipped it back to its usual place on the edge of her shirt. Thank God for habits!

Sticking the hard rectangle of plastic in her teeth, she worked her way back down again. With the badge, she was able to snag a bit of the grille enough to reach it with her other hand and pull it mostly closed. Hopefully they wouldn't look too closely at the ventilation shaft above them when they came looking for her. It would pass a quick inspection. Maybe.

Scooching back, Caitlyn contemplated her next move. She could explore the rest of the duct and see where it led or she could wait here to see what the thugs were going to do next.

If she did find a way out, would she have the strength to get out anyway? Her arms were shot, her muscles burned in pain, and even her abdominal muscles ached. She didn't relish the thought of sliding on her stomach through dust and dirt and heaven only knew what else.

Of course, if she stayed put, she could easily get caught by an errant sneeze should someone walk into the room. Neither option looked very appealing. Caitlyn wished she could see her watch so she'd know what time it was. Had Mac come for her? Had they already killed him? How long she'd been unconscious, she had no idea. The day was so mixed up in her mind, it seemed like months had passed since she woke Jim up that morning.

Poor Jim, he'd blame himself for taking her to work. And if he didn't, Liam or Tom would. Then they'd all blame Mac for getting her involved in the first place.

Oh Mac. What would this do to him? They wouldn't let him live if he came for her, but his innate goodness wouldn't let him stay home. Would Tom be able to convince him not to sacrifice himself?

Probably not.

She thought back to the article she'd read about him saving a roomful of newborns from a drug addict. He was a hero. It was a trait that went bone-deep in him. Caitlyn had no doubt he'd blame himself for this mess and try to save her himself.

"Please God, please, keep him safe. Keep them all safe," Caitlyn prayed. It was the only thing she could do.

Chapter Twenty

The streets leading to the warehouse were eerily deserted. The streetlights—what few remained unbroken—had come on in the gathering dusk. Mac's neck prickled with danger. This was what he lived for, wasn't it?

It was his job to put his life on the line for others, that's what he did. But it had never meant so much before. One screw up, one little mistiming and Caitlyn would be dead. He no longer gave a shit what happened to the city. The pictures and Miguel's testimony were enough to bring an investigation into the mayor's office. It was up to Hartford's police and fire department to save their city tonight. His focus was Caitlyn and only Caitlyn.

"You're sure you're set with this? It's not too late to try something else." Tom looked at Mac through the darkened interior of the car. Liam followed a few miles back in a beat up van that held the tape recorder and GPS—global positioning satellite—equipment. As long as they left Mac his shoes, Liam would be able to track him.

"Like what? Do you have an army stashed somewhere that you didn't tell me about?"

"How can you joke? I have to decide between my sister and my partner. And I'm not even sure either one of you will make it out alive."

"It's not your decision to make, it's mine." Mac faced Tom. "Just know I'll do anything, *everything* to keep Caitlyn safe."

"Even at the risk of your own life?"

"Absolutely."

Tom looked startled and opened his mouth to say something, but never finished as a body went flying across the hood of his car.

"What the hell?" Tom slammed on the brakes.

"Get down!" Mac pulled Tom down just as a gun blast shattered the window. Glass exploded over them in a glittering rain. "Drive! Drive!"

Tom stepped on the gas and floored it, keeping his head as low as possible. "What was that all about? I thought they wanted you?"

"That's not Carlos' man, look, he's wearing blue. He's a 525. It's begun."

The farther into the city they got, the more insanity reigned. Store windows were smashed, dumpsters spewed oily, black smoke and flames. Cars were turned over and were being stripped of their parts faster than Mac could imagine. Hell had been let loose on the city.

And he was on his way to see Satan himself.

"Let me off here. I'll be all right."

"Are you kidding me? Those aren't toys those kids are carrying. Those are real guns out there. You'll be killed before you take two steps."

"I'll be safer on the street than I will a sitting duck in the car. Turn around and tell Liam to stay back as far as he can. Mobilize as many teams as possible. Have them ready to move in when I give the word and not a moment sooner. I'll stay in contact through the tap."

"Watch your back and don't take any stupid chances." Tom rounded a corner into a narrow alley.

"You too." Mac reached out and clapped Tom on the shoulder. "I'll get her back, don't worry." Mac rolled out of the car and blended in with the shadows.

Adrenaline coursed through his veins and every sense was hyper-alert. His ears strained for any signs of company before he slipped off through the night. He was only two blocks from the warehouse, and if Miguel could be believed, he'd be able to get there through a series of back alleys.

Using all his training in urban warfare, Mac skulked his

way over fences and behind run-down houses. He avoided the lights from the fires and kept to the shadows. Most of the people were either in hiding, or moving off to better pickings. This area was poor and had little to loot. If Liam and Jim had things in place, the mob wouldn't get much farther.

Mac skirted the flaming wreckage of a car turned upside down and stepped into the shelter of a doorway as a gang of boys hardly into their teens rounded the corner. They ran to the burning car and started throwing garbage and soda cans into the fire. Had this insanity taken over the entire city?

Just a few more buildings to go. He could see the bulk of the warehouse against the full moon. His gut warned him of someone's approach right before his arms were grabbed and pulled painfully behind his back.

"The Man's been waiting for you. He said we get to kill you when it's time." The voice in his ear belonged to one of Carlos' bodyguards, Rocco. What little brainpower he possessed was wrapped up in a sick desire to kill and maim. Great. If Rocco was around, that meant that Carlos wasn't far. Another goon stood silently by his side, waiting for Mac to fight for his freedom.

Now why would Carlos be sticking around when his people were on the streets hauling in as much loot as they could carry? It didn't make any sense.

Unless he was after a bigger prize.

Could Carlos be making a move to be the Man? He'd have to keep his eyes open and see what played out when he got into the warehouse.

The two thugs dragged an unresisting Mac through the street and into a loading bay of the beat up warehouse. He spotted men with automatic rifles guarding the entrances to the building. Apparently it was okay to destroy everything in sight, as long as it didn't belong to Carlos.

"So, Diego, we meet again." A lighter flickered and Mac smelled the acrid smell of Carlos' favorite cigar. "Or should I call you Mac?"

"You can call me whatever you want as long as I get to see Caitlyn O'Toole." Mac didn't struggle or try to fight against his captors.

Carlos nodded and Rocco punched him in the stomach, knocking the wind out of him. "You're in no position to make demands. You'll see the girl when the Man says you will. And that won't be until you've handed over the evidence. Pat him down," he ordered the thugs.

Carlos' bodyguard ran his hands roughly down Mac's legs and chest, patting down his arms and checking his groin.

"He's clean."

"Where's the evidence, Diego?" Carlos looked nervously over his shoulder towards an office in the back.

"In a safe place. You didn't think I was stupid enough to bring it with me now, did you? Come on Carlos, you should know me better than that." Mac held back the groan of pain from the punch to his gut. Bile rose in his throat, but he kept his face blank.

"Then the girl is dead."

"I don't think so. If she doesn't make it to her brother's house in the next hour, the pictures I took of you and the mayor go directly to the D. A.'s office, the governor, and my boss at the FBI."

"Too bad you won't be alive to appreciate it." Carlos threw down his cigar. "Eliminate him."

"Not so fast, Carlos. I have a few questions for Mr. McDougal. You weren't thinking of letting him go without giving me a chance to talk to the man who infiltrated your organization so easily now, were you?" Mayor Nadowny walked into the bay like he was entering his throne room. He had a swagger in his step that told Mac he thought he held all the cards.

Good. Let him keep thinking that. It would give Liam plenty of time to pull his forces together and grab him.

"Mr. Mayor." Mac nodded mockingly.

"I'd like to say it was nice to see you again, but considering the circumstances..." Nadowny trailed off meaningfully.

"Where's Caitlyn?"

"She's resting after her ordeal. I'll bring you to her shortly. As soon as you give me the evidence you've gathered in your investigation."

"As I was telling Carlos, I didn't bring it with me. Once you let Caitlyn go, I'll direct you to the film and the disk that has my notes and reports on it." That was a complete lie. Mac had given all his reports verbally to his boss in order to maintain his cover.

Nadowny didn't look surprised at the pronouncement. "I figured you wouldn't follow the rules, you feds never do."

"How did you spot me?" Mac asked, buying time.

"Easily. Carlos gathers finger prints from all his members and I use the computer right in my office to find out if the member is an agent, such as yourself, or just another punk looking to make a quick buck."

Carlos twitched at the condescension in his voice, but didn't say a word. Mac noticed his hand hovered near the pocket of his jacket though. Did he have a gun in there? Probably.

"My prints should have come up as Diego Torres." That still bothered him. Did Nadowny have a mole in the Bureau too?

"They did, but you forget, I know who Diego Torres really is. When those prints came up I asked for a picture of you, which was easy enough to get with all the camera phones around. Once I made the match, Carlos was supposed to take care of the rest. Pity he didn't get that done before now, but that's easily corrected."

He sure as hell hoped not.

"Come, we'll go find your friend, then you can direct me to the evidence. You'll understand if I don't let either of you go until the evidence is found."

Mac didn't even answer. Nadowny was getting too much enjoyment out of all of this.

"If you'd follow me." The mayor turned and walked towards a set of metal stairs.

The two thugs pulled Mac roughly, almost wrenching his arm out of his socket. Carlos remained below. He was definitely up to something. With all the confusion, how hard would it be for the mayor to take a stray bullet? That was more Carlos' style. He wouldn't attack openly, he'd wait until Nadowny's back was turned, then shoot him.

So why did he want the evidence so badly? To cover his

own ass or to use against the mayor? Not that it mattered, the pictures were even now being specially delivered to the FBI and the D.A.'s office. Hey, if they weren't going to play fair, why should he?

A narrow row of rooms ran against one wall of the cavernous warehouse. The place looked one stiff breeze away from completely falling apart. Most of the rooms they passed were filled with huge boxes covered in dust. Miguel had said this was where they stored the guns, but all those boxes couldn't be guns. What else could they be storing in here? Drugs? There'd be enough pharmaceuticals to get every man, woman, and child in the city high as a kite.

What else was going on here?

The little procession stopped at a room at the top of the stairs. Nadowny rapped sharply on the door. "Miss O'Toole, I've a visitor for you," he called out in mock cheerfulness as he unlocked the door.

Nadowny threw it open dramatically. The room was empty.

"What sort of game are you playing?" Mac asked, fear congealing in his gut. Was this why Carlos wasn't with them? Had he taken Caitlyn for his own bargaining chip?

"Carlos!" Nadowny thundered, storming into the room. He kicked at boxes and tipped the desk over.

"Where is she?"

Carlos came running up the stairs, puffing with exertion. "What?"

"Where's the girl?"

"In here." He looked around as if she'd magically appear somewhere.

"Obviously, she's not. What the fuck have your men been doing? Did they let her out?"

"No way, man. She was knocked out from that punch he gave her." Carlos nodded his head at the goon on Mac's right.

Mac made a mental note to get even for that. If Caitlyn had been hit hard enough to knock her out, her jaw could be broken. His heart ached for the pain she must be going through.

"Well, she's not unconscious now. Get your men and

search the building from top to bottom. She has to be here somewhere."

"I only got a few guys here, the rest are out in the city grabbing anything they can carry and smashing anything they can't," Carlos grumbled.

"Then I guess you're going to have to get off your ass and help them. She's a witness, you fool. Her testimony is just as damaging as his."

So much for letting her go in exchange.

Carlos stomped out of the room and called instructions downstairs to his men. Mac was tied roughly to a chair and left by the tumbled desk. The two thugs who'd been holding him moved boxes and searched for Caitlyn.

When all the boxes were shoved in the center of the room and it was obvious Caitlyn wasn't hiding behind any of them, Nadowny swore and stalked out of the room. The goons followed, locking Mac in.

As soon as the door clicked behind them, Mac shuffled his way to the nearest box and rubbed the ropes against a rough edge. This would take forever, but it was better than sitting there and worrying about Caitlyn.

Where had she gone? And how had she done it? He prayed half forgotten prayers she'd escaped and was even now on her way to Jim's house.

A thump came from overhead and a suspiciously feminine sneeze followed. Mac rubbed harder on the bonds that held him. He didn't know where Caitlyn was hiding, but if she was in one of those boxes stacked up high, she could easily fall down and get crushed. When the thugs had moved them around, it had taken all their strength to shift the stacks. Those boxes could kill her if they landed on her. Not to mention what damage the fall would do.

"Mac? Is that you?"

"Shhh, yes it's me."

"Is the coast clear?" she whispered.

"For now. Stay put and I'll get you as soon as I get free. Where are you?"

The ventilation shaft high overhead shuddered and

squeaked as the grille swung open. "I'm up here."

"How the hell did you get up there?" Mac's wrists started to burn from the friction. They'd bleed before long.

"I climbed up the boxes and crawled in. Sort of."

Mac closed his eyes. The knot of fear in his gut grew bigger. "Never mind, I don't want to know after all. Can you get out of the building through there?"

"Yes and no. The ducts just go straight over the rooms here, and I can get in the room next door, but I'd still have to get past the guys at the bottom of the stairs. There's an office underneath the room you're in. I heard people talking in there before I climbed up here."

"No one's there now, they're all searching for you. What's left of them, anyway."

"How many are out there?"

Mac heard more shuffling and thumping from above. What was she doing in there? "I don't know. There were four guarding the doors, and two more guarding Carlos and Nadowny. I think I saw a few more hanging around. So probably twelve tops."

"So, what if we do a bait and switch?"

"*We* aren't going to do anything. You're going to hightail it out of here. Your brothers have things in place, they're just waiting to know you're safe." Hopefully they caught that on the tape and could stop worrying.

A white shoe poked out from the shaft, then another. Caitlyn's feet flailed around in the air until they hit one of the boxes that had been shoved near the vent.

"For the love of God!" Mac didn't know whether to close his eyes and block out the image or keep them open in case she fell. "Over towards me more. You're on the very edge of the box. Be careful! Christ! That box isn't on there all that well."

His heart lurched in his throat with every slip of her foot. Mac aged ten years in the time it took for her to find stable footing.

"Heck, this was much easier than getting in."

"Uh huh." Mac held back a groan as the stack of boxes wobbled too and fro with every step Caitlyn took

"There. That wasn't so bad, was it?" She jumped off the last box and brushed dust off her hands before running over to him. Her face was filthy with dirt marring her porcelain skin, and a bruise bloomed along her left cheek. He'd get the bastard back for that.

"Hold on, I'll see if I can untie the knots. I wish they hadn't taken my trauma shears, those would've come in handy right about now." She shook her arms out as if she was in pain.

"Are you okay?"

"A few bumps and bruises, and I'll probably have a black eye for a while, but other than that I'm doing fine. Ask me again tomorrow when all the muscles I've abused today start to ache."

Mac just hoped they'd be alive tomorrow.

Caitlyn leaned down and kissed him lightly on the lips before scooting around and going to work on the ropes that held him tight.

"What was that for?"

"For luck, because I missed you, and because I didn't want you to come and risk your life, but you did anyway."

"I'd risk anything for you. Anything." Her hands stilled for a minute, and Mac wished he could see her face.

"Part of me is doing the Cha Cha right now, and the other part of me is saying you'd put your life on the line for a perfect stranger too. That's just the type of person you are."

"Bullshit."

"Oh? Did you have a relationship with any of the babies in the hospital? Or their mothers?"

"That was different. That was my job at the time."

"And this isn't? Face it Mac, you're a hero, it's in your blood."

"Whatever. Right now I'm more worried about your blood and keeping it inside you. We need a plan to get you out of here."

"I have a plan, if I can ever get these darn knots untied. You stretched them so tightly I can't get a grip on them."

"If I create a distraction, do you think you could slip out of here and make your way to the nearest police station or fire house?" Mac asked, trying to relax his wrists and not pull the ropes even tighter.

"Sure, but why don't we wait and do it together?"

"Because I need to know you're safe while I go after Nadowny."

"Hold on, I think I've got some wiggle room, keep your hands relaxed," Caitlyn said, ignoring him. "There. Got it."

Mac felt the ropes drop from his wrists and the painful prickling of circulation returning to his hands. He shook them out and rolled his shoulders to ease some of the strain the position had given him.

"Here, let me help." Caitlyn took one hand and rubbed it briskly between her own. The tingling heat was excruciatingly painful, but passed quickly.

"Thanks," Mac said when both hands were back in working order.

"Always on the job, what can I say?"

"Say you'll get the hell out of here." Mac looked into her whiskey brown eyes and knew he couldn't live with himself if something happened to her.

"I have a better idea. Why don't we do a bait and switch? I'll act as bait and let them chase me in here. You knock them out as they come through the door."

"No." Just the thought of those goons chasing after her with guns made his knees weak.

"Do you have a better plan?" she asked, hands on her hips.

"Yes, I go after them and you get out of here."

"That's a great idea, except for one thing. How are you going to get out of the room? The door's locked, and the only way out is through the ventilation ducts. You have to take the shaft to another room that isn't locked to get out. Think you can do it?"

"Sure, if you can do it, I can."

"I don't have a half healed bullet hole in my side."

"It hasn't slowed me down so far," Mac lied. Just the thought of climbing into the shaft and crawling around in such a confined space made his side ache.

"Fine, why don't you climb up and try it? If you can get up there you can help me in and I'll be on my way. But if you can't, I'll slip out, unlock the door and we'll try my plan. Deal?"

"Deal." Mac would get into that damn shaft if it killed him.

Chapter Twenty-one

Caitlyn watched Mac struggle to hide the pain he was in as he climbed up the stack of boxes to the ventilation shaft. If anyone could will his body to do things it wasn't physically ready to do, it was Mac. Her heart lurched every time he winced in pain, but still he continued on.

Damn it. Why did he have to be so stubborn? Why couldn't he let her help him? Okay, to be fair, she didn't have any experience with this sort of thing. But still, her plan would work if he could get over his protective streak.

Mac had made his way to the top of the pile and was balancing precariously under the grille. Her first trip up would have been a lot easier if the boxes had been that close to the vent.

Yeah, she should have asked the goons to come and move the boxes a little closer to help her escape.

"Shit!" Mac swore a blue streak and clutched at his side. While she'd been lost in thought he'd reached inside the shaft and tried to pull himself higher. Obviously, he was unsuccessful.

"Ready to give up yet?" she called up cheerfully.

"I just need to catch my breath. You stay close to that heating vent and see if you can see what's going on below."

She bit her tongue and didn't tell him what he could do with his orders. Maybe if she was looking through the grate on the floor she wouldn't be panicking with every sway of the boxes. What the hell was in them anyway?

The vent on the floor was old and rusty, like everything else in the building. She scrunched down next to it and twisted her

216

head this way and that to see if she could see anyone. Supposedly the mayor and his crew were looking for her, but she didn't see anyone. Maybe they were out on the streets with everyone else?

Caitlyn fretted about her brothers. What was going on out there? Had their plan worked? She'd gotten in touch with a lot of the off duty nurses who said they'd spread the word, but had they done it soon enough? She bit her lip again, then winced in pain. Her face still throbbed from the punch and she had a goose egg on the back of her head from where she'd been hit in the car.

Cripes, they were the walking wounded. Mac's side was still sore, her head was sore, how the hell were they going to get out of here?

Another stream of curses came from above and Caitlyn turned to see what caused this one. Mac's face was ashen from pain. He couldn't get inside the shaft without pulling himself up with his arms, which pulled on his abdominal muscles and probably hurt like a bitch.

He climbed down slowly, the boxes swaying with his steps. Caitlyn didn't say anything, just watched his face for clues to what he was thinking. Sweat dotted his forehead and his eyes looked almost glassy with the pain he was in. Stupid man. Did he have to almost pass out before he would admit defeat?

Apparently.

"Well?" she asked finally.

"Fine. You're right, is that what you wanted to hear?"

"No, but it'll do for now." She stood and dusted off her hands. "So, we'll try it my way?"

"With one exception. You open the door and I'll go after them. I want you out of here."

"Mac, think clearly for a minute. You have to stop looking at me like a female and start thinking of me as a partner. There is no way you can do this alone."

A muscle in his jaw twitched and Caitlyn knew he must be grinding his teeth. Tough noogies. He had to face reality, and that was he couldn't do it alone.

"I don't want you to get hurt. I—I can't tell you what I went through knowing the mayor had you here. It about killed me

217

thinking about you locked up and hurting."

Caitlyn's heart did a slow tumble in her chest. He might not realize it yet, but his feelings went a lot deeper than just a quick roll in the sack. Too bad they weren't exactly in a position to explore this new development. She'd make sure they lived long enough to have this conversation again.

"Oh, Mac. I know what you mean." She reached out for him, then pulled her hand back. She had to be tough. "But we have to get out of here, and we have to stop the mayor and Carlos before they destroy everything. I don't know why they're doing this, but I won't let hundreds of innocent people get killed because you're afraid of what will happen to me. And I won't let you do it either."

Mac spun and kicked the chair he'd been tied to, sending it flying across the room. "I hate this!" His eyes were fierce.

"You don't have to like it, you just have to do it. Now suck it up. I'm going up there. I'll knock on the door twice before I open it so don't hit me when I come in."

"You're outta here the first chance we get. Understand that now. As soon as you unlock that door, I'm calling in the troops. Then I'm going after the mayor and Carlos by myself. And you can go to your brother's house and stay put."

Yeah, like that was going to happen. She wasn't leaving him alone if they got out of here. Not if, *when* they got out of here.

"Fine," she lied. She'd fight that battle after they got out of the room.

Mac ground his teeth in suppressed fury as Caitlyn disappeared from view. The pain in his side had died down to a dull ache, but there was no way he'd be able to get into that shaft. Even if he could have pulled himself up, he'd probably have gotten stuck in the bend. He was just too big to go crawling around ventilation shafts.

Snap out of it! He couldn't sit here and wallow in self-pity. He had to be ready when Caitlyn opened the door. He also needed a weapon. Mac searched the room for anything he could use to knock someone out. A crow bar lay in a pile of dust partially hidden by some boxes. That would work nicely. He swung it a few times, getting a feel for how much mobility he had with his aching side. Not bad.

Where was Caitlyn now? How many rooms was she going to have to get into to find one with an unlocked door? Mac paced the room slapping the bar into his palm lightly. How many men were still here? Had Liam had a chance to get the reserves into place?

So many questions and not one damn answer. Where was Caitlyn? What if she got hurt getting down? She could be lying unconscious or in pain on the floor of another room and he'd never know. Mac growled in frustration.

What had happened to his objectivity? His distance? He'd been in situations more dire than this and never fretted like an old woman. Christ, this sucked. He paced some more.

If she took much longer, he'd use the crow bar to hack his way out of the room. This waiting sucked. It suddenly occurred to him that this was what spouses went through while their loved ones were on assignment.

God. How did they stand it? Year after year, the waiting and not knowing if they were dead or alive. No wonder the divorce rate among agents was so high.

Was that a knock?

Mac hustled over to the door and strained his ears. He saw the handle wiggle.

"Mac, I can't pick the lock. It's more complicated then the ones Tom taught me to pick."

Tom taught her how to pick locks? He'd have to ask his partner about that one.

"What type of lock is it? I didn't get a good look at it when they brought me in." Idiot. He had been so worried about Caitlyn, he hadn't paid attention to the door."

"I don't know. It's not a dead bolt, but more complicated than a bathroom lock."

"What do you have for tools?"

"I scrounged some screwdrivers from another room. I'm using the smallest one to try and tweak the tumblers."

"We don't have time for that. This is what I want you to do.

See if you can unscrew the handle itself. Then you should be able to get at the insides and either unlock it or poke the mechanism out."

"Okay, I'll try."

Mac looked at the handle on his side of the door. It was an old lock, so his plan should work. Should.

Sweat dripped down his back as he unconsciously counted the seconds ticking away. How long could she fumble with the lock before someone came up to investigate? How much time did they have to screw around before their luck ran out?

"There." Her whisper came seconds before the handle fell off in his hand.

Mac pulled the door open and crept out into the hallway. Caitlyn's face was dirty and her shirt had a tear in it, but her eyes twinkled with the success of her mission.

"Let's get out of sight quickly. I don't want them spotting us before we're ready." Mac pulled her behind him and they crept down the stairs.

The warehouse was deserted. Where was everyone? Weren't they supposed to be searching for Caitlyn? What the hell was going on?

"I'm going to call in reinforcements." Screw her plan, he just wanted her safe. There weren't that many men around now. The guys Liam had lined up should be able to take them out and get Caitlyn to safety. He dragged her behind a box and pushed her down. "Liam, send them in."

"Who are you talking to?" Caitlyn asked, looking around.

"Don't worry about it."

Minutes dragged by like hours and no one came. Could the battery in the tap be dead? Maybe they ran into trouble. Mac had to figure they were on their own.

"Nothing's happening," Caitlyn said, stretching her legs.

"No shit. Looks like we're on our own."

"Then I guess we'll have to go with my plan. We can't wait around here forever. We're going to get caught eventually. Don't you think it's better to go after them with a plan than just wait here to get caught?"

No, he didn't, but he was running out of options. He had to

get out there and find the mayor and he couldn't do that if he was worried about Caitlyn. "Fine," he growled.

"You don't have to sound so pissy about it." Caitlyn stood and followed him deeper into the warehouse.

They found a nook where Mac could lie in wait. Divide and conquer. "I don't know where everyone is. You might want to start near the bays first. Don't get too close, let them see you, then run like hell. Try to keep as many boxes between you and them as you can so they can't get a straight shot at you." It was damn hard to hit a moving target, but he didn't want to take the chance one of the gun-toting goons would get lucky.

"Okay, I'll let them see me and chase me and you'll pop them." She turned to go, but Mac stopped her with a hand on her wrist.

"Don't be a hero. If there's a chance for you to get out, take it."

"Don't worry about me, just be ready to pop them as I come running by." She gave him a peck on the lips and slipped quietly away.

Yeah, right. He'd stop worrying about her when he stopped breathing.

How long would it take for Caitlyn to locate one of the guards? Even if they were all off searching for her, the guards at the bay should still be in place. If she could pull them away, Mac could get his hands on a weapon too.

He gripped the crow bar tightly. It would feel good to take some action instead of waiting. Straining his ears to catch the slightest sound, Mac crouched low in his hiding place and tried to focus on one step at a time. After they stopped the remaining men here, he'd find Nadowny and Carlos.

The sound of shouting and running feet came quicker than he expected and he waited for his target. Caitlyn tore around the corner and ducked behind him. Mac's muscles tensed in anticipation as the bandana wrapped head came into range.

One quick strike with the crow bar and the thug dropped to the ground like a puppet whose strings had been cut.

"Quick, get his gun." Mac pulled the bandana off the man's head and used it to gag him. Yanking the shoelaces out of his high tops, Mac tied up the victim's hands and dragged him behind a row of boxes.

Caitlyn held the automatic rifle in front of her like it was a poisonous snake. She was breathing heavily, but otherwise looked okay.

"Did you have any trouble?"

"No. He was actually walking into the building when I spotted him. I kicked a can on the ground to get his attention, then weaved between the boxes like you told me until I got here. He didn't even take a shot."

"Good. Did you see any more guys out there?"

"Nope, but like I said, he was on his way in when I saw him. I'll check outside this time."

"Be careful. Try to find out how many are out there before you get the next one's attention."

She rolled her eyes at him. "Man, want me to wrap him up in a bow while I'm at it? Some people are never satisfied."

"Hey, I'd be much happier doing this myself. It was your idea you know."

"Yeah, yeah, whatever. I'll try to skulk around a bit first this time." She took a deep breath and slipped off again.

Mac went back to his unconscious gang member to try to get a better look at him. He looked familiar, but Mac couldn't put a name with the face. No matter, he didn't need to know the guy's name to arrest him.

So far he hadn't seen any of the guys he shared an apartment with in the warehouse. They must be on the streets already. How many of them would die today? All it would take would be one wrong move from a rival gang and the bullets would fly. The uneasy truce that had held off the violence between the gangs would last only as long as there was enough loot for all of them. As soon as two punks wanted the same thing, all bets were off.

And with so many guns around, it was only a matter of time before the blood ran in the streets. What kind of sick mind did this? Nadowny had to know that the body count could number in the hundreds when this was all done. How could he give so many guns to kids not old enough to drive and expect them to stick to his rules?

Or did he? Was he using the confusion of the looting for some other purposes? Mac wracked his brain, what was he missing?

A rapid succession of gunshots echoed through the warehouse and Mac's heart leapt in his throat. His pulse raced as he prepared for the next victim. Caitlyn skidded around him, panting with exertion. Mac didn't have time to do more than glance at her to see she was okay before the first of two thugs came into range.

Mac clocked the first one on the head and he dropped, but that gave the second one warning, and he pulled the trigger on the rifle. Bullets whizzed past Mac's head and bounced wildly around the room.

Ducking for cover, Mac reached for the weapon slung over his shoulder. He didn't have time to aim, but shot back wildly. Wood splintered as the bullets slammed into the boxes surrounding him. Mac crouched down again and waited for the return fire.

Without warning, gunfire sounded behind him. Caitlyn held the other goon's rifle and shot at the thug in front of them. The gang member's body jerked and convulsed as the bullets penetrated it. Blood spurted everywhere and the gun dropped from his hands seconds before his body fell next to it.

Caitlyn's face was deathly pale as she pointed the gun at the ceiling. Mac knew what she must be going through. Killing a man was never an easy thing, but for someone used to healing, it would be even more devastating.

He scrambled over to her and took the gun from her unresisting hands. As she began to tremble he pulled her close to his chest.

"I—I killed him," she sobbed.

"You had no choice. It was either him or us." His heart ached for her, but they didn't have time for her to deal with the guilt that came with taking a human life. That would have to come later—if there was a later.

"Oh my God. I killed a man."

Mac slung his gun back over his arm and used both hands to grab her shoulders. Giving her a rough shake, he waited until she looked him in the eye. "Listen, I know this is hard for you, but we don't have time for you to fall apart. Are there any more out there?"

Caitlyn looked startled at his roughness, but it was enough to help her regroup. Wiping her face with her hand, she sniffed back her tears. "I didn't see any more. I checked the best I could, but I think this was it. I heard these two complaining that everyone else had run off and they were the only two who wouldn't get any of the goods. I think Nadowny and Carlos are out there somewhere too."

Her eyes still looked a little wild, but at least she'd stopped crying. "Nadowny is running, I'm sure of it. With you on the loose and the evidence we have, he's probably halfway to the airport now."

"What do we do about them?" Caitlyn nodded to the two unconscious men on the floor.

"Leave them here for the cops to pick up when this is all over. Come on, let's go."

Mac shielded Caitlyn with his body as best he could. She averted her gaze from the bloody body on the floor. Her survival instincts would kick in soon and she'd black this out until her mind had time to process it. Hopefully reality would hold off until they were safe.

"Where are we going?" Caitlyn asked as they slipped out of the warehouse into the darkened street.

"We'll head for the station, you'll be safe there."

"Where will you be?"

"I'm going after Nadowny."

Sirens wailed in the distance and smoke hung heavily in the air. They rushed through the streets, not even bothering to stick to the shadows. He had to get Caitlyn to safety and get Nadowny. That was all that mattered.

A muted roar grew louder as they rounded the corner. There were no streetlights left and the pall of smoke in the air dulled the moon's glow. What was that noise? Mac pulled Caitlyn behind him. He slowed their pace and listened for any clues as to what was happening.

As they neared the center of the city, the sirens grew louder and the smell of pepper spray in the air stung his eyes, nose and throat. Mac turned down a side street to escape the spray.

"Pull your shirt up over your nose and mouth," Mac ordered.

The roar grew in intensity, and as they exited the street, Mac saw the reason for it. Charging down the street was a hoard of screaming, crying people. Police in riot gear chased the thundering mass straight at Mac and Caitlyn.

They had to get out of there or they'd get trampled. "The fire escape. Come on, I'll give you a boost up." Mac dragged her to the nearest ladder and crouched down so she could use his thigh for a step. "Get up to the roof and get as far away as you can."

Caitlyn stopped climbing and looked down at him. "I'm not leaving without you."

"Get to your brother's!" Mac ordered as the mob rushed towards them like a tidal wave.

He lost sight of her as the press of panicked bodies swallowed him up.

Chapter Twenty-two

Caitlyn's breath came out in labored pants as she ran across another roof. The stitch in her side was unrelenting, but she wouldn't stop. She had no idea where she was, just that she had to keep going. The last she saw of Mac was his stubborn face telling her to run as the swarm of bodies overtook him.

How could she find him again? He said he was going after Nadowny. Did that mean he was heading towards the airport? Where were her brothers? Caitlyn bent over and tried to catch her breath. She stumbled to the edge of the roof and looked over, trying to figure out where she was.

Fires dotted the streets as far as she could see. Smoke billowed up, distorting her view. All the landmarks were hidden from her and she felt lost in the night. This was the last building in the row—that much she could tell. There was no choice about it now, she had to get down and take her chances on the streets.

With shaking knees, Caitlyn searched for a fire escape ladder. Some of the newer buildings didn't have them all the way up to the roof. If she couldn't find one, she'd have to skip back across the buildings until she found one that did. Her legs ached at the thought.

Just as she was about to give up, she spotted the guardrails that led to the ladder. Swinging her leg over the side, she scampered down the rungs as fast as she could without slipping. If she lived through tonight, she'd never climb a ladder again.

Her feet dangled in the air for a moment before she jumped to the ground. The force of the landing vibrated through her aching body, but she had no time for that now. She had to get help for Mac.

Scanning the street for a sign or some clue as to her location, she headed for the corner. Bond Street. Damn, she was far from home. And all alone.

Caitlyn jogged as best she could towards the center of town. A police car turned towards her, driving without his lights on. She raised her hand to flag him down, then hesitated. What if it was one of the mayor's men and not someone she could trust? It could be someone she'd known all her life or it could be someone trying to kill her.

She dodged for cover behind a tumbled pile of garbage cans. The car came slowly closer. What to do? Who could she trust? Fear and indecision tumbled around in her head, clouding her judgment. Was the car slowing down?

Sweat dripped down her back. If only she could see something. If she could see the driver she'd know, but the night shrouded his identity.

"Caitlyn! Are you out there?" The loud speaker on the car echoed between the buildings.

It was Liam. Relief washed through her. She ran out from behind the garbage and almost fell into the street in front of him. Liam slammed on the breaks before he hit her and jumped out of the car, scooping her up in his arms.

"Where have you been? We've been searching for you since we lost contact with Mac."

"You had contact with Mac? How? When?" She was so confused.

"He had a tap in his shoe, but the battery died. The GPS is still working, but that only gives a general location."

"Can you use it to find him again? We got separated when the mob came towards us."

"I don't know. Tom has the van now, we'll go back there and see if we can find him."

Caitlyn climbed into the passenger seat and locked the door. Her hands shook as she buckled herself in. Please God, let Mac be okay.

తు

A drop of either sweat or blood slid slowly down Mac's cheek as he tore open the first box he came to. After fighting his way—literally—out of the mob of terrified people in the streets, he'd found himself right back where he started. A block away from the warehouse.

Now that Caitlyn was safely on her way to her brother's house, he could focus again. And he wanted to know what was in all those boxes piled high. Finding an abandoned cell phone, he'd placed a call to Tom's cell phone and got his voice mail. He'd left a message for Tom to check the train station, bus station and airport for Nadowny since he couldn't follow him through streets thronged with people and pepper spray. Besides, he wanted to investigate the warehouse instead.

What were Carlos and Nadowny so anxious to protect? He suspected guns and drugs, but wanted to know for sure. The top of the box finally yielded to his efforts and he tossed the crow bar down to dig through the packing materials. His hand hit another box and he yanked it out.

Ripping the top off, Mac found a mound of bubble wrap. Bubble wrap? What the hell? He unwound the object from the yards of plastic until a tiny clay pot was revealed. Mac didn't know squat about pottery, but this seemed old and sort of South American in design.

Was Nadowny smuggling art out of Mexico with Carlos' help? Mac dug through the rest of the box and found four more carefully wrapped packages. Grabbing the crow bar, he hacked away at another box until he got that top off too.

This box didn't have packing materials in it—it didn't need to. Stacks of money in neat rows stared up at him from inside the box. There was easily half a million dollars in tens and twenties just sitting there. No wonder he had machine gun wielding punks guarding the doors. If anyone ever found out what was in here, the place would be ransacked in seconds.

Disgust curled through him. Mac had lived in one of the poorest parts of the city for months and saw how people struggled for survival. And all the while Carlos and Nadowny were sitting on enough money to feed every man, woman, and child.

Rage burned through him red and hot. Little kids turned to the gangs to make money so they could eat and ended up getting shot in drive-bys. Mac wanted to take the crate of money and throw it out on the street for the taking, but he couldn't do it. First, it would make the rioting going on right now look tame in comparison. Secondly, he needed the evidence to nail Nadowny and Carlos to the wall for a good long time.

He'd need backup at the warehouse. Cameras, finger printing kits and big trucks to haul the evidence away. A phone, where was that damn cell phone he'd used before? Mac scrambled through the discarded packing materials looking for the cell phone. A glint of silver caught his eye and he pounced on it.

It was a camera phone too! That was a bonus. Mac clicked pictures as fast as he could. They wouldn't come out great in the dim light, but it was better than nothing. When he was finished taking pictures of the money and pottery, he dialed Tom's number again. He'd leave him a message to get evidence crews in here, then take some pictures of whatever evidence was in the office.

As he dialed Tom's cell, he headed towards the office and was almost run down by a moving van charging through the wide bay doors. Rolling to the side, Mac dove for cover, dropping the phone in the process.

"So Mr. McDougal, we meet again." Nadowny climbed out of the van with a gun pointed at Mac's chest. "How did I know you'd be here?"

"Just lucky, I guess." Mac held his hands out in front of him. The crow bar was in reach, but wouldn't do much good against an automatic rifle.

"Luck has nothing to do with it. Nothing. Sit down in that chair while I think of what to do with you now that my plans have gone awry."

Mac walked slowly to the chair and sat, not making any sudden movements. He prayed the phone was transmitting or he'd be in deep shit. The mayor didn't look all that stable. If Tom answered his phone, and Mac could hold out long enough, backup would be on its way.

Nadowny yanked Mac's arms behind him and tied them together with a plastic wire tie he pulled out of his pocket. Pain shot up from his wrists to his shoulders, but Mac refused to utter a sound.

"A tough guy, huh?" Nadowny smacked him on the head as he stood behind him. "I'd love to prove how quickly I could tear that bravado down, but unfortunately I don't have the time. I have some packing to do."

"Don't let me stop you." *Come on, give me something to hang you. Go ahead, brag.*

"You won't. You may think you've stopped me, but this is just a minor set back. I'll move my operation to Mexico and start all over again. I have contacts down there, you know."

"No, I didn't realize you were a multi-national organization," Mac said, stroking his ego a bit. For reasons he'd yet to comprehend, the bad guys always felt the need to brag when they thought they had him down. Maybe they wanted an audience since so much of their best work was hidden? He didn't know why but they always spouted off, at various levels of truthfulness, about what they'd done once they had Mac on the ropes. Mac just prayed someone would be able to get the information.

"There's much you don't know. I bet you thought I was just an opportunist, taking a kickback from the gangs and pocketing the money. Didn't you?" Nadowny grunted as he heaved a box onto a dolly and pushed it towards the van.

"The thought crossed my mind." Mac watched as Nadowny picked certain boxes over others and shoved them towards the van. There was no way he could get even a quarter of the boxes in there. Which ones did he think were the most important? The money or the artifacts?

"I'm sure it did, and that's what I wanted you and those other idiots to think. Carlos and the rest of his ilk put their pedestrian motives on me and I let them believe it."

Mac said nothing, just waited for Nadowny to continue. His shoulder blades twitched as the mayor disappeared behind him for a bit. Would he kill him before or after he packed up?

Nadowny came back into view, pushing more boxes towards the van. "Are you wondering where you were wrong yet?"

"I don't think I was wrong. I think you're no better than the two bit punks you used," Mac goaded.

Nadowny's face twisted in anger, but he reined it in quickly. "I won't let you distract me with your insults. But I will tell you how wrong you are...eventually." He laughed and disappeared again.

Where the hell was the backup he asked for? God, with his luck Tom wouldn't check his messages until tomorrow. Christ on crutch.

Several more boxes were stacked near the van before Nadowny stopped for a rest. Mopping his brow with a handkerchief, he leaned against the van and stared at Mac.

"So, have you figured out my plan yet?"

"Maybe. You contacted the three gang leaders and united them with promises of police protection and more money—if they did things your way. They listened and compartmentalized their activities and stopped killing each other. Once they'd stopped in-fighting, they made money hand over fist, of which you got a cut."

"Pretty good, so far."

"I'm not done yet. At first I thought you orchestrated the rioting so that you could call in the troops and look like a hero in time for the next election. But now I'm thinking you had other plans in mind. Something to do with smuggling stolen artifacts perhaps?" *Come on, come on, give me something here.*

"Very good. I'm sure the FBI will miss your intelligence when you're dead. The riot served two purposes. First, it gave the gangs something to look forward to in way of a reward, therefore keeping them under control more easily. Second, it was a great cover for moving the materials I'd gathered here over the last six years."

"Too bad those same people are now going to loot this place and take all your stuff before you can get rid of it."

"Never."

"We had the police mobilized long before your mob hit the street. It won't be long before they come back here. Too many of your guards know about it."

Nadowny swore and took a step towards Mac with his fist raised.

Mac braced himself for the blow, but Nadowny stopped himself.

"Very clever, Mr. McDougal, but not clever enough." He turned and began loading the van. "You think too small. I had much bigger plans. Have much bigger plans."

"Besides stealing from the poor and addicted? How do you sleep at night knowing your money comes from junkies and prostitutes?"

"Very well. And I'll sleep even better in the Governor's mansion."

Ah, so that's where this was headed. He wanted to go for the big time. "I see. Campaigns are expensive, so you figured you'd finance it with drug money."

"You fool, that's only part of it. As Governor I could control so much more, expand my operation over the entire state. I'd have more points of entry for my goods and make millions. Billions! With guns, drugs, and phony artifacts coming in from South America from different venues, I'd have enough money to go for the presidential nomination in a matter of years. I'd be the next political darling and the city would love me for it."

"Are you crazy?"

"Like a fox. After this riot, I'd make a tearful pledge to clean up the city. Once I took out the principle leaders in the confusion, I'd replace them with my men. They'd keep the violence down and pull in enough money to keep the gangs from infighting. I'd look like a hero."

"Except you hadn't planned on Carlos not telling you about me until I'd gathered enough evidence to bring to a judge. I was his main drug dealer long before I joined the gang. He didn't send you my prints right away, did he? He waited so you wouldn't know about the deal he had working on the side. The money he made from me, he kept, and I bet, used to buy more guns. Do you really think he was going to listen to you? I'll bet he has people after you right now."

Nadowny looked over his shoulder quickly before he caught himself. His face filled with rage as he faced Mac. "Shut up! Just shut up!"

Lord, please let someone be listening to the phone. Please have gotten this all on tape. If he had to die, at least let Nadowny get nailed to the wall as a result. Mac's hope for rescue had diminished with every box the mayor loaded into the van. Either his call to Tom hadn't connected and they weren't hearing any of this, or they didn't have the manpower to spare to help him. Either way, time was running out.

A flash of movement behind one of the boxes caught Mac's attention. Was someone else there? And were they friend or foe?

"So how are you going to kill me? Leave me tied to a chair with a bullet in my head? Just another victim of gang violence?"

"That would be too quick. I want you to think about your folly for a long time." Nadowny held a gasoline can in his hand and splashed it around the room. "It's a shame to lose all these weapons and drugs, but they'll keep the fire burning nice and hot for you. Don't worry, you'll pass out from smoke inhalation before you feel the flames licking at your feet."

Mac saw another movement by the van. Sweat dripped down his back, even as hope rose in his chest. If it was a friend of Nadowny's, he would have made himself known already, wouldn't he?

"I think I'll start the fire in the office. Must get rid of the evidence you know. By the time the fire makes its way to you it should be really cooking. And who knows? Maybe you'll get lucky and get shot by one of the boxes of ammo exploding before the fire gets you."

"One can only hope." Mac had to keep his attention off whoever was by the van.

Nadowny laughed as he made his way to the office. As soon as he was out of sight, Mac felt hands fumbling with the plastic tie behind him.

"Crap, I need to get a knife, hold on," Caitlyn said from behind him.

Chapter Twenty-three

Caitlyn felt Mac's hands tense and heard his gasp of surprise, but she didn't have time to reassure him. She thought she saw a knife lying on the floor of the van when she stole the keys, but it was dark and she was trying to be quiet, not take inventory. Scurrying as quietly as she could on shaking legs, she ran to the van and fumbled around in the dark until she found the utility knife on the floor.

"What the hell are you doing here? Where's Tom? Is backup coming?"

"Don't move your hands, I might cut them by accident. There isn't much room here."

"Would you answer me instead of worrying about the damn ties?" he hissed.

"Tom is busy rounding up the gang leaders with Miguel's help. Liam was patrolling the streets looking for me, but is now arranging backup. I think they're on the way. I left while they were still arguing over the best way to save you."

Idiots. They were so preoccupied with who was going to do the rescuing they weren't listening to what was going on.

"I take it someone answered Tom's phone," he said wryly as she cut through the bonds.

"Eventually. Come on, by the time we get out of here they should be on their way."

"There's a phone here somewhere, grab it."

"Why? We'll get another phone."

"Because that one has all the pictures on it."

The smell of smoke drifted towards her and panic churned in her gut. Caitlyn had a nice, healthy fear of fire after being a first hand witness to the devastation it could cause. She looked frantically around the room for the stupid phone so they could get out of there.

Mac shook his hands a bit as he stood unsteadily to his feet. Dried blood crusted over a cut by his eye and a bruise bloomed across his temple.

"What happened to you? You have blood on your face." Caitlyn tugged at his hand to get him moving towards the exit, but Mac kept looking around the room.

"I have no idea. I got hit so many times trying to get out of the mob, it must have been from that."

"Yeah, I saw you go down. I'll bet you have a lot more bruises than what's showing now. Would you come on? Let's get out of here! What are you waiting for?"

"I'm not leaving without Nadowny. You go on and wait outside for me."

"Are you out of your mind? Let the police get him, they're on the way." Caitlyn grabbed his hand again.

"No. He's slipped away too many times, I'm not letting him escape."

"He could have already left out another exit. He started the fire. With all the boxes in here this place will go up like kindling!" A shiver of fear slithered down her back.

"He's not going to leave without the van. That has all his money in it."

"Too bad for him, I've got the keys." Caitlyn waved the keys in Mac's face. "Now will you come on?"

"I'll take those, thank you." Nadowny pointed a gun at her and she froze on the spot.

It was the same type of gun she'd used on the guard. She knew exactly how much damage it could do, too. Bile rose in her throat as she remembered blood spraying everywhere and the body convulsing as it hit the ground.

Mac snatched the keys from her hand, drawing Nadowny's attention to him instead. "You mean these keys?"

Caitlyn's attention snapped back to the present as Mac

threw the keys across the room into the jungle of boxes.

Nadowny let out an inarticulate scream and turned the gun on Mac. With a cry, she dove for cover. Bullets sprayed overhead, ricocheting wildly. Mac was behind another box and she couldn't see him.

What should she do? If she tried to run, Nadowny would see her. If she stayed where she was, either he'd find her eventually or the fire would.

More shots rang out overhead. Sparks shot off the metal lights on the ceiling, and Caitlyn felt panic clawing its way up her throat. She had to bite her lip to keep from shouting in fear.

Caitlyn crawled slowly away from where the last shots were fired. Maybe if she could get around him, she could knock him out or something. She still had the knife, but wasn't sure she could stab him hard enough with the short blade to disable him. Slitting his throat was an option she didn't want to consider except as a last resort.

Just the thought of taking a life in such a deliberate manner made her soul shrink in fear. She just didn't have that in her. At least she didn't think so. If it were Mac's life on the line, she'd find the strength to do whatever it took to save him.

Bullets riddled the box to her left and she hunkered down with her arms over her head. Caitlyn had to bite her lip to keep a whimper of fear from escaping.

"You can't hide forever. If I don't get you, the fire will."

"Yeah, but it'll take your van with it," Mac called from the far wall.

Nadowny shot in his direction and Caitlyn heard a rush of air as the gasoline caught fire.

"That was stupid. Now the whole place is going to go up in flames, including you."

Caitlyn watched in horror as the area where Mac had been standing exploded. Where was the mayor? Where was Mac? She peered out between the boxes, trying to find an escape path before the flames spread to her.

"I don't care. As long as you're dead." Nadowny pulled the trigger and waved the spray of bullets back and forth where Mac had been until the gun clicked empty.

Before he could reload, a crow bar flew out of nowhere and struck his hand, knocking the gun out of it. Mac charged Nadowny, slamming him in the stomach with his shoulder and wrestling him to the ground.

Punches flew as Mac pounded Nadowny repeatedly. Caitlyn crept closer to help Mac if she had to—or to pull him out before the flames got to him.

Mac's face was distorted in fury as he pummeled his victim. He was so focused on beating the snot out of him that he didn't notice Nadowny's hand creeping down.

Almost in slow motion, Caitlyn watched the mayor pull a small handgun out of his jacket pocket.

"No!" she screamed and dove for Mac without thinking.

Her shoulder slammed into Mac's chest, knocking him to the side. The bark of the gun deafened her as shooting fire tore through her other shoulder.

Caitlyn's shout tore Mac out of the red haze he'd been lost in as soon as he had the mayor under his fists. He looked up in time to get bowled over by her and feel her body shudder as a gun fired.

"Caitlyn!" he screamed, shaking her.

"Nadowny... gun. I'm fine." Her face was deathly pale and her breaths came in rapid pants, but at least she was still breathing.

Mac rolled her off him and flinched as he saw the dark blood pump slowly from her shoulder. Nadowny stumbled as he tried to stand. He fumbled around looking for the gun, which he must have lost when Caitlyn slammed into them. Rolling towards him, Mac used a scissor kick to lock up his legs and take him down.

The thunk of Nadowny's head hitting the floor was drowned out by the roaring and crackling of the flames. The entire building was going up around them.

Carefully lifting Caitlyn off the floor, Mac draped her over his shoulder and bent to grab Nadowny by the collar. He hoped to God the thugs they'd knocked out and tied up before had managed to get out before they were burned alive.

Smoke billowed from boxes all around him, distorting his vision. Mac choked as a wave of heat blew past him. Where was the exit?

There had to be a way out of here. He turned his head back and forth and forced himself to think. Caitlyn's life pumped out of her while he waited. There. To the left there wasn't as much smoke.

Mac dragged Nadowny behind him as he wove through the maze of boxes towards the cooler part of the building. The bay doors were all open, adding oxygen to the flames growing rapidly behind him. If he could just get to the bays before the flames got to him—

His entire body ached, but he pushed it aside. Mac coughed and stumbled, but kept going. Nadowny started to struggle, but Mac ignored him. *Just get out, just get out.*

Heat chased him as he fought to carry Caitlyn to safety. The open doors acted like a chimney, drawing the smoke and flame out and over him. It would be a race to see what came first, the exit or exhaustion.

He would not give up. Nadowny's foot caught on the edge of a box and Mac was tempted to leave him, but he couldn't do it. "Move your foot or lose it," he barked out and kept walking, dragging Nadowny with him.

The steep stairs of the loading dock beckoned him. Mac could hear sirens screaming in the distance. Already the first fire engines were pulling in behind the surveillance van Liam had been driving.

"Over here!" Mac shouted, lunging for the stairs, almost falling down them as he struggled with the extra weight he carried.

Tom, Liam, and Jim poured out of the van and ran towards him. Jim reached to take Caitlyn off his shoulder.

"No! I've got her. She's been shot, we need an ambulance."

"You're falling over. Give her to me and I'll get her to the hospital."

Mac didn't argue, but kept moving away from the building and across the street. Tom waved off his brother and hauled Nadowny up instead, freeing a hand for Mac. Jim stopped arguing and barked commands into his portable radio.

"How badly is she hurt?" Liam asked, worry clouding his eyes.

"Small caliber gun, close range, in the shoulder. I don't think it hit an artery, but it's bleeding pretty badly."

She hadn't moved since he picked her up, and he couldn't tell if she was still breathing.

"Where's the fucking ambulance?" he shouted.

"It's coming, it's coming." Jim reached for her again, but Mac held him off and pushed his way through the crowd that had gathered to watch the warehouse go up in flames.

The three O'Tooles and Mac formed a phalanx and plowed their way through the people. Mac was ready to walk all the way to the hospital if the ambulance didn't get there soon enough.

Before such a desperate action was necessary, the ambulance careened around the corner, lights flashing and sirens blaring. Jim yanked open the back doors before it had even come to a complete stop, hauling the stretcher out of the back and pushing it over to Mac.

"You have to let her go now. I'll take it from here."

Mac laid her gently on the stretcher, his heart in his throat. He couldn't lose her now, he just couldn't.

Medics pushed him out of the way, starting IV lines in her arms and slipping an oxygen mask over her face. Jim shouted orders as they strapped her to the stretcher and pushed it into the back of the ambulance.

The doors slammed shut and the rig pulled carefully out into the street. Mac wanted to shout for them to rush, to get Caitlyn to the hospital before it was too late, but he bit it back. They knew what they were doing and Jim would make sure she got the best care possible. The rest was up to God.

"Come on, the chief wants to make sure there are plenty of witnesses when he reads Nadowny his rights. Doesn't want to take any chances of him slipping through the loopholes. We'll go to the hospital as soon as that's over with." Tom pulled him out of the street and back towards the crowd gathered around the police cars.

"How can you be so calm? She's your sister, for Christ's

sake."

"Don't you think I know that? Don't you think I want to be inside that ambulance with her right now?" His jaw clenched and his face showed the angst he was going through. "But what good is it going to do her to stand around and get in the way while people who know what the fuck they're doing work on her? I have to trust that Jim will do whatever it takes to save her while I do my job and make sure the bastard that shot her doesn't get away."

Mac knew he was right, but that didn't make it any easier to deal with. All he could see was her ashen face, almost as white as the sheets she was laying on, as the stretcher pulled away. He'd do his job and make sure Nadowny didn't get off on a technicality, but for the first time in his life his mind was anywhere but on the job.

News vans were already pulling into the area, and helicopters circled overhead like urban vultures, their noise adding to the confusion. Mac followed along in a daze. The adrenaline that had carried him this far had run out and he was ready to collapse where he stood.

"We found Carlos in his car with a bullet in the back of his head. Several other gang leaders are missing too. I expect the body count will go up as the day wears on." Tom slipped his shoulder underneath Mac's arm to prop him up.

"How much of Nadowny's confession did you get over the phone?"

"All of it, pal . All of it. Even if it's not admissible in court as evidence, it's more than enough to convince the judge to let us search his records."

"Good luck. Most of the evidence is going up in flames now." Mac looked around at the fire fighters battling the blaze. They were in a defensive formation, not so much fighting the fire as preventing it from spreading to the surrounding buildings.

"I'm sure he left a paper trail. Swiss bank accounts or something. Don't worry, we'll find it and nail him."

Mac was sure he'd care again when the shock and fear wore off, but right now all he wanted to do was find a quiet place to wait for word of Caitlyn.

Tom held him up as they made their way through the crowd surrounding the squad car. Liam snapped handcuffs on the mayor as the chief read him his Miranda rights from a card in front of him. They were taking no chances on a sharp lawyer getting him off because his rights weren't read correctly.

Light bulbs flashed and spotlights shined on them as Nadowny was shoved unceremoniously into the back of the car. Mac's cover was blown for good now. His face would be on every paper in the northeast, and around the world once the wire services got a hold of the story.

And he couldn't have cared less.

The car pulled away with Liam driving and the chief in the back with the mayor.

"Let's go to the hospital. We can take care of the rest of the stuff later." Mac and Tom worked their way to the van. Every muscle, bone and tissue in his body ached and he couldn't wait to collapse. His mind had gone almost blank and it was a struggle to stay upright.

"I think while we're there we might want to have you checked out too. You're not looking too good, partner."

Mac nodded numbly and reached for the handle on the van. Another police car pulled up behind them, blocking the van in. Tom and Mac turned as one to see who needed them now.

An officer got out of the car. His hat was low over his brow and Mac couldn't get a look at his face.

"Do you know him?" Mac asked Tom. Something about the way he moved triggered something in Mac's memory, but he couldn't remember what.

"He doesn't look familiar, but there's a lot of Hartford cops I don't know. Could be a friend of Liam's who wants to know how Caitlyn is."

They waited for the officer to introduce himself as he walked closer, but he remained silent. Just as Tom stepped forward to hail him, Mac saw the cop's hand reach for his gun.

"Get down!"

Mac and Tom dove in different directions as shots exploded into the night. The sound of gunfire spooked the already wired crowd and people scattered, knocking each other over and adding to the confusion.

The cop came after Mac, who was trapped against the van. He reached blindly for some way to defend himself and only came up with sand. Throwing it in his face, Mac bought himself time to maneuver and kick out at the cop's kneecap. Bone ground against bone, and the cop dropped to the street with a scream of agony.

Tom ran over and put his gun to the cop's head and disarmed him. Mac got up gingerly. Blood oozed from multiple scrapes on his arms, and more body aches made themselves felt.

"Do you recognize him?" Tom pulled off the hat that had covered his face. Revealing a jagged scar across his cheek.

Oh yeah.

"It's Nadowny's body guard. He's no cop."

"Looks like he'll be joining his boss in jail tonight then. Where'd you get the squad car, buddy?" Tom asked as he handcuffed him.

"I want to talk to my lawyer."

"Absolutely. You'll need him." Tom looked up at Mac. "Call this in. We need to find out if he stole an unoccupied vehicle or killed the cop that was in it."

Mac ground his teeth in frustration. He knew it was important to take care of this, but he wanted to be with Caitlyn. His head spun as he reached for the microphone attached to the radio in the car.

Tom hauled his prisoner to his feet and opened the back of the squad car.

"I think you can cancel that call. I know what happened to the driver." Tom pointed to the back seat where Liam's friend Mark lay trussed up in his underwear like a roped calf.

"At least he's not dead," Mac said before the night spun around him and the world went gray, then black.

Chapter Twenty-four

Mac shifted uncomfortably in the hard plastic chair of the family lounge. He felt like he'd been hit by a truck, but didn't want to take the painkillers the doctor had given him. With everything else that had gone on in the last twenty-four hours, the pain was about the only thing keeping him awake.

Tom sprawled across two chairs, snoring softly, and Liam paced the tiny waiting room, jiggling the change in his pocket. Empty coffee cups littered the room and Mac's stomach grumbled. He should probably grab a snack or a nap like Tom was doing, but he just couldn't. With his luck, as soon as he went to the cafeteria the doctor would come in with news.

Jim and Maggie had come in twice already to give them updates. Caitlyn was in surgery, the bullet had lodged in her shoulder blade, which may have saved her life. If the gun had been a higher caliber, it would have shattered the bone and ripped open an artery.

The hospital overflowed with people waiting to hear about loved ones injured during the riots. A triage tent had been set up outside the emergency room and the Red Cross had set up stations where family members could go for information. The advance warning Caitlyn had given had kept the chaos to a manageable level. Mac thought it was ironic that the life she saved by calling in her friends was her own.

All eyes turned as the door opened and a doctor dressed in surgical scrubs walked in. When she spotted Liam, her eyes widened and she walked over. Mac nudged Tom who woke quickly and stood.

"I take it you're all Caitlyn's family?" she said, trying to cover a yawn.

"Yes," Tom said, speaking for all of them.

"I'm Dr. Patel, I performed the surgery on her shoulder."

Liam shifted uncomfortably but didn't say anything. The doctor avoided looking at him and focused mainly on Tom. She was a tiny thing, petite and probably no taller than five feet three inches. That she stood close to a foot shorter than the three men surrounding her didn't seem to affect her in the least. There was an interesting by-play going on between her and Liam, but Mac was too numb with worry to figure it out.

"How is she? Is she going to be okay?" Mac couldn't take the suspense.

"She made it through the surgery with flying colors. Her arm is going to be immobilized for a while, and I want her on bed rest for at least two weeks, but she'll live. As long as she doesn't get any secondary infections, she should be back to her old self again before you know it."

"When can we see her?"

"She's in recovery now, Jim's sitting with her. Once a room opens up on the trauma floor, they'll move her in there and you can visit with her briefly. She'll be pretty disoriented for a while from the blood loss and anesthesia, so you might want to wait until tomorrow. It wouldn't hurt for all of you to get some rest and take showers before you come back. She won't know you're there anyway." Dr. Patel looked pointedly at Mac, who still had dried blood caked on his face.

"I just want to see her, even if she doesn't know I'm there. If I can see her for a minute, I promise I'll go home and wash up before I come back."

"You can see her for one minute, but don't disturb her. I want her to rest for as long as she can." She turned and motioned them to follow her.

The recovery room was dimly lit and quiet. Harried-looking nurses monitored several beds as well as patients in lounge chairs along one wall. Jim sat in a curtained off area next to a bed. Tubes and wires ran in a tangle over Caitlyn's face and body.

She lay so still beneath the sheet. Jim moved out of the

way so Mac could squat by the side of the bed. He was afraid to touch her. She looked so pale and fragile.

"Rest easy, sweetheart. I'll be here when you wake up," Mac murmured, more for his benefit than hers.

Caitlyn's eyes fluttered open slightly, but didn't focus before they slipped closed again.

"I'll be back soon." Even though it tore his heart in half, Mac moved away from the bed and let Tom and Liam have a turn.

He waited in the hallway for Tom to finish. Thank God she was okay. He hadn't blown it. There was still a chance for them, if she'd listen to him and believe what he said.

Mac snorted to himself. Would she believe him? He'd spent so much time telling her how they couldn't be together and how important his job was to him. How he wasn't the family man sort of guy. Why should she believe him now? He sounded fickle even to himself.

"I'll make you believe, Caitlyn. I'll do whatever it takes." His head swam again.

Tomorrow, or rather later on today, after he had a chance to grab a few Z's and a shower, he'd come back and wait with her. Even if he couldn't tell her how he felt, at least he'd be near her to reassure himself she was still alive.

Tom came out into the hall and took a drink from a water fountain before joining him. "We can go as soon as Liam gets done. He doesn't have a car here either."

"Okay." Mac weaved a bit on his feet.

"Are you all right, buddy? I don't want you passing out on me again. Did the doctor really say you could leave? Or did you sign yourself out?"

"I'm fine. The doctor said it was just a reaction to the knock on my head and breathing in too much smoke. Some fluids and rest and I'll be good as new."

"I notice you didn't answer the question."

"I didn't have time to wait for some overworked doctor to sign discharge orders, if that's what you're asking."

Tom grabbed his shoulder. "Then you're going right back down there. I'm not having you drop on me again."

"Hold up, would you? Look, they told me to get some rest and replace my fluids and gave me some painkillers. If we go back down there, we'll be there forever. The ER is overwhelmed as it is. I can rest just as easily at Jim's place as I can there and I'll drink a gallon of water, okay?"

Mac was counting on the fact that Tom didn't like hospitals any more than he did to keep him out of the ER. Tom looked at him skeptically for another minute, then relented. "Get a drink while we're waiting for Liam."

"Yes, sir." Mac gave him a mock salute and crossed to the water fountain.

As he turned his head to get a drink, he caught a glimpse of Liam talking softly to Dr. Patel in the alcove of a doorway. Mac averted his gaze quickly, but not before he saw Liam brush his hand over the tiny doctor's cheek.

Well, well, well. Looks like there's a little something more going on there than Liam let on. Dr. Patel was attractive enough from what Mac could see in the baggy green scrubs and cap. She had almost black eyes and a pert little nose to go with her dusky skin and jet-black brows. Very interesting.

Mac finished his drink of water and walked back where Tom waited. He wished Liam all the luck in the world with his love life. Lord knew he'd need it.

∞

The first thing Caitlyn noticed when she came out of the fog she was in was the noise. Someone's IV line alarm was beeping. She'd have to get that. Her arm felt like it weighed a hundred pounds and she was so disoriented. She couldn't seem to open her eyes. Why was she at work? What time was it?

"Shh, it's okay. Go back to sleep." Caitlyn felt a hand squeeze her fingers gently, then the world went dark again.

The next time she woke, her head was a little clearer, but pain throbbed from her shoulder through her whole body. Even her fingernails hurt. She tried to sit up, to relieve an ache her back, but she couldn't use her left arm.

The memories came back like a movie on fast forward. The

warehouse, the mayor, Mac's face snarling in rage. The gun. She'd been shot, she remembered that. The mayor had pulled a gun from his jacket pocket and Mac was so focused on punching him that he wasn't paying attention. She hadn't thought more than to get him out of the way and stop the gun. Did she really shove him out of the way? Looking down at her arm wrapped tightly to her chest she realized she must have. And gotten shot for her efforts.

Where was Mac now? She looked around the room and spotted Tom in one of the chairs, sound asleep. That man could sleep through the apocalypse.

"Tom," she croaked. Her voice was raspy from disuse. How long had she been out of it anyway?

"Huh? What?" Tom woke with a start and shook his head as if to clear it. "Hey. You're awake."

"More awake than you, I bet. How long have I been out?"

"About a day and a half," Tom said, coming over to help her sit up. "Are you in pain? Do you want some more meds? I'll call the nurse."

"Yeah, that would be good. My arm really hurts." A day and a half? What'd she miss? "What happened? I don't remember anything after the warehouse catching on fire. Did they get the mayor? Is Mac okay?"

"Hold on, I'll tell you everything, just let me tell the nurse you're awake. They'll want to take more vitals I'm sure. Someone's been in here every twenty minutes poking at you," he grumbled.

"It's their job. What's wrong? Did they interrupt your nap?" Caitlyn teased, reaching for the cup of ice chips by the bed. Her mouth felt like it was coated in fur.

"Very funny. Just see if you're laughing when they start poking at you now that you're awake."

Caitlyn smiled in good humor. If Tom was grumbling about not getting enough sleep, things couldn't be too bad. She was dying to ask him about Mac, but held her tongue. She'd get the whole story when he was ready to tell it and not a minute before.

A nurse she didn't recognize bustled in and made some notes on the chart at the foot of her bed. After seeing if she needed anything, she quietly left the room.

"Finally. Now tell me everything."

"Okay, I don't know what you know, so if I'm repeating things, bear with me."

Caitlyn nodded for him to continue.

"We figured out that Nadowny was involved with Carlos about five minutes too late to keep him from grabbing you. It turns out the chief was running his own undercover operation with Miguel, which was why he was involved."

"I'll bet Liam's relieved. He really respected the chief." Caitlyn had been worried about him.

"Yeah, it's a load off his mind. There's still some dirty cops, but Miguel has fingered most of them, and I'm sure the rest will be weeded out after all the evidence has been sifted."

"Go on," she urged. She hoped they caught the one who ran her license plate.

"Nadowny called, giving us two hours to gather what evidence we had in exchange for you."

"Yeah, I remember that. I told you not to do it."

Tom snorted. "Oh sure, like that was going to happen. Will you stop interrupting me?"

"Fine." She rolled her eyes.

"Okay, so Mac shows up with a quick tap in his shoe. He's telling us everything that's going on in the warehouse and we're recording it. Meanwhile, the chief has pulled out all the stops and called in mutual aid from every department he can call, page, or email."

"What happened with the mob? When Mac and I got out of the warehouse, they were coming back towards us. I heard some of the gang members saying they were headed downtown near the shops for better looting."

"I'm getting to that. Since we knew what, approximately, was going to happen, we had forces in place to prevent the looting. The area near the warehouse got hit worse than we expected, which is why we didn't have any backup for Mac. They were overwhelmed. It's really too bad, because those folks are the ones who can least afford to replace their stuff." He shook his head. "Anyway, the rest of the city is pretty much undamaged. Some broken windows and flipped cars, but nothing too major."

"How'd the hospital do? I called in as many people as I could, but I ran out of time before I got grabbed."

"From what I could tell, they were busy but handling it. Maggie should be stopping by any second, you can ask her."

Caitlyn nodded as Tom filled her in on the mayor's arrest and the subsequent arrests that were coming in.

"The news media is losing their collective minds. Every day there's another screaming headline. Poor Mac has been on the cover of almost every newspaper in the country."

"How is he doing? He'd gotten pretty banged up himself and his wound wasn't really ready for that much activity."

"He's fine, got a little loopy from breathing in too much smoke, but after some sleep and some fluids he's fine. I'm sure he'll be in here soon too. He's been here almost every other minute since you came out of surgery."

A little thrill went through her at his words. She tried to squash the hope burning in her chest, but it wasn't easy. Just because he wanted to make sure she was okay didn't mean he wanted to hang around forever. Still, he could have taken off, making a million excuses.

"What about Liam and Jim? Are they okay? I remember Jim in the ambulance, but it's kind of fuzzy. And the last time I saw Liam was when he brought me back to the van."

"Where you should have stayed, then you never would have been shot."

"But if I had waited for you all to do something, Mac would have been dead."

"We had to go through proper channels. If we went barreling in there without the warrant in place, anything we got as evidence wouldn't mean squat."

"Were you able to get anything? Nadowny started the fire in the office."

"Yeah, Miguel snuck into the warehouse and stole the van before it caught on fire."

"Would've been nice if he could've helped me out while he was there," Mac said from the doorway. He held a bouquet of roses and a colorful balloon.

Caitlyn's heart dropped straight to her toes and right back up again at the sight of him. His face was a mass of bruises, but the blue eyes sparkled at her just the same.

"Are those for me?" she asked, feeling shy all of a sudden.

"Uh, yeah. I thought you might like something pretty to look at when you woke up. Guess I was too late."

"Hey, she had me. I'm better looking than a bunch of stupid flowers." Tom stood and winked at her.

Mac gave him a meaningful look and Tom hesitated a moment before bending down to kiss her on the forehead. "I'm going to grab a cup of coffee and some lunch before Mac strains a muscle glaring at me."

"Thanks," she said, kissing him on the cheek.

"No prob." He nudged Mac in the shoulder on his way out and shut the door quietly behind him.

Mac shifted uncomfortably from foot to foot before he crossed the room and put the flowers on the little table near her.

"How are you feeling?" he asked, sitting on the edge of the bed.

"A little rough around the edges, but okay." She really wished she'd had time for a quick swish of mouthwash before he came in.

"You had me—us—really worried for a while. You lost a lot of blood."

"I'll be fine. You got us out of the fire." The memory of the trip out of the warehouse was a blur of smoke and heat and pain. She couldn't remember details, just a vague fear for her life and Mac's.

"I would've been a goner if you hadn't stopped Nadowny from shooting me, so I guess that makes us even. Did Tom fill you in on everything that happened?"

"Pretty much. I'm sure I'll have more questions later, but for now I'm just glad everyone's okay."

"There'll be a lot of shake-ups for the next few months." Mac stopped talking and held her hand gently.

They looked at each other in silence for an awkward minute

before Caitlyn couldn't take it any more.

"So, Tom tells me your picture is all over the newspapers. Have you gotten calls to make the rounds on the night shows?"

Mac smiled wryly. "No, that isn't exactly encouraged in my line of work."

The hope that had flared when he walked into the room began to dim. "Yeah, I guess it's hard to be an undercover agent if you're on Letterman."

"No kidding." He took a deep breath and gripped her fingers more tightly. "Look, there's a lot I want to talk to you about, and I'm sure this isn't the right time for it. You've just woken up and you're probably in a lot of pain, but if I don't say it now I might not get the chance."

Caitlyn felt fear congeal in the pit of her stomach. Here it comes, the brush off. She'd run out of time to change his mind. A lump formed in her throat and she fought back tears. She would *not* cry. If nothing else, at least she'd have her pride. Cold comfort, but better than looking like an ass. Steeling herself, she pasted a smile on her face. "Go ahead."

Mac looked at her, opened his mouth to speak, then shut it again. "This is harder than I thought. I never wanted to hurt you, and here I almost got you killed."

Drawing it out was hurting worse than any bullet wound could. "Just say it Mac, I'm tough, I can take it."

"You're not tough. You're sweet and kind and have a heart that wants to save everyone, including a beat up agent like me."

"I'm sure my name has already been placed on the list for canonization," she snorted. He made her sound like Little Miss Goodie-Two-Shoes.

"I wouldn't go that far, but you deserve someone a lot better than me."

Every word sent another dart of pain into her. Oh God, she knew it was going to hurt, but not like this. Where was the nurse with her pain meds? Maybe a nice shot of morphine would stop the ache in her heart too.

"But I can't give you up."

"What?" Her gaze caught his. What was he saying?

"I know I'm going to sound like the biggest hypocrite that

walked the face of the planet. I mean, I kept telling you how wrong I was for you and how I wasn't a 'happily ever after' guy—"

"But?" She was afraid to misunderstand his words and have her hopes dashed all over again.

"But, I—I love you. I don't want you to be with someone who deserves you. I want you to be with me."

His face was open and more vulnerable than she'd ever seen it. His love and fear were laid out for her to see.

"You had to tell me this when I can't even lift both arms to hug you, didn't you?" Tears fell from her eyes as the emotions she'd been fighting back filled her.

"I told you my timing sucked." He smiled at her and brought her hand to his mouth for a kiss. "Are you going to put my out of my misery here? I've been sweating this speech for hours."

Butterflies danced in her belly and her heart flipped over slowly. "I love you, too. I have since that first night together, but I didn't want you to feel trapped."

"I might have. I never thought I was cut out for a family life. I figured I'd work undercover until I either retired or got killed. I'm good at what I do."

"I know. But now your cover's blown."

"To hell and back. I'll never work undercover again."

"And?"

"And, although I might miss the adrenaline rush now and then, or even the challenge, I won't miss hiding in dumpsters or sleeping with one eye open for months at a time. And I definitely won't miss losing myself in my cover."

"I kind of like the person you are right now," Caitlyn said. She knew she was smiling like a loon, but couldn't seem to stop.

"I'd take a few less aches and pains, but I'm pretty comfortable in my skin now too." His smile was just as goofy so she didn't feel so badly anymore.

"What happens next?"

"There'll be months and months of dispositions and testimony. Legal maneuvering and deals on both sides—"

"I mean with us, doofus. With you."

"I've been offered a job as Director of the Northeast Region of the FBI. I wanted to have our talk before I agreed to anything though."

"Is that something you'd like to do? Working behind a desk is going to be a lot different for you."

"It sure will. I'll be doing a lot more behind the scenes and directing of covert operations. That appeals to me. I'll also be involved in directing a program to control the gang population in cities, and that really means a lot to me."

"I'm not surprised. You'd know about the problems first hand after this assignment." He still wasn't telling her what she wanted to know. He'd said he loved her, but what next?

"That I do." He stopped talking again and just looked at her.

Was she going to have to drag it out of him? "Ah, where does that leave us? I don't want to misunderstand things, so why don't you spell it out for me?"

"Quite the romantic, aren't you?" he teased.

"Mac!"

He leaned down and kissed her nose, then drifted lower to kiss her lips lightly. "I want to be with you forever, to eventually have a family and a house and a yard for all the strays you bring home," he murmured against her mouth.

"Oh." She kissed him back, pouring all the joy and love that filled her into the kiss. "But I think from now on I'll stick to stray dogs."

"For the love of little green apples! How many times am I going to walk in on the two of you in bed?" Tom groused from the doorway.

"If you learn how to knock instead of barging in, you could avoid it in the future," Mac shot over his shoulder, kissing Caitlyn again just for good measure.

"But where's the fun in that?"

Epilogue

Aurora Patel contemplated moving the two feet to the left that it would take to reach the coffee pot, but couldn't work up the energy. Twelve straight hours on her feet with one small break for food before she was called back into surgery made the very thought of moving again repugnant. Her hands were red and raw from the harsh antiseptic she used to scrub the germs off, and her back screamed in pain.

And she'd get to do it all again tomorrow. Yippee. Ah, the glamorous life of a surgeon, what more could she ask for? A back massage would be nice. And maybe a week in the tropics.

Was the coffee worth the effort of moving? Aurora looked at the pot. It had maybe an inch of dark black sludge sitting in the bottom. Nope, definitely not worth moving for. But if she got up now, maybe she could use the momentum to carry herself out the door and to her car. It was a short ride to her apartment, and then she could take off her shoes and lay down for eight blessed hours.

Okay, on the count of three she'd move. "One—two—" the phone on her hip rang before she could get to three.

Crud.

She had to answer it. She was still in the hospital and therefore still available if there was an emergency. Please don't let there be an emergency.

"Patel, here," she answered with as neutral a tone as she could muster. Pleasant wasn't happening.

"I know where you are." The sinister voice rasped through the phone, sending chills down her back.

"Who is this?" Aurora sat up straight.

"I know where you are, and I'm watching you, doctor." The last was said as more of an insult than a nod at her title.

"What do you want?"

The caller disconnected before she got an answer.

Aurora's hands shook, and she was afraid the trembling would travel through the rest of her body in seconds if she didn't do something. Almost without thinking, her fingers dialed a familiar number.

A number she'd sworn never to call again.

"O'Toole."

"Liam, it's me. It's starting again."

About the Author

To learn more about Arianna Hart, please visit www.ariannahart.com. Send an email to Ari at ari@ariannahart.com or join her Yahoo! group to join in the fun with other readers as well as Arianna! http://groups.yahoo.com/group/friendsofari

He found her handcuffed to his bed. Can they unchain her memories in time to save her life?

Lost But Not Forgotten
© *2007 Mackenzie McKade*

When pharmaceutical researcher Alexis Knight returns home from the Amazon jungle in a quest to reclaim the year of her life lost to amnesia, she discovers a host of changes have taken place in her absence. Not only has the shy, geeky boy she knew years ago transformed into a virile, confident hunk, he's bought her family home and is in the process of turning her late mother's bedroom into a den of iniquity.

When Jake O'Malley finds spitfire Allie handcuffed to his bed, accused of breaking and entering, his first thought is that his dreams have been served up to him on a platter. Then he realizes she's not acting when she says she doesn't remember the past year, nor her own mother's death.

As Jake eases Allie past her grief, her journey to reclaim her memories entwines with an exploration into the world of BDSM. Just as their psychological duel to dominate heats up, they make another, more chilling discovery.

There's a reason Allie lost her memory—someone wants her dead.

Available now in ebook and print from Samhain Publishing.

Enjoy the following excerpt from Lost But Not Forgotten...

Crap. Allie hightailed it toward her bedroom, shutting the door just before Jake burst from the bathroom.

The pounding on her bedroom door startled her, but she didn't move.

"You little witch. Open this door." Jake didn't sound too happy.

"Serves you right," she shouted at the closed door. The pipes in the house had always been a little finicky. She had learned that much as a child. Too many times, she had begun to bathe just as her mother started the dishes. The result was hot or cold water—never anything in between.

Truth was she could use a cold shower about now. It had taken all her strength not to accept what Jake offered, a night in his arms. Even now, her body burned with need.

Allie's heart raced as she leaned against the locked door. >From the other side, Jake shook it so that she felt the tremor clear to her bones.

"Allie, let me in," he growled.

"Beat all you want. You're not getting in here." Vibrations from his pounding continued to shake the door. Abruptly, they stopped. Allie harrumphed. "Giving up so soon?" A chuckle of satisfaction rose and died as quickly.

She shouldn't have taken her temper out on Jake. Everything that had happened recently was overwhelming. She was in trouble—big trouble.

Jake had been good to her mother—good to her. He didn't have to let her stay here. Truth was this wasn't her house. But that hadn't stopped her from making an appointment to meet with her mother's lawyer tomorrow.

The click of the lock sent her into action. "Oh, shit!" Allie flung herself against the door, but it was too late. Jake rushed through still only wearing the towel low around his hips. The inertia sent her backward and she fell on her ass. Pain radiated up her spine.

"Sonofabitch!" *That hurts.*

Before she could rise on her own, Jake yanked her to her feet, firmly against his solid chest. The lines on his face were hardened, but his eyes were not.

Damn man was enjoying himself. Her anger flared anew, racing like a wildfire across her cheeks.

He gave her a little shake. "I ought to jerk you across my lap and beat your ass."

She glared at him. "You wouldn't dare."

Jake released her, except for the iron grip he had on her right arm. "The hell you say." He began to drag her toward the bed.

Planting her heels into the worn carpet, she balled her freed fist and swung.

With lightning speed, he caught the punch and slammed her back against the wall. The air in her lungs gushed out on impact. She recovered quickly, countering with a raised knee to his groin that missed its mark. Just in time, he swung away only returning to pin her flat against the wall with his unyielding body.

Trapped. She couldn't move—couldn't breathe, except for the spicy, masculine scent that assailed her.

Damn. He was good. He knew her way too well, anticipating every defensive move she made.

"Release me or I'll—"

In a surprise response, he stole her threat away with a punishing kiss.

There was no gentleness in his touch. Teeth meshed with teeth. His invasion was demanding, forceful, as his tongue pushed past her tight lips. Fast and skillfully, he tasted every inch of her mouth.

Her struggles for release were futile. He was bigger—stronger—and his body covered hers like a shield.

This definitely wasn't the boy she knew.

Allie whimpered, caught between anger and the slow burn he stirred inside her as he ground his hips to hers. His arousal pressed tight against her belly. His masterful kiss plucked the strings of her desire, pulling her deeper and deeper under his control.

But he wouldn't win, she swore to herself, even when his warm hand slid between the folds of her silky robe. Yet when his fingertips worked past her camisole to cup her breast, she silently screamed, *No! You won't win—*

Her breath caught as he squeezed her nipple.

Sweet pain splintered through her breast as he increased the pressure. The radiating sensation filtered through her globe, heading down south to tighten low in her belly.

Anger and need collided, releasing a fresh wave of desire between her thighs.

It had been forever since she'd made love, felt her body satisfied.

The truth was she needed to be held. With everything that had happened, Allie needed a strong man's arms around her more than anything.

Before Allie could change her mind, she wadded her hands in the towel around his waist and pulled. The deep rumble in his throat only heated her blood more. Her fingertips weaved through his light dusting of chest hair. Within seconds, he had her devoid of her robe, camisole, and panties, her heavy breasts against his moist chest.

For a moment, he didn't speak and only stared at her breasts. The desire in his eyes stoked the fire inside her.

Again, he captured her lips in a fiery kiss, hungry and fierce. His smoothed his palms slowly up the outside of her thighs, then moved inward. She inched her legs apart, waiting breathlessly as he skimmed closer to her pussy.

A deep growl vibrated next to her neck sending a shiver through her.

His fingers played across her skin. Every place he touched sparked with life.

His gaze was hot—sultry.

She released a squeal as he pushed her back against the cool, stucco wall and lifted her off her feet.

"Wrap your legs around my waist." His voice was a dark seduction, so demanding.

She locked her ankles behind his waist, pressing his erection hard against her wet folds. Before she could weave her arms around his neck, he captured both wrists in one large hand and held them high above her head. He looped his other arm beneath her ass. His body did the rest to keep her suspended.

"Jake—"

She tried to suck in a much-needed breath, but he took that moment to shift his hips and drive his cock deep inside her.

"*Ahhh...*" she groaned. Jake was so large it took a moment for her body to soften and receive him. When he moved deeper, filling her completely, all thought, not to mention argument, fled from her mind. Her only coherent reflection was how wonderful he felt buried inside her. Then he began to thrust, not gently, but hard and fast.

Oh God. It was heavenly.

Allie had never had a man fit her so perfectly—one who made her pussy hum as he did, moving in and out of her body. Every muscle tightened with delight, every nerve ending came alive.

Stinging rays shot up her chamber. "Jake!" she screamed, writhing against him. Hands pinned above her head, she jerked for release, but it was useless.

He slammed into her body with a force she felt at the back of her womb. Her orgasm moved closer and closer. She needed what lingered just out of reach, driving her insane, as her breasts rasped against his chest.

"Come for me," he rumbled.

When Jared Romero gets shot the only person he can turn to is Macayla Sullivan, but will she risk her heart—and her life—to help him?

Take Your Medicine

© *2007 Arianna Hart*

After escaping from an abusive relationship, Macayla has no interest in tying herself to another man, even if he is drop-dead gorgeous. Unfortunately, Jared doesn't understand the meaning of the word no and breaks down her defenses as fast as she can put them up.

When Macayla saves Jared's life, little does she know that she's putting her life—and her heart—in danger.

This book has been previously published.

Available now in ebook and print from Samhain Publishing.

GET IT NOW

MyBookStoreAndMore.com

GREAT EBOOKS, GREAT DEALS . . . AND MORE!

Don't wait to run to the bookstore down the street, or
waste time shopping online at one of the "big boys." Now,
all your favorite Samhain authors are all in one place—at
MyBookStoreAndMore.com. Stop by today and discover
great deals on Samhain—and a whole lot more!

Samhain
Publishing ltd

WWW.SAMHAINPUBLISHING.COM

Printed in the United States
116608LV00002B/83/P